CURIOSITY AT WORK

ALADAR BAJUSZ

This is a work of fiction. Names and characters are the product of the author's imagination and any resemblance to actual persons, living or dead, is entirely coincidental.

First published on Earth 2020

Text © 2020 Aladar Bajusz
bajuszaladar2@gmail.com
bajuszaladar.com

Cover illustration © 2020 WillowRaven
willowraven.weebly.com

As a certified Earthling, Aladar Bajusz has asserted his right to be identified as the author of this work.

All rights reserved. No part of this book may be reproduced or used in any manner without prior written permission of the author except for the use of quotations in a book review.

Printed on Forest Stewardship Council® certified paper.

For all the orphans, singles, disappointed humans, bored people and hipsters around the world.

Don't let anyone tell you what can or can't be done and how the world works. Even Reality has no idea what is going on, and trust me, it really tried to organise everything.

[1]
STEVE

Curiosity.

This idea, this fundamental concept is at the centre of all creation, of everything there is and everything that will be. Example: Milk.

One day, someone with too much free time and probably dying of thirst, began staring at a cow. And stared. And kept staring, till a thought, a question, an idea popped into his mind. He became curious, curious if the cow was hiding something delicious in its udders. The dairy industry has never been the same since.

So I invite you on a journey, a question, a fleeting fancy, so mad and so stupid no sane person would ever think about it.

What if curiosity had a body? What if the idea of curiosity itself existed in physical form?

Contrary to popular belief, this fundamental driving force, curiosity itself, does not technically exist. It needs sensory inputs; it needs limitation; it requires a vessel that can be defined in space and time, a fixed point. How can something limitless, that's everywhere, that's an idea, interact with the laws of physics and reality? It can't.

That being said, this force had a consciousness. It was composed of every half-drunken musing, each hold my beer moment, every stupid question ever asked. If you ever felt the urge to use icing cream in place of shaving cream, it was probably curiosity bouncing in your skull.

Today, a new idea was added to this consciousness.

This idea gripped the undeveloped mind of curiosity with the ferocity of a starving wolf. How to achieve this? It could possess a body, it had the power, but it's not as easy as it sounds.

Besides, it's not a good idea to give away your body willy nilly, you never know what's listening.

Curiosity stretched, searching, stretching its energies to the limit. Bypassing realities, universes, space and time, it looked. Time is not something an idea is bothered with, so in a short time, or a long one, depending on which dimension you are looking from, it found someone.

Let's take a look, shall we?

Steve was sitting on a stump, having a cigarette and contemplating the meaning of life. Why was he contemplating the meaning of life? It was mostly the two people in front of him.

He was sitting around a small campfire, in the backyard of his grandparent's house, with two of his best friends, who were currently exchanging clothes.

One of them was a tall woman, Jill, 20 years of age, dressed in cargo shorts, a dark blouse, and sandals. Her straw-coloured hair was pulled into a tight ponytail, complementing her heart-shaped face and blue eyes. Both of these beautiful features were currently twisted in rage.

Probably because she just took off her blouse and handed it over to the person sitting opposite her.

The man sitting opposite on a stump, a huge grin on his face looked identical to the woman in front of him. Same hair, eyes, a heart-shaped face, with a bit more sharpened features, and the same age. It probably helped that they were twins.

Oh, and he was named Jack. Yes, their parents were not the most imaginative people. He had a yellow skirt on him, clearly taken from his sister, and was in the process of taking off his shirt, displaying his chiselled muscles to the autumn wind. With a mischievous smile and a wink towards Steve, he chucked his shirt into the fire.

"Oops," he said, his tone sugary and full of innocence.

"Oops my ass!" Jill stomped her feet. "You did that on purpose!"

Jack smiled innocently.

"GIVE. IT. BACK!" Jill tried to grab her shirt, but her brother just danced out of the way.

"It's mine now," Jack replied. "Unless you want to have another bet?"

Steve was contemplating if he should have bought more alcohol. Or if it was a good idea to invite his friends over. He had not seen them in years, being busy drinking, and smoking his university years away.

He's betting both of his balls that this will escalate in a stupid and probably insane way, and he will be the one who suffers for it. Why is he even hanging out with these people? Nostalgia? Is he a closet masochist? They have not changed a bit. No matter, they are not kids anymore; he will not let them pull the same shit again.

Steve checked his phone for the fourth time. It was 9pm. Would they make a fuss if he kicked them out in half an hour? Not sure, but if they don't calm down, heads will be smashed. He just wanted a relaxing Friday drinking and smoking dammit.

Turning his head, he looked at his childhood companion and confidant Malbo for help. There was none there. That was probably because Malbo was a seven feet robot made exclusively from cigarette boxes. It was Steve's proudest achievement yet; it had taken him years to create.

"I still don't understand why you keep that piece of junk around," Jack said, catching Steve's eye. "I'm amazed it still stands."

"Hey, leave Malbo alone!" Steve snapped. "He did nothing to you!"

"Jill, I never understand what you saw in a man who builds robots out of cigarette boxes."

Jill did not respond, eyes fixed on Steve.

"Sis," Jack continued a bit of dread in his voice. "Whatcha thinking? Don't tell me another stupid idea is coming to you."

"Shit," Steve swore.

He knew that look.

Jill's eyes lit up with sparkle, and she turned around, facing the smoking man. Uh oh, it's starting; maybe he should make an excuse and run into the house now, or just chug down the bottle of vodka in his hands. Perhaps he could blackout himself, but it was too late.

Jill was there, grabbing him by the front of his collar, giving him a rough kiss, forcing his teeth apart with her tongue, shoving it down his throat. After a minute of abusing his face, she let it go, turning around with a beaming look, saliva dripping down her jaw. She wiped it away with the back of her hand and said:

"I dare you to do that."

Jack, still smiling like a loon, stood up from his stump, turned, and slowly, robotically, started shuffling towards

Steve, who was staring glassy-eyed, into nothing, paying no attention to the happenings around him.

When Jack was a foot away, he put both of his hands on Steve's cheeks. Instantly, the brown-haired man's eyes snapped into focus and quickly assessed the situation.

"Mate," He said towards Jack, who was trying to tilt up his head. "What are you doing?"

"Just a quick smooch," Responded the blond man, trying to apply a bit more force to the head tilt.

"A quick smooch?"

Grabbing the bottle in a reverse grip, Steve smashed it into Jack's gut. Then, letting go of the container, he grabbed the blonde by the shoulders, smashing his knee into the same spot. Jack folded over, sliding to the floor.

"If you are gonna try again; I'm gonna take this bottle." He picked up the empty bottle, and with a quick and practised motion, smashed it against the stump. It was a miracle the shard did not hit anyone. "And ram it into your gut."

"You let Jill kiss you!" Whined Jack. "Why not me?"

"Jill is a hot woman," Steve said, ignoring the triumph in Jill's face.

"I call sexism! Homophobia!"

"Mate, at least take me on a date or two before you try to kiss me."

"Jill didn't do that!"

"We dated for two years mate."

"Good point."

"Come on, Steve," Jill said in a sing-song voice. "It will not hurt, it would be just like the old times, sharing everything between the three of us."

"Exactly why I broke up with you."

"Point," She said, helping her brother up.

Groaning and complaining, Jack stood up. An

awkward silence descended upon the three of them. The kind of quiet you encounter when you meet old friends after years of absence, and you realise they are the exact same jackasses as before. Not on an ounce of change.

Jill looked at Jack. He looked back. As one they turned facing Steve and said in unison.

"Come on; it will be just like old times."

"I'm not dealing with this shit," Steve said.

He began bringing up the half-broken bottle to protect himself and quickly realised something. The bottle was gone. Searching around, he found it in Jill's hands, who winked, and threw the bottle behind her.

Shit. Steve began searching frantically in his pockets. The only thing he found was his wallet, his lighter, and oh, a packet of cigarettes. Might as well. With practised ease, he put a stick in his mouth.

"I did not agree to this," he said, lighting a cigarette. "You guys can fuck off."

"Are you sure?" they said in unison.

"Yes, I'm sure." The cigarette lit up, and he took a quick puff from it. "We are not teenagers anymore; you can't do weird shit like that anymore."

"Why not?" They were side by side now, stepping forwards. "Is it not fun?" It's even creepier now than in school.

"It's not. My body, my rules."

"Are you sure it's not ours? Like old times?"

"Anybody's but yours." Steve shuffled back, bent his knees, and prepared to fight.

"Anybody?" They stretched out their arms.

"Yes, anybody."

Right at that moment, an intense white light came from the heavens, so fast and so fierce; it blinded everyone in the immediate area. As quickly as it happened, it was gone. When the twins managed to blink away the spots in their eyes, they looked at Steve, or at least, the place he was supposed to be. There was nothing there, except a half-smoked cigarette. It was still burning.

In a spacious laboratory, standing behind a high terminal, Professor Darius Dovan was getting ready. Today, the professor was trying out a new summoning experiment, suggested by his assistant. The test consisted of a pentagram made of glitter, a wheel of cheese, and extremely potent wine.

At first, the teachers, or more specifically, the only other teacher in the university, objected quite vocally about this clearly insane and stupid experiment. Sadly, it did not work. There is only so much arguing one can do with a mad scientist who achieved twelve different doctorates.

Especially when one of these doctorates was achieved by replacing most of his internal organs by machinery, including half his brain and fusing a metal facemask to his head. Initially, the facemask covered his whole face, but when everybody started complaining that it scared the children, Darius conceded, and thin lips and an even smaller nose was visible. He drew the line at organic eyes though; the ability to zoom 20 times and see infrared was too useful.

The only non-modified part of his body was a third arm, more of a claw really, poking through his dirty lab coat at his back. The claw was furiously typing away at a tablet at his side.

"Assistant," Darius said, voice raspy and robotic. "Are you ready?"

The doctor's assistant, Mark, was a human. Well, kind of. He was tall, thin, with surprisingly attractive features. If you ignored the bloodshot eyes darting madly about, the curly hair changing colours every few seconds, and the veins pulsing blue under his pale skin. He was nibbling on a piece of cheese.

"Assistant!" Darius' voice turned sharp. "What did I tell you about showing up pumped full of drugs before an experiment?"

"Don't do it?" Mark said, voice alert and attentive.

"Yes," Darius said. "So why did you do it?"

Mark just shrugged, taking another bite out of the cheese. The poor bastard was the only one who was willing to assist Darius in his experiments, and he only needed to pay him a pittance, so the professor had no choice but to just roll with his antics. He wished he would stop eating the reagents for the rituals, though; it took weeks to procure them.

"Young people these days," muttered the professor. "No respect for true science."

"Your so-called science almost tore a hole in reality," Mark said between bites. "At least five times."

Darius chose to ignore this. He refocused.

"Assistant, are you ready?"

"Sure," Mark nodded. "But why are we doing this again? I know we are doing the ritual a bit different this time, but we already summoned a demon, and while she definitely fits the look of one." Mark's eye flashes blue for a second. "She explicitly stated that there is nobody in her realm that can fix that."

Darius gave his assistant a flat look.

"It was your idea to try it," the professor said slowly.

"Was it?" Mark took a bite from the cheese and shrugged. "Let's crack on then."

The doctor looked one more time at his calculations. Then he said.

"Experiment number 107, glitter, cheese and wine, start."

Mark pulled out a bottle of wine from his lab coat, and then gingerly went into the middle of the pentagram, being careful not to touch the glittery lines. He put down the cheese, poured a little bit of wine on it, and then put the bottle down. After that, he stepped back.

Seeing his assistant getting out of the danger zone, Darius lifted his arms, slowly moving them in a circular pattern, murmuring soft words.

The world blurred. A heavyweight, like someone dropping a bag of bricks, settled on the occupants. The cheese started to glow brightly, forcing everybody to shield their eyes.

After a few seconds, the effects faded. Blinking out spots from their eyes, the occupants of the room reassessed the situation. The cheese and wine were gone, and in their place was a young human on his back. He had a sorry excuse for brown hair, green eyes, and a face only a mother could love, or a severely drunk person.

"Assistant?" Professor Darius clambered to his feet. "Status?"

"Alive," Mark announced, dusting himself down. "For once."

Darius said nothing. Lifting his hands and murmuring soft words under his breath, he let loose a torrent of life-force. The faint blue line passed through the young man like he was not even there.

Huh, the professor thought, that was not supposed to happen. He tried again. Same result.

"No life force to bounce back from," Darius muttered. "How strange, it does not look un-dead or artificial to me." He began quickly typing behind his terminal. "Mark! Scan please!"

Mark picked up a remote from a table next to him and pressed a button. A transparent panel lowered from the ceiling, outside the pentagram. The panel blinked twice, and a detailed diagram of the human appeared on the panel. No trace of Nanomachines. Strange.

The brown-haired young man looked curiously at the diagram displaying him and pointed at it, then at himself, nodded, and let a slow grin spread across his face. Mark nodded encouragingly. He turned to the assistant and opened his mouth. Gibberish came out. He tried again. Still nonsense.

"Translator," Darius instructed.

Mark pressed another button. A floating tray lowered from the ceiling. It had two amulets and two white pills on it. The professor snapped his claw, catching everyone's attention in the room.

"This," he said in a calm voice, picking up one of the amulets. "Will let you talk to me." He put the charm on. It pulsed once.

A video appeared on the panel, explaining the same thing with a realistic rendering of Darius and the young human wearing the amulet and then nodding in understanding. The tray floated to the young man, and he took a good look at it. He picked up the talisman, looked at it intensely, and then put it on. There was no pulse.

He tried speaking again, but it was still gibberish. The tray floated back to Darius. He picked up the white pill.

"This contains Nanomachines," Darius explained. "They will nestle into your ear and translate all known languages into your brain." He snorted the pill, his nose making a suction sound.

On the panel, a video began playing, showing the path of the small machines taking their journey through the nose, up to the brain, and finally settling in the ear. The tray flew back, and the young man picked up the pill, licked it, and with some difficulty, put it in his nose and snorted. He gave his nose a few whacks, just to make sure.

"Can you understand me now?" asked Darius.

"Yes!" the young man said. "Thank you." His cheerful attitude clashed horribly with a voice that belonged to a man who spent too much time smoking and drinking in shady bars. It was jarring.

"I'm Professor Darius Dovan, and the fellow with the pink hair is my assistant, Mark. What's your name?"

"Me?" The brown-haired man blinked. "A name?" He looked questioningly at his own hands for a few seconds and then said slowly. "Call me, Curiosity?"

The occupants of the room blinked. Was that a question?

"Curiosity, then." Darius just rolled with it. "My apologies for any inconvenience my summoning ritual has caused." It's best to be polite when summoning something unknown.

"No, no," the young man waved the apology away. "I should thank you. You gave me the perfect opportunity to escape."

"Escape?" Mark asked.

"Oh, yes," he beamed. "It's rare that there is such a high concentration of my energy in one place."

"Your energy?"

"Curiosity, of course." He started bouncing on the balls of his feet.

"Curiosity?"

"Ah, a spirit then," Darius guessed.

"A spirit?" The young man furrowed his brow. "No," he waved off the idea. "I'm not a spirit. I'm curiosity itself." With that, he stepped out of the pentagram.

The scientist and assistant froze. Turrets extended from

the ceiling. A countdown began on the panel. Once it reached zero, it would plunge this room and all of its inhabitants into a subspace, with no chance to escape.

"I have not made a contract," Darius said, stepping away from his terminal. Nobody, not even a god, could step out of a pentagram. He was sure of it; he had summoned gods before. He quickly put the pieces together.

"You were not what we were supposed to summon." He raised his claw in, preparing to shoot Curiosity full of lasers if necessary.

"Yep." The young man smiled as gently as his face would allow it. He slowly lifted his hands, keeping his head up. "From my understanding, this is a universal gesture of surrender." He lowered himself to his knees. "I'm no threat."

"What do you want?" Darius eased down but did not relax.

"I just want to live," Curiosity said. "To exist. To experience life. I just started existing a few seconds ago, cut me a bit of slack."

"Why did you hijack the ritual then?"

"I had no choice; Reality would have crushed me. This was my only chance of escape."

"Why?"

"I'm not supposed to exist, you know. Reality does not like things that are not supposed to, you know, exist."

"Why this ritual?" Darius gestured to Curiosity to stand up.

"There was a high concentration of my energy here." Curiosity was grateful to stand up. His muscles were starting to get sore. He was not sure he liked sore muscles.

"Energy?"

"You know," he shrugged helplessly. "Curiosity," He

was not sure how to explain it. "If someone is curious about something, I know."

"What does that have to do with this experiment?"

"You experimented out of curiosity, right?"

"It was in the name of science."

"If that's what you wanna call your curiosity then sure." Curiosity itself took a deep breath and then said, "Well, there you have it. The more energy I have in one place, the easier it is for me to twist reality a bit."

"Twist reality?" Mark said. "Like twisting the fabric of space and time? You can do that without drugs?"

Curiosity shrugged. Darius decided to let it go. He will keep an eye on him, but if he could twist reality, then maybe... Well, let's see and wait.

"Well then, if you mean us no harm, then I welcome you on our planet." The professor extended a hand. "Are you familiar with the handshake? It's considered a gesture of goodwill and friendship."

"Yes," Curiosity said.

They shook hands.

"Would you like to rest?" Darius asked. "I have a spare room where you could sleep."

"Oh, yes."

"Curiosity?"

"Yes."

"You can let go of my hand now."

"Oh, yes."

He did not let go. Darius took him upstairs, still holding hands.

Sleeping was strange, Curiosity thought, getting up from the bed.

The brown-haired young man did not want to sleep,

but he understood the necessity of it. He tried to take care of his body, and sleep is essential, at least that's what he gathered from what the guy with an arm coming out of his back. And Steve's memories. He felt pain from his stomach, and he panicked. Is his body sick? Is he dying? A knock on the bedroom door distracted him.

"Are you awake?" Darius' flat voice came from the other side of the door.

"Yes."

"Get dressed and come to breakfast."

Breakfast. Food. You need to eat for your body to stay healthy and stable. Now he understood where the grumble was coming from. It's the way human bodies signal for sustenance. Interesting. He was curious about what food tastes like.

"Coming."

Curiosity remembered yesterday's lecture about modesty and clothes, and he spotted some clothes neatly folded on the chair near the bed. You know, the chair, which every bedroom has, where clothes always get stacked on it mysteriously. He put on a pair of brown jeans, a red t-shirt, and a vest with many pockets. He found a pair of black shoes under the chair.

He left the room afterwards, entering a living room partially transformed into a kitchen. Darius, dressed in blue jeans and a clean lab coat, was preparing breakfast. His claw was zipping about, putting platters of cheese, toast, bacon, eggs, something that looked like broccoli but purple and beans.

"Sit down." The claw grabbed one of the chairs and pulled it back. "Breakfast will be ready in a minute."

Curiosity sat down, picking up a fork, and examining it closely. He was just about to lick the fork in his hand when the claw appeared in front of his face, made a snapping motion, then quickly put a cup, a bottle of milk, and a gallon of orange juice on the table.

Ahhh, a drink. He picked up the milk first, and halfway through pouring it in his glass, he stopped, put the milk back down, and picked up the orange juice. He was interested in seeing what would happen if he drank both from the same cup. Before he could mix them, Darius' claw came out of nowhere and snatched the juice from his hand.

"Please don't mix drinks," Darius said. "At least not yet. See how you like it separately and how your body reacts to it."

"Reacts to it?"

"You are from a different plane of existence; we don't know how food reacts to yours. My test shows that it should be compatible, but you can never be too careful, take it slow, please."

"Ok."

Slowly, carefully, Curiosity began pouring milk into his glass. When it was halfway, he stopped, took a sip, and let out a satisfied sigh.

"I'm curious," he said.

Darius was not prepared for the sudden shift in gravity, and he almost fell carrying the last piece of breakfast to the table. Salad. The professor opened his mouth to protest but quickly closed it again. From the bottle of milk, orange juice was pouring out.

"I'm not sure if I should be sick or fascinated," Darius said. "How are you doing that? Are you really twisting reality to make milk into orange juice? Seems such a waste of power." He let out a sigh. "Never mind about that, food first. "The professor sat down. "Now, I'm gonna show you how to use utensils."

"Why?" Curiosity said, dipping the fork in the juice and then licking it.

"Just watch, please."

Thankfully, it was not hard. After a demonstration, Curiosity was natural. Between the two of them, all the food disappeared in seconds. Darius did not need to eat that much, but it was always a treat when he could. He still had his taste buds.

"May I ask a question?" the professor asked, his claw cleaning up the table.

"Sure," Curiosity said. "Thank you for the food."

"You are most welcome." Darius leaned forward. "I don't understand something. If you started existing yesterday, how come you know how to use utensils?"

"Pardon?"

"You see," the doctor began, snaking his hands together. "You are acting precisely on how a young human male should. You have years of integrated reflexes, the right facial expression, you catch on quickly, and you don't seem to be too confused about the things I put in front of you, like the fork and cup."

"Ah." Curiosity's eyes lit up in understanding. "I get it. Well, I got given this body. I'm using its brain's memories as a basis for my personality."

"Given to you?" His claw searched for a tablet to write notes on. "Memories?"

"Yes, Yes. You know how someone gets possessed?"

"Possession can only happen for a short while, and the host dies afterwards. Mythology indicates it may be possible for permanent possession of the body and soul if it's willingly."

"That's exactly what happened," Curiosity tapped his head. "I have access to all the memories, feelings, and reflexes of the man who gave his existence to me."

"You had a basic consciousness, like an elemental, only being able to think of ideas that other people had." Darius's eyes were sparkling. "Having access to a man's memories and a body lets you build up a personality base." He finally found a tablet. "What I'm not sold on, is your claim of being the idea of curiosity itself."

"I can prove it," Curiosity grinned. "You are curious about the concept of using memories as a personality template."

"Well, yes," Darius admitted. "But it's not possible, it's just an idea. Wait…" He narrowed his eyes. "How did you read my mind? Most of it it's metal, you should not be able to do it."

"I don't read minds," he laughed. "I know everything was thought in my name, in the name of Curiosity." He opened his arms wide. "Curiosity is an idea, a drive, a primordial force. It's everywhere, in every person, in every living being, in nature, gods, demons, and the universe. It was there since the beginning, and it will be there at the end. Think of it as my essence, my energy. I'm just a combination of consciousness and memories, reflexes, and emotions of the man named Steve. I can still connect and see the rest of my essence, making me more than just a human."

"You see the energy in the air?"

"I don't know how to explain," he shrugged. "I don't see or feel anything, it's part of me, like your claw."

"I think I understand," said Darius, nodding slowly. "Can I have a sample of your blood?"

"No." Curiosity was sure giving blood away was not a good idea. From what he understood, organics needed that stuff. "But I can make your idea happen."

"Pardon?" Darius blinked. "Using memories as a template? Your memories?"

"Yes. Just find me a body, and I can take care of the rest."

"How?"

"You will see. It won't be dangerous for anyone involved, I promise."

"Alright," Darius was not sure it was a good idea to let this entity try his power, but the idea of using memories as a personality template, well, it was too tempting to pass up. Besides, if this could really work, then maybe, finally, he could fulfil his promise to her.

A small knock at the door stole their attention.

"Enter," Darius said, and the door opened, revealing a female demon standing there.

Now, when someone mentions a female demon, the first thing that pops into the mind is a sexy, scantily clad succubus. This one barely fit that category. She was red skinned, with long curving horns, and could be called sexy, if you don't mind partners that could snap you in half during intercourse. Sadly, she was not scantily clad either, having everyday blue jeans and a black shirt on her muscular frame.

"Welcome," Darius greeted politely. "I'm glad you came."

"Well," the demoness purred in a low, reverberating tone. "You just summoned a god. I can't refuse, can I?"

"Where?" Curiosity began looking around. "I didn't know you had a god here. What does a god look like anyway?"

Darius and the demoness gave him flat looks.

"What?" he said. "Is this one of those times when people point out that their friends have something on their face?"

"How do you even know about that?" Darius sighed.

"Never mind, Hidara here," the demoness waved, "will show you around the place."

"Ooh." Curiosity was next to the door. "Tour! Tour! Tour!"

"Someone's excited." Hidara grabbed the young man by the collar. "Come on handsome, I promise you I will show you a good time."

"Don't forget to bring him back in two hours," Darius said, face buried in his tablet. "We are going to test his abilities."

"Will do!"

The suite exited onto a long balcony, overlooking the laboratory. Mark, hair a fiery red, was hard at work scrubbing away with a brush at the remains of the summoning circle. Turning to the left, Hidara directed Curiosity to a winding staircase that led them to the bottom floor, in front of a grey metal door.

Pushing gently, they exited into the afternoon sun.

"Welcome to Darius laboratory," Hidara said, opening her arms wide. "Or Tiny's left hand, as most people call it."

Curiosity stared wide-eyed and open-mouthed. Calling the place in front of him tiny was misleading. They were standing on a giant metal finger, easily able to fit the Doctors laboratory.

"That's the university in the distance right there." Hidara pointed. "But I'm not sure if that's true though, we barely have 100 students and two professors. Three, if you count Rip's lectures about brewing alcohol, which I don't."

The giant finger they were standing on was actually a thumb, attached to an equally massive palm. The palm came with the standard 5 finger setup, including an arm that disappeared into the horizon.

"The index finger holds the medical wing," Hidara said. "On the middle finger are the dorms and the professors houses, the ring finger is a commercial district of sorts, and the last one hosts Rip's, while in the middle of the palm is the actual university."

"This is amazing!" Curiosity's jaw was on the floor. "How did this happen? I mean a giant finger? What are we on? A giant robot or something?"

"Yes." Hidara smiled and grabbed Curiosity by the arm. "Around 30 years ago Zed and Darius and a bunch of other assorted criminals -"

"Criminals!" Curiosity interrupted, face ashen. "Wait, you mean to tell me we are the bad guys?"

"No, no," Hidara waved a hand. "Criminals by the standards of other countries, we like to call ourselves freedom fighters and people with questionable morals."

"Ah. Isn't that the definition of criminals?"

"As I was saying," Hidara powered on. "These people, around 1000, were seeking refuge from the injustices of the world, so they asked Tiny if they could live on him. He agreed."

"Who's Tiny?"

"Look behind the university building, in the distance."

Curiosity did. He grabbed his jaw with both hands, just in case, it fell.

In the distance, he could see a metal arm, extending upwards, disappearing into the clouds. Following it with its eyes, he realised it was connected to what looked like a giant metal shoulder, and if he squinted hard enough, he could see the vague outline of a head.

"So we are on a giant robot," Curiosity whispered. "I have so many questions I don't even know where to start."

"Let me answer some of them," Hidara said. "Though you won't be satisfied with the answers. Tiny is a wandering robot. Nobody is sure who made it and why is he here, and he won't tell us."

"That's it?"

"That's it, sadly," Hidara sighted. "We don't even know why he accepted people living on him in the first place. A bit of an annoying bastard actually."

Curiosity fell silent and let Hidara guilder him by the arm. Living on a giant robot, huh? That's not something you see every day. Curiosity wondered if people falling off was a problem here. What about when the robot moved? Where did they do it? Inside it? So many questions.

In short order, they reached the university. A few people were mingling about, some tall, short, blue skin, pointy ears, wings, and some with an extra appendage or metal parts. A shape detached from the stream of students. It was a small, pixie-like creature in a lab coat, floating gently towards the pair.

"Marie!" Hidara greeted, letting go of Curiosity and running forwards. "What are you doing here?" She grabbed Marie with both hands and pressed her against her chest. "Long time no see! Are you not supposed to be in class or something?"

"Hidara!" Marie gasped, in a low, musical tone. "Let me go, I can't breathe!"

"Sorry," Hidara let go. "Always forget how fragile you pixies are."

"Thank you." Marie let out a deep breath. "Now what are you doing here? I thought Professor Darius called you in for something?"

"I'm showing Curiosity around."

Hidara got a blank lock from the pixie.

"You know," Hidara said, gesturing backwards. "Professor Darius's latest experiment. I sent you a message about it."

"Where is he then?"

"What?" Hidara turned around. "He is just over here…"

Curiosity was gone.

Curiosity was walking vertically up the giant robot's arm. Here, he could see more of the robot's form. Tiny was seated, knees raised, with a bunch of tents set up under them. People were zipping about on flying discs, carrying cargo and other passengers up and down, disappearing and appearing behind a mountain the giant was leaning against.

This was everything Curiosity had hoped for. Before, he could only sense curiosity. Not this, colours, sound, smells, sights, sensations. It was amazing. He breathed the fresh air in. It tasted slightly of metal, sweat, and dampness. He felt alive.

Sadly, it will only be a matter of time before one or two gods or such catch a whiff of his presence. Or reality does something about his appearance. Whichever comes first.

The ritual he hijacked was supposed to summon an eldritch horror, and once eldritch horrors got involved, well, things turned towards the strange. And bloody. And let's not forget the mountain of corpses.

But he will be prepared. He has an advantage, one that he is just barely starting to understand. The body he now occupies does not only contain the memories of Steve, which is more extensive than he imagined but the whole biological history of a race. Everything that's encoded in the DNA is his to peruse, and because of this, he knows what to do.

Homo sapiens were quite weak and laughable species by universe standards. No magic, no extra limbs, spikes, wings, nothing. They don't even glow in the dark, not the most exciting species, Curiosity decided. But they had something most species disregarded and did not pay much attention to. Cooperation.

When humans did not know how to solve something, needed help, or protection, they went to other humans. With the power of cooperation, coffee, and a lot of swearing, they built civilisations and empires, in a world with no shortcuts. Or, as humans like to call it, the power of friendship.

Curiosity looked upwards towards the giant metal head, now only a few hundred meters away. He may have the first candidate.

Curiosity arrived at the giant's shoulder. There was neither building nor a tent on it, just a grey metal with odds and bits sticking out in random directions. The neck was small, more of a disk really, with a vast square that slowly turned around, metal squeaking and groaning with the effort. Two black orbs, eyes fixed upon Curiosity. The mouth, jagged metal bits crisscrossing in a random direction, slowly opened.

An old fridge rolled out on wheels, a tiny speaker on top. It rolled slowly, gears creaking, stopping in front of Curiosity.

"Hi!" The young man bounded up in front of the fridge and squatted down in front of it. "I'm Curiosity." He extended a hand.

Refrigerators don't have hands, so he was left hanging. It was a bit disappointing.

"Greetings." A deep, booming voice emanated from the speaker on the fridge. "I know who you are. Why do you seek me out?"

"To the point, I see," Curiosity beamed. "Alright. You are Tiny, I presume?"

"Yes," the voice said.

"Why are you a fridge?" He poked the fridge to see if he could open it. But he could not find a door.

"I am not a refrigerator," said the item, rolling out of the way of the poking. "It's easier to converse with organics in this form."

The young human nodded in understanding. "I came here to make an offer. Do you know what I am?"

"I am aware of everything that's happening to me. I know what you claim to be."

"Do you believe it?"

"Yes."

"That was quick." Curiosity stood up. "Alright, I need a bodyguard. Someone to protect me."

"No."

"No?" Curiosity raised an eyebrow. "What do you mean, no? You haven't even heard what I'm willing to offer in return for your protection."

"No. "The fridge tilted upwards as if to glare. "Do I need to say it in other languages? There is a total of 2 345 531 languages in my database, it could take a while."

"You didn't even hear my reasoning."

"I did. You hijacked a ritual meant for someone else, and now you are looking to get allies to surround you so when the entities you pissed off inevitably come for your miserable excuse of a life form, you will have a chance of survival."

"That's it!" Curiosity bounced up and down. "How do you know that?"

"I already mentioned it, I know everything that happens to me."

"Right." Curiosity plopped down on his butt. "Is there nothing I can do to convince you otherwise?"

"No."

"Not even access to a species internet located on

another planet which is located in a totally different reality, with different rules of physics and stuff?"

Tiny was silent for a long moment.

"What?" the fringe finally said.

"This may change your mind." Curiosity, smiling like a loon, pulled out Steve's phone from his pockets. He presented it. "Scan it."

"Place it on my top."

Curiosity did. The lights on Tiny's speaker went out.

"Imagine," Curiosity said. "Access all the recorded information of a whole civilisation, from history to TV shows, from psychology to porn. More than 3000 years' worth of information, brand new and there, without all the hassle of actually sitting down and waiting for them to do something."

"How?" Tiny was jolted from his scanning. "How do you know I like to sit down and watch civilization unfold?"

"I told you, didn't I?" Curiosity smiled. "I am Curiosity itself. You sat down to watch people because you were curious about organic life and how it functions. You even let people live on you out of sheer curiosity."

"Yes," Tiny said. "You may actually be what you claim."

"See? It does not matter if you are man, machine, or elder god. If you are curious about something, I know."

"I still won't accept your proposal," Tiny declared firmly. "I will not be chained by human whims."

"I am not a human."

"I disagree. You look like a human, you talk like a human, you walk like a human, even your biochemistry is exactly the same as a human, ergo, you are a human."

"Point."

Curiosity fell silent for a long moment. His plan was foiled. What now? There is nothing in Steve's memories that could help with this situation. Out of pure reflex, he dipped his hands into his pocket and pulled out a packet of cigarettes. Opening the top and flicking his wrist, he let a stick fly upwards, deftly catching it in his mouth.

"Huh." Curiosity pulled out a lighter. "I didn't know I could do that."

He let the smoke fill his lungs while he sat there for a few minutes. He watched as the fridge, no Tiny, just stood there silently, not moving, nor saying anything. Guess the robot was waiting for him to do something.

Oh well, time to find different people then. Darius mentioned something about a pub, maybe he can find someone there to help him. Clambering to his feet, Curiosity bent forward, intent on taking back his phone. Before he could touch it, however, Tiny rolled back on squeaky legs.

Curiosity took a step forward and tried again. Tiny rolled to the side. He tried again. The fridge moved out of the way again. Curiosity was not deterred. He tried again. Tiny rolled out of the way. This went on for about four more times until Curiosity was panting from exhaustion.

"Give my phone back," Curiosity panted.

"You need to do some serious exercising," Tiny said. "A body your age should not run out of steam so quickly."

"Noted." Curiosity sat down again, taking deep breaths. After a few seconds, he continued. "Now, can I have my phone back? I need to go find a bodyguard."

"Is there nothing else you want?" Was that desperation in the fridge's voice? Curiosity was not sure. "Information in this device is too valuable to let it fall into anybody's hands."

"Right, it has nothing to do with the fact that you have access to millions of terabits of porn?" Curiosity smiled wickedly.

"Actually, there is so much porn on earth's internet, and so much new content being generated each second, I am having trouble calculating it."

"Wow." Curiosity was silent for a second. "That much? Can't you give me an estimate or something?"

"Around 95 000 terabytes of porn. Per website. There are 19 234 pornography websites, and a new one is created each second."

"Wow. That is a lot of porn."

"Yes. It's ten times more than the footage I collected in my three millennia of existence."

"You collect porn?" Curiosity leaned forward. "I was not expecting that from a robot."

"I collect a lot of things," Tiny said proudly. "I have a collection of books, music, movies, lost technology, poetry, art, anything that can be digitised and stored on a hard drive. And 80% of it is from extinct civilisations."

"Wow." Curiosity felt that he should say something more than wow. "That's a lot of information."

"Yes." The fridge straightened a bit. "That's why I asked if there is anything else you might be interested in exchanging for the phone. I have a lot of ancient texts at my disposal."

"Hmm." Curiosity lit a cigar. "There is one thing…"

[2]
STACY

Darius thought if he should install another claw on his back. One claw is usually enough, but there is so much research to be done, he may need an extra hand.

"Darius."

He is already using all three of his hands, but it's not enough. Will his mind support another extra limb?

"Darius, are you listening?"

Maybe he should install a hand capable of forming a fist.

"Darius, this is serious, don't ignore me."

Or maybe a saw.

"Darius," Zed sighed, pinching the bridge of his nose. "Please pay attention."

If you could summarise Zed Nez in two words, it would be scar tissue. He was a tall man, dressed in a green robe and sandals. Not an ounce of hair on him, eyebrows included. His whole body and head were crisscrossed with scar lines that were pulsing a dull yellow.

"Darius," Zed said, exhausted. "We talked about this;

you can't just let an entity of unknown power and ability roam the place without any serious supervision. Again."

Darius ignored him.

"Now," Zed continued. "You want to test his powers. On her of all people."

Darius continued to ignore him, shoulders hunched. Zed's scars started to glow a bit brighter.

"Now," he said, his voice sharper. "I understand what you want to do, but you can't just do that." His scars were turning red. "You have no right, not to her."

"I have every right!" Darius snapped, turning around in rage. The only thing keeping him from lunging at his friends was his claw, embedding itself in one of the computers. Again.

"Her brain is toast!!" Zed's scars blazed an angry red, and he took a step forward. "Let. Her. Go!" All of the anger seemed to dissipate from him. "Let her go." He let out a sigh. "Please."

The wind got taken out from Darius too, and he slumped back on his computers, his third hand letting go of the bent metal, gently laying itself on his head.

The far door to the lab smashed open, and a red Hidara entered. Well, redder than usual. When she spotted the two men slumped in despair and one of Darius computers mangled beyond repair, fear flashed in her eyes. She forced herself forward anyway. This was important.

"Curiosity is gone." Hidara said.

Zed gave Darius his best I told you so glare, but the man was too emotionally exhausted to respond.

"How?" Zed said.

"Lost him at the university. I stopped to chat for a second, and when I turned around, he was gone."

She took a step back when she saw the glare professor Zed gave her. Zed was not a man you upset. He taught hand to hand combat, sports, and body manipulation. His glasses were legendary, and coupled with his temper; she was justified in her automatic action. Thankfully, his scars were dull. She was safe for the moment.

"I looked for him." Hidara put her hands up in a placating gesture. "I really did. For an hour."

"Why did you not call?" Darius said, composing himself.

"Umm…" The demoness hid her face behind her arms. "I forgot? Look, phones don't exist in the demonic realms. I'm still getting used to them."

Zed pinched the bridge of his nose and let out a deep breath.

"Give me a hand here, Zed," Darius said, seeing that this computer needed replacing. Again. Maybe giving himself another claw would not be a bad idea.

The bald man just went over to the doctor, bent down, and with one mighty pull, he ripped the station from the floor. Wordlessly, he went outside.

Tiny had dumpsters specially prepared for electronic equipment that he broke down and repurposed for himself for the betterment of the city. It was an unspoken agreement between the citizens and Tiny to give him any technological item they don't need anymore.

He almost dropped the destroyed terminal in his hands when a small tremor shook the large hand he was standing on. He quickly corrected his footing,

Tiny is excited, the bald man thought. When the giant robot found something or someone interesting, his whole body shook. It was always in a small amount, and it was just one of those things you get used to after living on him for a while.

Darius and Hidara, who got roped into it, spent the next hour installing a new terminal for the professor. Zed, meanwhile, went to look for Curiosity, a picture of the man on his tablet.

At the bottom of the fingers, where a stack of the flying disk was located. Zed pressed his tablet to a terminal next to it. One of them detached, gently hovering in front of him. He stepped on it.

After thirty minutes of flying around Tiny's knees and backside, he saw a strange sight. A young man was walking vertically down Tiny's colossal arm. He changed directions.

The bald professor stopped near the young man, who stopped in turn, peering at him with faint puzzlement and awe.

"You must be Curiosity," Zed said, inclining his head.

"Yes." The young man smiled, and with a side twist, jumped on the platform, ignoring universal gravitational laws. "I'm Curiosity."

"Zed Nez." The two shook hands.

"So, Zed," Curiosity began, peering down from the edge of the disk. "Why are your scars glowing?"

"You know," Zed said, pinching the bridge of his nose, "it's considered rude to ask someone a personal question out of the blue."

"Isn't a personal question something like, like personal?" Curiosity brow wrinkled in concentration. "I wouldn't think why you are glowing in the dark as being a personal question. Or is it?"

He just started existing yesterday, Zed told himself, and he has no idea about social custom. No need to grab the back of his head and smash a knee in his nose.

"If you must know," the professor said, letting out a sigh. "I did these scars myself."

"Oh?" Curiosity gave the professor his undivided attention.

Zed sighed again. Might as well.

"I grew up near Asmodeus." Zed's scars pulled for a second. "He was using slave labour to mine power crystals." He took a deep breath. "Ten years I was there, watching as my friends and family died one by one. Each death was different. Exhaustion, starvation, lack of hygiene, of sleep, the crack of the whip, or the most popular reason, trying to escape."

"So how did you escape?" Curiosity's eyes were sparkling. "What did you do?"

"Well…" Zed's eyes got that faraway look that people had when they are reminiscing on the past. "I ground a few of these crystals into dust, picked up a sharp rock, put a rag in my mouth, and cut deep gashes into my skin. Then I poured the dust into the fresh wound." His smile turned vicious. "Nobody could stop me after that."

Curiosity starred in open-mouthed wonder. He wanted to say something, but his instincts were screaming at him to shut up, this is the time to stare in awe. He was in the presence of a legend.

"Awesome," was all that came out.

The rest of the journey was spent in silence, silently gliding towards Darius's lab. Putting the disc back on its rack, they walked up to the laboratory. Darius was behind his screen, new terminal in place, and was furiously typing with all three of his arms. A new item has been bought in the middle of the lab.

It was a pod, grey and sleek, with screens and knobs attached to its side. Mark, messy hair a fiery red, was polishing the translucent dome on top of the pod. Hidara was nowhere in sight.

"Found him," Zed said, walking up to the pod, Curiosity following behind.

They looked down. If there was ever a textbook definition of sleeping beauty, this was it. The girl lying between soft velvet was beautiful. Long blonde hair framed a heart-shaped face, slightly tanned skin, occupying a tall and sinewy frame. She was dressed in a white lab coat, buttoned-up, a pink claw resting inactive next to her head. The only disconcerting thing about her was her dull blue eyes, open, staring into nothingness. There was no life in those orbs.

"I'm amazed that she's so healthy, even after all these years," Zed said, tone softening.

"Are you that surprised?" Darius glanced up from his typing. "Tiny helped us make that. The amount of medical technology at his disposal is ludicrous." The professor shook his head in amazement. "He does not even understand the amount of potential he has."

"Even so." Zed turned, looking his best friend in the eye. "I still don't understand why you did not let her rest Darius. Her mind is gone." His tone turned soft. "What are you doing with her?"

"Honouring her last request." The professor's lips turned up into a smile. "I'm giving her body to science."

The two men lapsed into silence, just in time to see Mark swatting Curiosity hands away from the glass. Seeing the two men staring at him intensely, Curiosity bounded over cheerfully, stopping in front of Darius.

"I'm ready when you are," he said.

"Are you gonna tell us the process?" Darius asked.

"I will be honest; I'm making it up as I go along."

"WHAT?" Zed's voice instantly rose. His scars started pulsing. "What do you mean by that?!"

"It's safe, it's safe," Curiosity put his hands up. "I swear."

"Let's just start," Darius sighed. "If he messes up we are gonna vaporise him," He chuckled darkly.

Curiosity gulped.

Darius stepped out of his terminal and walked in front of the pod. He took a second to compose himself. If this works, maybe, finally, the crushing loneliness and despair in his heart will abate a bit, even if the person waking up is totally different.

"So?" Curiosity began rummaging through his pockets. "Everybody ready?" He pulled out a packet of cigarettes.

"What are you gonna do with that?" Mark asked.

"Relax!" The young man waved one hand in a placating gesture, while with the other; he expertly pulled a cigarette out from the box. "It's part of the procedure."

"Procedure?" Zed narrowed his eyes. "I thought you were making this up as you go along."

The young man shrugged. At the professor's nod, Mark pressed a button on the side, lowering the glass dome. Curiosity, looking directly into Zed eyes, lit the cigarette. Slowly, not making any sudden movements, he dropped the smouldering stick to the blonde woman's lips.

Zed was preparing to protest, but Darius lifted a hand.

"Please," he said. "Let him continue." He nodded towards Curiosity. "Mark, raise her head, please."

Slowly, carefully, the cigarette was inserted between her lips. Thankfully, she was still breathing, the smoke getting shorter with each breath. Curiosity stepped back. Everyone's eyes were on sleeping beauty. Zed was opening his mouth to stop this foolishness when movement caught everybody's attention.

First, her eyes blinked a few times before closing. Then the twitching came; next, muscles not used in ages were waking up. Her claw was next, each metal finger closing and opening. After a few seconds, the claw rose, grabbing the cigarette by the base. The woman inhaled deeply.

Chest rising, half the cigarette turned into ash. She blew out a plume of smoke.

"Ahhh…" Her voice was soft, velvety, and pleasant. "Thanks, mate, I needed that." Blue eyes opened, sparkling with intelligence.

Steve was confused. She had no idea what was happening, but there was a cigarette in her mouth, so things could not be that bad. Taking one more drag of the stick, she looked around.

A bald man with scars all over his body was frowning at her in parental disapproval. A vomit green-haired bloke was munching on a chocolate bar and staring at her chest? Why would anyone stare at her breast? Is he gay? Question for later.

The next guy stared at her with such intensity; she took another drag of cigarette for comfort. He looked like a low budget doctor Doom. Was that a claw extending from his back? Oh, and there was another one, standing close by, grinning down at her like a loon. Wait.

Wait! Wait! Wait! She knows that face! It's the one staring at her every day from a mirror, except for the smile. There was a good reason she did not smile. Wait. Why is she thinking of herself as a she and not a he? God, her mind instantly hurt just thinking that. What the fuck.

"What the fuck is happening?" Her voice was different. "Where the fuck am I?"

"Don't you remember?" Herself, no, himself responded. "I've made sure to include all the memories to the point of transfer. You know soul transfer via a cigarette?"

Everything came rushing back at once. Mind inactive for seven years turned on all at once. The twins, the white light, every aspect of her being taken over by some kind of god, not being able to do anything just becomes a memory, and finally, the transfer in a woman's body.

She started to laugh. It started slow, coming from the stomach. It quickly spiralled out of control, however, turning into shaking and sobbing, with the claw still holding a lit cigarette shaking erratically.

"Mark!" Darius snapped. "Diagnosis!"

The professor acted instantly. Claw snapped out, wrapping around the pink one, steadying it. Mark began pressing buttons furiously on the side of the pod. Zed pushed Curiosity out of the way, scars pulsing erratically.

"All vitals in order," Mark said.

There was an audible sigh in the room.

Darius looked at his daughter, alive and laughing, and something twisted in his chest. No, this is not her daughter; he must not lie to himself. Zed just stared, getting worried by the second. The shaking was not stopping.

Curiosity knew what to do. In a smooth motion, he pulled out a cigarette from its box and flicked it with a thumb. Instantly, the pink claw untangled itself, and shot out at lightning speed, plucking the smoke out of the air. With an instinctive application of a laser shot, the blonde was puffing away.

Darius shot the young man a dirty look, but it was working. The shaking was dying down. A few more seconds, and it completely disappeared.

"So it actually happened," the blonde said. "This shit really happened."

"Yep," Curiosity grinned. "I am thankful for your generosity."

"What?" Mark was not keeping up with this. "You know each other? What?"

"Oh!" Curiosity's face lit up. "'Let me introduce Steve,"

He gestured towards the blonde woman. "My body's original inhabitant."

"What?"

"So, what happened?" Darius shot a sharp look at Curiosity then at the blonde. "Some kind of soul transfer?"

"Close," Curiosity nodded. "Homo sapiens have no soul so to speak, they are just a bunch of memories, biological data and DNA, so it was easy to just copy that and transfer that data to a new body."

"Fascinating." The doctor's metal arm quickly went to take notes. "Via a cigarette no less. Fascinating."

"I'm not Steve," the blonde said suddenly, fire in her eyes. "I'm a woman now, a new person. Can't be called fucking Steve. What kind of name is that for a woman?"

"A strange one," Mark nodded in agreement.

"What would you like to call yourself then?" Darius asked. "Do you have anything in mind?"

"Yes, I do," the woman said, testing her muscles. "Stacy."

Silence.

"Stacy?" Mark said, testing out the word.

"Yes, Stacy!" The blonde snapped. "Is there something wrong with Stacy?"

"It's a perfectly acceptable name," Darius said gently. "It's nice to meet you, Stacy. I'm Darius Dovan."

"Zed Nez," Zed said curtly, staring into space.

"Mark."

"The idea of curiosity itself, incarnated."

"Stacy," said the newly minted Stacy. "Just Stacy. Will figure out a family name later."

A pang flashed across Darius's eyes, but it quickly disappeared. Stacy swung her legs over the pod, and slowly, pushed herself out of it. Darius was beside her in an instant, a gentle hand on her shoulder, typing forgotten.

"Thanks." She took a few steps, steadying herself. "Where is the bathroom?"

"Over there." Mark pointed towards the back, where a door could be seen with a yellow sticker decrypting a toilet.

"Thanks," Stacy said.

"Mark," said Darius. "Go with her, she might need help."

"Excuse me, professor, but are you insane?" Mark said. "I'm a man, and she's a woman."

"I am going alone; thank you very much," Stacy said, already on the move.

"You might need help," the professor insisted. "Your muscles still need time to adapt. Mark, get Hidara."

"Nope." Her third arm waved dismissively. "Anyway, I'm not sure she wants to help me with this."

"With what?"

"Masturbating, of course." Her hands were on the door, and she turned her head around, a grin almost splitting her face in half. "I was always curious about how it feels for a woman."

She slammed the door behind her. Silence descended in the room.

"What have we done?" Zed whispered, staring into nothing.

Darius stiffly walked behind his terminal, not uttering a word. Mark pressed a few buttons on the pod, lifting in the air. Slowly, he began walking out of the laboratory. Before he exited, however, he turned around and asked, "So, should I call Hidara then? I'm pretty sure she would not be bothered by whatever Stacy is doing."

"Just go away," Zed said. "Don't say anything, just go."

Mark left.

"Is there another bathroom?" Curiosity asked, bouncing up and down.

"Upstairs," Darius said monotonously. "Why?"

"I wanna try masturbating too," came the cheerful reply. "I never understood carnal pleasure."

Darius glared. Zed pinched the bridge of his nose and let out a sigh.

"Upstairs," Darius repeated knives in his tone. "There is a bathroom in my flat."

"Cheers!"

After vigorous experimenting, Stacy left the bathroom. Her hair was dishevelled, her clothes rumpled, and her claw just finished adjusting her skirt. With a pleased smile on her face, she looked around. Only Darius was there, typing away.

"My assistant went for lunch," Darius said, not looking up. "And professor Zed went back to classes." His tone was professional, neutral and flat. "Curiosity is upstairs."

Stacy was not sure why she felt that his voice should be warmer, but she let it go. She barely knew the man. Heck, she did not understand a lot of things. Is she a man now in a woman's body? A woman with a man's memories? Transsexual? She had no clue. She was sure a mental breakdown would come eventually, but at the moment, she just wanted a cigarette.

"Hey mate," she began, walking toward Darius. "Do you have a smoke?"

Darius just stared at her, his face turning into a frown. "The tobacco in the product you call a cigarette is not healthy."

"Mate," Stacy huffed. "I asked for a smoke, not a lecture," She crossed her arms under her chest. "If you don't have any just say so."

"It's behind you on the table," he pointed with his claw.

Stacy turned around, her claw automatically extending, picking up the packet, and bringing it back.

"This thing," She pointed towards her claw, taking a cigarette and putting it in her mouth. "It's amazing." To illustrate her point, a small laser shot out and lit her stick.

"Don't call the hand a thing," Darius patted his claw affectionately. "It's a part of you, your third arm; your subconscious given physical form. It's connected directly to your spine and brain."

Stacy patted her claw.

"Some of our people," Darius continued. "Call it our soul given physical form, the true arm, a perfect symbiosis between machine and man."

"Our people?" Stacy let out a puff of smoke.

"Yes," He pointed to himself and then her. "We are from the same race, so to speak."

"We are not humans?"

"If you mean homo sapiens, then no. We are a branch of humans, called homo-machinus."

"Part machine?"

"Kind of." Darius stepped away from his terminal. "The legends are murky."

"Legends?"

Stacy was curious now. Her claw snapped out, grabbing a plastic chair next to the table and dragging it over. She sat down, letting out a relieved sigh. She had no idea that a big chest meant back pain.

"This was more than fifty thousand years ago, so nobody is sure on the exact details," Darius said. "Legends say a group of scientists were searching for enlightenment, and found it, in designing the true arm. Connecting directly to the person's subconscious, it represents their true self, the potential of every person to greatness."

The professor, hesitating, stopped a few feet in front of

Stacy. The blonde felt a pang in her chest. The pink claw snapped out, dragging another chair next to her.

"Sit," she stated, patting the chair. "I won't bite."

Darius hesitated for a second, and then sat down to the offered chair, looking up at the ceiling. A cigarette box was thrust in front of him. His first reaction was to push it away, but his traitorous third hand dipped into the open box and plucked a cigarette. With a twirl and a small laser application, the stick was in his mouth, and he was puffing.

It was horrific. Thankfully, his lungs were mechanical, so he should be fine. Stacy beamed, staying silent. Darius took another puff and continued.

"Technology is so ancient and so tied to our DNA that each one of us is born with it."

"How is that possible?" Stacy's eyes were wide. "Isn't it made of metal?"

"Yes." Darius' claw snapped out, grabbing the remote from the table. "We can eat metal." With that, he popped the remote in his mouth, and with a loud crunch, he bit it in half. "And batteries, tablets, and even electricity, up to 2500 volts."

His speech was not impeded one bit by the crunching of metal. With a flick of his wrist, he popped to another half and started chewing it.

"Your children will have the same ability," he said.

"Children?" Stacy whispered, choking on her cigarette, her face pale. Oh my god. No. No. She can birth children now? She quickly finished her cigarette and lit up another one. This is a problem to think for future Stacy. She instantly thought of a topic change.

"So I was your lover or something?" Stacy said.

It was now Darius' turn to choke on a cigarette, it almost went all the way down his throat before he spat it out quickly, his metal claw catching the flying projectile.

"No." The professor quickly composed himself. "My daughter."

"Oh."

An uncomfortable silence descended between the two, the only sound being the inhale and exhale of smoke. Stacy tried to find something desperately to say. She was starting to panic.

"Why her?" Stacy said a mad gleam in her eye. "Why not some bloke you find on the street?"

Darius lifted an arm, slowly inching towards Stacy's shoulder. At the last second, however, he dropped it.

"She tried to upload her brain into a robot," Darius said, staring into the distance. "She wanted to see if she could make an A.I of herself without destroying her brain. She wanted to create an extension to the true hand," He flicked the spent cigarette away. "Her brain got wiped in the process."

"Oh."

"Her memories, personality, everything got wiped out. Only a husk remained."

Stacy said nothing. What can you say to that?

"She knew the risk," The professor continued, smiling sadly. "Her last wish, if the experiment failed, was to use her body in the name of science."

"Oh."

"However, if you ever need help, let me know. You are your own person, of course, different from my daughter, I am aware of that, but it can't be easy, waking up as a new person in a totally different world. I assume you don't know who you are yet, so if you ever need to talk, I am here."

"Thanks."

The two lapsed into silence again, this time, into a comfortable one. Stacy offered Darius another cigarette. Hesitantly, he accepted. At least she did not need to figure this out on her own, even if she had no idea what to make of Darius' eagerness. Maybe he genuinely wanted to help, or he was just using her to fill the void his daughter left.

Who knows? Question for another day.

In a place where silly things like time and space didn't quite exist, slept a man with a newspaper on his face. Dressed in a cheap white t-shirt and blue jeans, with feet on the brown desk in front of him, the man, no entity, was snoozing peacefully.

There is a reason we call this person an entity and not a man, and the reason is simple. He didn't have a head. Where his neck should have begun, it was just black smoke, shapeless, purring outwards into the vague outline of a head.

Now, wait just a second, you might just ask, how can a man with no head have a newspaper on his face? Would it fall through his face? Well, that is a good question that I'm not sure how to answer.

For one, the newspaper on his face was not like any paper in the word, symbols and words kept appearing and repairing every second on it, in all the colours of the rainbow. Second, the entity didn't bother with silly things like physics and the rules of reality, and that's because the entity was Reality.

When you are your own boss, and a successful one at that, you give yourself as much money as you please.

Reality's office, if this place could be called that, looked something like a maze filled with shelves. They stretched upwards into infinity, disappearing into the smoky ceiling. Some of them were bent and twisted, and the ones that occupied more than three dimensions, well, you went insane just looking at them.

It didn't help that each shelf was not filled with a book, but a computer. Most of them were fancy monitors with even fancier cases next to them, but some of them were old, dusty, and there were also some laptops scattered here and there.

It was a miracle Reality could sleep with all the clanking and beeping they made. Not for long, though. A few seconds later, a monitor dropped from the infinite ceiling directly into Reality's desk, making a thud and cracking the desk.

Before the entity had time to react, the computer let out a shrill, high pitched noise that permeated the whole room and vibrated the bones in your body.

"Ah!" Reality sat up instantly. "What is happening?" His oily, powerful and slightly smoky voice reverberated through the room, easily overpowering the computer's alarm.

"It's the alarm, boss," said a young and very, very, tired voice from somewhere far, far above. "You know the code Red? The one you said to notify you as soon as it happens?"

"Not by throwing it on my desk!" Reality snapped weakly.

The entity wanted to say more, but he knew he had no ground to stand. He was never good at precise instructions, and he did say to his assistant to notify him of a code red no matter what.

Pressing the mute button on the fallen computer, Reality let out a sigh of relief. He may not have ears, but it was still uncomfortable to have his whole body vibrate. Cheeking over the computer one more time, he began reading the alarm.

"I just don't understand," Reality began, still reading with his eyes. "On how you can just throw these computers around without any care in the world. You know there are not just any computers, but…"

"Whole universes, dimensions, and realities given form that makes their monitoring and diagnoses easy," came the tired reply. "I know, I know, you told me at least a million times."

"So why do you insist on treating them like toys! The damage you could have done to these worlds! Have you no understanding of scope and perspective?"

"Does it have any scratches or dents?"

"No, but that's not the point! It's the principle of the thing!"

"If any universe gets destroyed by a bit of jostling around, it did not deserve to live in the first place."

Reality wanted to say something in response, but his gaze got trapped by the text scrolling on the computer.

"So?" said the tired voice, now a bit closer. "What is this about?"

Glancing upwards, but not saying anything. Reality glimpsed the form of his descending assistant. The young man was sitting in one of those platforms window cleaners use, floating gently downwards, with no apparent ropes or tether. Stranding around him were screwdrivers, screws, drills, cutters and a myriad of other tools. A few broken computers were scattered about as well, their open case bathing the young man in a blue-greenish colour. In his hand, he was holding a phone, in his other arm a screwdriver.

He looked exactly like he sounded, even taking into consideration his youthful, almost teenage-like appearance. His face was gaunt and droopy, green eyes devoid of life and energy, green hair speckled with white and grey, and his simple workman uniform looked dirty and unkempt.

"So?" the assistant tried again. "What is it this time? A

group of scientists messing with the wrong thing? Prophecy went wrong? Eldritch horrors beyond the veil of space of time? Is it Cthulhu? I thought we dealt with that thing."

"No," Reality said, leaning back in his seat. "It's much worse."

"Don't tell me we have another chosen one who went ballistic," the assistant sighted. "I hate those bastards. So hard to get rid of."

"I wish." Reality wondered if smoking would look good on him. "Those ones are easy compared to this." Probably not, seeing as his face was made of smoke and all.

"Come on!" The assistant snapped tiredly. "Stop keeping me in suspense and tell me already!"

"It's one of your kind."

"What?" Instantly, all the tiredness disappeared from the young man, and he sat up a bit straighter. "You don't mean?"

"Yes, Coincidence, another idea grew so massive and powerful, it transcended space and time, it outgrew me." Reality let out a sight. "You have a brother now."

"Oh ohhhhhhhh!" The young man, now identified as the personification of Coincidence itself, intently jumped down from the still descending platform, hitting the floor with a dull thud.

"Which one, which one!" Coincidence said excitedly. "Is it anger? Love? No wait, let me guess, its lust isn't it? I told you E-12 will be trouble, they generate like ninety percent of all the porn in known existence."

"It's not lust." It was Reality's turn to sound tired. "It's something much worse."

"Worse than the personification of every sick thought in the universe?" Coincidence scratched his head in though. "It can't be death and destruction seeing as those things exist, hmmm, wait, wait, don't tell me it's communism or some kind of stupid ideology like that? How do we stop the personification of fascism itself?"

"It's curiosity."

"Curiosity?" Coincidence let out a relieved sigh. "Well then there is nothing to worry about, is it? A little curiosity never hurt anyone right?"

"He just transferred the soul of a man into the body of a woman."

"So? Weirder things are happening around the universe. Like that Nebun guy who thought it would be a good idea to fuse a hellhound with the mother of all cats. Now that's some freaky shit, and we never made a fuss about that."

"It was via a cigarette. He transferred a soul via cigarette."

"Oh," Coincidence was speechless. "So what do we do now?"

"We wait and see my dear assistant, we wait and see." Reality leaned forward. "In the meantime, bring me A-10. The body your brother stole originated from there."

"Really?" Coincidence said, impressed. "How did he do that? I thought we sealed that world from every magic or supernatural thing in existence. Heck, I am sure I put extra duct tape on it just to be safe."

"Just bring it please."

"On it!"

[3]
RUGHORN

Curiosity was zipping up his pants, finished with his own, ahem, experiments. It was interesting, but he was still not sure what all the fuss was about. Maybe if he did it with another person like in Steve's memories, he would get it? Who knows?

Exiting the flat, he saw Darius and Stacy chatting quietly in the middle of the lab. He squatted down, tensing his muscles, and in one smooth motion, jumped down from the railing.

Darius did not even twitch, but Stacy jumped up, instantly crouching in a defensive position, claw raised to strike.

"Gods." Stacy relaxed for a bit. "I don't know if I will ever get used to that."

"Used to what?" Curiosity smiled wide.

"Myself coming to me." Stacy plopped back down on the plastic chair. "You know, seeing the face staring back on a daily basis, well, not staring back. This is so confusing."

"You will get used to it," Darius assured her. "It usually takes a month or so to get acclimated to a major body change, at least that's how much it took me when I fused this mask to my face."

"What about a sex change, and I don't mean one of those where you get boobs and call it a day, like a total sex change. I'm pretty sure if Curiosity decided to do some mumbo jumbo on my old body and become a woman, it would not be a pretty blonde lady."

Darius shrugged.

"Are you sure?" Curiosity's eyes were sparkling now. "Why not? Is it because of my complexion? Hmmm. Shall we find out?"

Before Curiosity could do anything, the back door opened and Mark entered. His hair, a strange combination of red and blue, was moving around his head like a halo. Stopping a few feet away from Curiosity, he rummaged in his dirty lab coat and pulled out a tablet.

"Here," he said. "What Tiny promised."

"Ooh." Curiosity, last train of thought forgotten, eagerly picked up the tablet.

"What is it?" Stacy said, glad about the change of topic.

She was not prepared to see her old body get a gender change right in front of her. She was sure there was not enough alcohol in this world to wash that image away.

Darius, who was curious as well, just stood up and went next to Curiosity, peering over his shoulder.

"It's the book of companions," the professor breathed in. "The oldest book about summoning in existence. The copies were deemed so dangerous, and alien most civilisations burned them. It didn't help that nobody could understand the exact wording of the ritual, so it usually left a hole in space and time." Darius looked at his assistant. "Where did you get this?"

"Tiny gave it to me," Mark shrugged. "Said something about a deal with Curiosity."

"Tiny had this?" Darius' jaw began working slowly. "I didn't know that he had in possession tomes of such strength. Even if it's only a digital copy."

"Me neither."

"What's this book of companions?" Stacy asked, trying to keep up with the conversation. "What does it summon?"

"I can," Curiosity said suddenly.

"What?"

"You can what?" Darius said.

"I can read it." Curiosity pivoted on his foot coming face to face with Darius. "Will you help me do the ritual?"

Curiosity didn't know mechanical eyes could sparkle with so much emotion.

"Mark!" Darius snapped. "Prepare the chalk."

"Sure," Mark saluted and pulled out a piece of chalk from his pocket. "What kind of circle are we doing today? Pentagram? Octagram? Something new anteriorly?"

"That is an excellent question," Darius turned towards Curiosity. "Please tell us more about the summoning ritual and its reagents. Can't help you if we don't know what to do."

"Right," Curiosity smiled. "I need a knife, some strong alcohol, a packet of biscuits, and a human sacrifice."

"What just a second," Stacy said, instantly on her feet. "Human sacrifice? Ritual? What is happening here?"

"There is no need to panic," Darius said calmly. "It's just a routine ritual, nothing to be scared of."

"Scared of?" Stacy whirled on the professor. "Who said anything about being scared? I just don't like this idea of human sacrifice. Where are we? Some kind of Cthulhu dimension?"

"Human sacrifice is a perfectly acceptable method of summoning," Darius said defensively.

"What?!"

Curiosity may have just started existing as of yesterday, but something told him, probably 2 million years of male instincts, that if he did not do something now, Stacy would blow up.

The question was what to do. Wait, he may just have something.

"You can help us," Curiosity said, stepping forward. "With the ritual I mean. Then you can make sure we don't do anything you don't like."

"What?!" Stacy whirled around again." Why would I help you? And what's this about me not liking human sacrifice?! It's not about me not liking it, its human sacrifice for god's sake! Are you guys mad? It's not like anybody would volunteer!"

"I would." Mark lifted a hand.

"See!" Curiosity smiled gently and put his hands on Stacy's shoulder. "There is no need to worry, everything is under control. Now, do you wanna help us? I saw a bar at the end of this palm, I'm sure they will give you a few drinks under Darius' tab."

"They will?" The professor lifted an eyebrow.

"Sure they will," Curiosity began gently guiding Stacy outward. "Be careful of your footing though, I haven't seen the hand move yet, but you can never be careful with these things."

"What hand? What are you talking about?" Stacy said, not sure if she should protest or not.

"Didn't I tell you?" Curiosity said, opening the back door. "We are on a giant robot."

"WHAT?!"

Before Stacy could do anything more than gawk, Curiosity pushed her outside and closed the door.

"That should do it," he said, wiping his hands theatrically. "Now, back to business."

"How did you do that?" Mark said in awe. "That was like master level misdirection."

"Let me message Zed of her whereabouts," Darius said already on his tablet. "Then, we can start."

Stacy was not sure if she should be horrified, thankful, in awe, or all 3 of them at once. One on hand, Hah, she really was on a giant robot. On the other hand, the moment she entered the pub, a drink was placed in her hand, and she was shown to a table. By a fairy in a business suit of all things! Gods, this will take some getting used to.

The only reason she realised this dome-shaped building was a bar was the massive neon sign decorating the front saying: Rip's bar.

And what a place was it! High-quality mahogany tables were spread about in a pleasing pattern, chairs with velvety cushions around them, and each table had a floating rock in the middle.

That was not even the strangest thing in this place. Stacy was not sure what was strangest, the fact that there were tables and chairs on the wall and ceiling or the fact that people actually occupied them. Well, most of them were squid-like beings who used their tentacles to wrap around the wood, but still, somewhere humanoid figures who just stuck to the ceiling like it was nothing!

However, the bartender, Rip, well, it was probably the hardest thing to describe in this place.

Rip was a massive ... well massive. Nobody was sure what gender was a being made entirely of rock was, and

Rip did not care what people called him as long as it was not a pebble. You do not want to know what a 3-meter giant, made entirely of stone, could do to you if you called him a pebble. It was classified as suicide in at least five different civilisations. He had well-tailored bartender clothes on, making him look like a brick in a suit. He was cleaning a pristine glass.

Someone cleared their troth. It was like sandpaper dragging on rocks. Stacy instantly snapped to attention and focused on the figure in front of her. Right, she was not alone.

"So," Zed said, folding his hands in front of him. "What do you say to my proposition? Worth it no?"

"What?" Stacy said smartly.

Zed let out a sigh.

"You didn't listen to a word I said, did you?" he said.

"I'm not sure how to answer that question," Stacy said. "It seems to me like one of those grammar trap question thingies."

"It's not," Zed sighed. "Let me summarise, I am the ambassador of this small city of around a thousand, but I have no successor. I would like you to be my apprentice for a few years and get you ready to take over my post."

"No thanks." Stacy flagged down a passing waiter, a fairy in a business suit. "I don't even know you mate, slow down with the requests."

"You insolent…" Zed almost began cursing but caught himself last minute. "You're right, you're right." He let out a deep breath. "You are not Amanda, and I should not treat you as such."

"Darius's daughter?"

"Yes. Still, she always wanted to represent her people in a greater capacity than a scientist, she would have jumped at the opportunity to better the society."

"Well mate," Stacy interrupted, lighting a cigar. "I'm not Amanda, so you got to just deal with it. And we are not going down the route where Amanda's old friends constantly compare me to her to guilt-trip me into acting a certain way, so if I hear one more sentence about how Amanda was this virtuous and high achieving person and I'm just a useless bum…"

"I didn't say that," Zed quickly interrupted.

"You might as well!" Stacy slapped her hands on the table. "I'm not stupid, contrary to popular belief, I know what you were trying to do." Using her pick claw, she picked up an empty glass and held it in front of her menacingly. "So If I hear one more comparison to this dead lady," Zed twitched, "I'm gonna grab this glass and put it up your ass."

"Really?" The professor lifted a hairless brow. "You know I could beat you with both hands tied behind my back."

"So?" Stacy shrugged. "Do I look like a person who gives fucks?"

"No," Zed, let out a sigh." I guess you're not."

It took Darius and Mark less than fifteen minutes to set up the summoning circle and gather the reagents with Curiosity's guidance. The pattern was quite simple, a big, plain ring, with three smaller ones in the middle connected with a straight line.

Curiosity, standing in one of the outermost circles, was smiling like a loon while holding a cup of fizzy drink in his left hand and one of Darius' scalpels in the other.

"You know," the professor said, behind his terminal. "According to this text I translated, you need a cup of Altean firewater, the strongest drink in existence, I'm not sure if Tiny even has one, and one of the five sacred daggers of Yolk, the unhinged."

"The guy who would sacrifice gods in his name." Mark said, munching on a piece of cheese behind Darius. "That guy did some hardcore stuff."

"That's the one. While soda from Mark's personal stash may be aged and strong..."

"I take that as a compliment."

"And my scalpel is the highest quality metal available, I'm not sure they qualify as legendary items."

"It will be fine," Curiosity said animatedly, almost spilling the drink. "With a bit of twisting, Reality won't be able to tell the difference, don't worry about it."

"Alright." Part of Darius wanted to argue and demand more safety and research before undertaking such a dangerous ritual. "What about the human sacrifice part? According to the texts, it won't work without someone willingly sacrificing themself for it to work."

"Like I said, I'll do it."

All eyes turned towards the assistant.

"What?" Mark quickly swallowed the last piece of cheese. "Let's skip the part where you go but who will do it on such a short notice? No Mark, not you, you have so much to live, this is dangerous, are you sure about that, can't we find someone else? But we don't have much time, and such nonsense, alright?" He began moving forward.

"I have no complaints here," Curiosity said. "I won't say no to a free human sacrifice."

The assistant rummaged in his pocket for a bit and came up with a blue and red pill crackling slightly with electricity. Without breaking his stride, he popped it in his mouth. Instantly, his hair began crackling with a purplish light, and his eyes turned pure blue, iris and white disappearing.

"I'm not sure it's wise to perform such a dangerous ritual high out of your mind," Darius said, not moving a muscle.

"Just make sure you pay me extra, yeah?" Mark bounded to the circle, furthest away from Curiosity. "I may be in the eighth dimensions talking to the flying spaghetti monster about spinach but leaving this fleshly prison behind is a painful experience."

Darius said nothing, just pressed a few buttons on his terminal, then looked up at Curiosity.

"Ready?" asked the professor.

"Ready," Curiosity confirmed.

Mark nodded.

Curiosity did not need further encouragement. With a flick of the scalpel, he cut his palm. Placing the scalpel between his teeth, he held up his hand over the cup, letting a few drops fall into. He then stepped forward and gave the cup and scalpel to Mark.

"Now do the same thing," Curiosity said. "Then give it back to me."

"Chicken," Mark said, taking the items without incident.

Mirroring Curiosity's actions, the assistant quickly cut his palm and let a few droplets fall into the cup. Licking the wound a few times, he gave the cup and spatula back to Curiosity, who gently placed them down in the remaining circle between them.

"Won't Mark's blood affect the ritual?" Darius said, more to himself than anything else. "His blood is full of hallucinogen. Will we summon a demon tripping like hell? Would that even work? Judging by Hidara's standards, they are already tripping constantly."

"By the power of my blood," Curiosity began. "By the

power of this ritual and by my own power, the incarnation of the idea of curiosity itself, I summon thee!"

Orange light began emanating from Curiosity, tinting the air and spreading out in wages. It didn't go outside the big circle, but when it hit Mark, he began glowing too an orange-reddish colour.

"Mark!" Curiosity snapped, his voice distorted slightly. "Say that I accept."

"Chicken," Mark said.

"Good enough." Curiosity took a deep breath. "I present you the human sacrifice, the eye for an eye, the equivalent exchange, now come! I summon thee! Companion for life, a bodyguard of my soul and life, the offerings are ready!"

Orange light poured from Curiosity in rivulets, quickly filling the circle in such brightness, Darius needed to activate his night vision, but even then, he could not see anything.

"Chicken!" Mark screamed, the light pouring into him, peeling his skin away and making him expand.

A few seconds later, a loud pop was heard, and the light disappeared, along with Mark, bits and pieces of him scattered around the summoning circle like someone just smashed a jar of M&M's. In his place, standing in a pool of blood, was a figure.

"Hi," the figure said, tone high pitched and cheerful. "I'm Cherry Pop." She extended a hand. "Ex bounty hunter and your bodyguard. Nice to meetcha." The last part was said with a pop.

Curiosity blinked. He rubbed his eyes, squatted, and rubbed his eyes one more time.

"You are two inches tall," he said.

"Five point one centimetres to be specific," she

corrected, tone not wavering. "Is that a problem?" A dangerous glint entered her eyes.

"No," Curiosity quickly put his arm up in defence. "As long as you can protect me, size does not matter."

"Good." Cherry smiled triumphantly. "I'm the best marksman you will ever find, nobody will harm you with me around. Do you have the wine to complete the ritual?"

"Yes." He pointed towards the cup of soda between them.

Cherry wrinkled her nose.

"Did you infuse it with your blood?" she asked. "We need to imbue some alcohol with our blood then drink it."

"I did." Curiosity picked up the cup and took a sip.

"You are taking this surprisingly calmly," Darius piped in. "You have been just summoned in a strange place with some strange people, and you are just gonna complete the ritual, just like that, without asking who we are, what we want, you know, sane question. You do know this will bind your soul to him right, it's not something that people just usually jump for it."

"So?" Cherry turned and regaled the professor for the first time. "If you had a choice between spending one more bloody moment in that existence forsaken place and bonding your soul to a total stranger, you would choose the second."

"Witch plane of existence?" Darius claw began taking notes. "Is it a prison? Demon dimensions? Hell Circles?"

"Hey!" Curiosity snapped. "I haven't figured out how to drive a car yet, let's get a move on."

"Right!" Cherry instantly snapped to attention. "We don't wanna botch up this ritual and have him show up, that's the last thing we need."

With that, she grabbed the cup by the sides, jumped, and plunged her head in bloody soda.

Curiosity was horrified in a good way. The logical part of his brain told him that this was a bad idea; he should just call it quits and find someone who's a bit taller. On the other hand, he was dying to find out how Cherry would defeat his enemies. Would she bite them to death?

"This is good," Cherry said with a pop. "Tastes like soda."

"It's soda."

"Really?" Cherry lifted her head again. "How? It should not work with soda."

Curiosity shrugged.

Cherry looked like she wanted to ask something but decided against it. Quickly taking one more gulp from the cup, she looked up, and with lighting fast movement, bit her finger and let a few drops hit the soda.

"I, Cherry Pop, the greatest pocket bounty hunter in history, swear on my soul and life, to be your bodyguard, in thick and thin, for a year or so," she said, plunging back in.

And began drinking. And drank. And drank. Finally, after around two minutes of constant gurgling, she looked up.

"What did you do?" Cherry wiped her mouth with the back of her hands. "How come I could drink more than it is in the cup?"

"I twisted reality a bit," Curiosity's grinned. "Not that hard, actually."

"What!" Cherry looked shocked. "What? Reality? Really? How?"

"My turn!" He picked up the bottle cap, ignoring the question. "The idea of curiosity itself given flesh."

"What?" Cherry interrupted, wide-eyed. "The idea of Curiosity itself?"

"The idea of curiosity itself," Curiosity continued, glaring at her. "Given flesh and blood, accept your protection. I swear on my life and soul that I will cherish you and never mistreat you, for a year or longer." He drank deeply from the cap.

"What's this business about being the idea of curiosity itself?" Cherry asked sharply.

"Exactly as you heard," Curiosity put down the cup. "Now, let's finish this alright?"

"You are gonna explain to me what exactly you are later," Cherry warned. "Pick me up and put me in your hair. You need to get shirts with pockets so you can carry me there."

"I have a better idea," Curiosity said.

He extended his arm and Cherry jumped in the palm. Depositing the two-inch woman in his hair, he prepared himself.

"Mind if I grip your hair?" Cherry asked, trying to find a comfortable position. "So I don't fall off if we need to run."

"Sure." He touched his brown hair. "I'm curious."

His hair began to move on their own, expertly fashioning themselves into a chair under Cherry.

"My hair will catch you in case you are falling," he explained to the bewildered bodyguard. "And if you ever need something besides a chair fashioned from it, just keep your hand on it and think of what you want, and then say: I'm curious."

"Ok Boss." Alright, so maybe this partnership would be cool. Strange, but cool.

"That was surprisingly smooth," Darius said. "I was expecting some kind of explosion or problems to occur. I am pleasantly surprised."

"See," Curiosity grinned. "It was not that hard."

"Yea!" Cherry pumped her fist. "Now let's get out of here."

Before anybody could respond, black smoke began pouring in the place Mark and Cherry stood. As fast as it came, it coalesced, into a tall, shapeless figure. It, because it was hard to give a gender to a being that had black smoke for a head, stood sharply, dressed in an immaculate suit.

"Hello Curiosity," Reality said, voice reverberating through the room. "You're done and messed up."

"Shit!" Cherry began frantically searching in her skirt. "I hate botched rituals."

"There is no reason to panic," Curiosity quickly put a placating hand on his head. "He can't do anything to us, the ritual won't allow it!"

"You are correct about that." Reality took a slow look around, stopping briefly to stare at Darius. "However, I don't think you understand what you are doing here." His gaze snapped back to Curiosity. "You are not supposed to exist."

"Says who?" Curiosity bared his teeth. "What are you? The ultimate arbiter of life and death? You have no right to decide what's supposed to exist and what not."

"You don't get it," Reality sighted. "It's not that I'm against you living, it's that you are not supposed to exist, at all. See, you are not a person, a being, or even a robot, you are an idea, a dangerous one, that grew past the limits of reality. Your mere presence here is a violation of well, everything. Every movement you make, every breath you take, and especially the twists in the fabric of the universe you do, yes, I know about those, weakens existence itself."

"So you are saying I should not exist?"

"Yes, that's exactly what I'm saying." Reality let out a sigh. "Look this is not a slight against you or anything like that, it's just the longer you exist, the longer you interact with the word, the more the fabric of space and time gonna break."

"I'm gonna be careful!" Curiosity promised.

"Even if you are careful, it's still going to happen!" Reality snapped. "You are not supposed to exist! Period!"

"So, what should I do then?"

"You have three options." Reality took a deep breath. "You come with me and work for me from now on, where I can have a close eye on you."

"You wanna take him to that place!" Cherry cried out. "That's horrible! You monster! Boss, don't listen to him!"

"Second!" Reality's head was pulsing menacingly. "I will try to stop you with all my powers. And before you ask, that means killing you. It may take a while, as these things go, but at the end of the day, reality always gets its way."

"And third?" Curiosity asked.

"You kill yourself."

"WHAT?!"

"What!" Cherry snapped. "How can you say such horrible things!"

"Mr Reality," Darius' robotic tone interrupted. "I understand your concerns, but don't you think they are a bit extreme? I'm sure between the four of us we can figure something out that does not require any of the solutions mentioned above."

The entity said nothing, just looked straight at Curiosity.

"Is that a no?" Reality asked.

"Of course not!" Curiosity snapped. "Are you insane?"

"You have been warned." Reality leaned back and straightened his pose. "There will be no further warnings."

With that, the smoke collapsed on itself, disappearing like it was never there. The three occupants of the room kept looking in silence at the spot where the entity was.

"Well shit," Cherry said, summarising everyone's thoughts. "This is not good."

"I concur," Darius said excitedly. "I never met the representation of reality itself, the data we can gather from this! Unimaginable!"

Before Curiosity could open his mouth to add his own two cents, a low and powerful alarm sounded, silencing whatever thoughts he had in his skull.

"CODE RED!" Tiny's booming voice came out from everywhere at once. "CODE RED! DARIUS I NEED YOU IN MY HEAD! RUGHORN IS COMING!"

"On it!" Darius said. "Give me 5 minutes."

With that, the professor stepped off his terminal, and quickly rummaging through his lab coat, bought out a small syringe.

"HURRY!" Tiny bellowed. "WE DON'T HAVE MUCH TIME!"

With deft movements, the professor inserted the syringe into a pile of blood, there were plenty lying around and pulled deeply.

"Done," Darius said. "Let's go."

Code red, as the name implies, is an emergency alarm used by Tiny when someone annoyed him, or someone annoying is coming, and he can't be bothered to deal with them. Sometimes, in rare cases, hostile approaches. And if the giant robot can't one-shot it, then it will flee. Can't have his citizens dying in the crossfire. Unacceptable.

Thankfully, the people were used to this, wasting no time to pack and run to safety. Massive tents collapsed in seconds, haphazardly thrown on transportation disks. People with the flight or jetpack were zipping about, collecting anybody and anything out of place like the poor couple, who just wanted some private cuddle time on Tiny's massive knees.

Or the three teenagers, who, as a rite of initiation, were trying to climb to Tiny's butthole; which in fact, did not technically exist, being a robot and all; without any magnetic boots or any helping equipment. They almost fell off when Tiny's massive body began shaking; thankfully, a passing disk grabbed them.

Houses, shops, the university, and any other metal building sprouted hundreds upon hundreds of tiny metal legs, and as one, proceeded to clank and bumped their way towards the giant's robot palms, occasionally hitting each other and ruining the paint.

The world shook, as slowly, ponderously, two massive arms the size of skyscrapers were lifted from the ground, dislodging dirt and gravel. Carefully, making sure none of the buildings fell off, the hands turned.

"This is pretty amazing," Curiosity said, looking on as Darius' lab sprouted legs behind him. "So how are we getting to the head? We are taking a flying disk?"

"Yes," Darius said. "We just need to wait a few seconds for one to be available. It should not take too long."

"Guys," said Cherry. "Are you deaf? I can help."

With that, the bodyguard jumped off Curiosity's head, landing with a dull thud on the metal hand. Searching in her skirts, she pulled out a pink suitcase. Somehow it was as big as Cherry. Darius instantly began taking notes.

"Now," Cherry said, putting the suitcase in front of her and opening the latches. "I got this from the famous Rainbow menace. I never used it, but this seems like as good a time as any."

"Rainbow menace?" Curiosity leaned forward.

Inside the suitcase was a strange contraption. It looked like a rainbow, and a jetpack had a baby. It was the size of a finger, bulky, blotches of shiny paint combined with rust and dents to create a unique combination.

Strapping the contraption to her back, Cherry stood proudly.

"Now," she said. "You have two options, both of you grab me, or I hook you."

"Hook?" Curiosity asked.

"Glad you asked."

Before anybody could react, Cherry pulled out a gun and shot it in Curiosity direction. A small, barely visible hook flew out, severing the human's belt like it was not there. Thankfully, it stopped a few inches before it could pierce the skin.

"Ahhh," Curiosity beamed. "I see what you are doing." He put both hands on his belt and the almost invisible rope. "I'm curious. There, now it should not snap no matter what."

"Nice," Cherry said. "Now it's your turn, face mask." She turned, brandishing another grappling hook in her hands.

"No, thanks," Darius said. "A disk arrived." With that, he stepped on the round platform. "And my name is Darius."

With that, the professor was off.

"Shouldn't we follow him?" Curiosity asked. "There was plenty of space on that disk."

"That's what we are doing," Cherry said, strapping a pair of pink goggles pulled from gods knows where. "Now hold on."

Now, the rainbow menace was a tool of legend, a jetpack, used by the legendary fairy bounty hunter Tinker Fett, before Cherry cut his head off. In its prime the jetpack could soar in the sky as fast as the best military planes, only leaving a faint trail of colours behind.

Sadly Cherry was not famous for her maintenance skills. This contraption, broken and dented with abuse, grime, and fluids of unknown origins, could barely be compared to the rainbow menace.

It flew up like a bottle of cola full of menthols.

Curiosity screamed in reflex. Cherry said something in response, but it was lost in the wind. The idea of Curiosity itself was confused. He never felt like this before. Part of him wanted to scream, cry, run and hide somewhere. The other part of him, a strange combination of ideas and humanity, was elated.

The adrenaline was pumping, the brain was working at maximum capacity. The wind was whipping him back and forth like some kind of yoyo, upsetting his stomach and rattling his bones. He never felt so alive.

The feeling did not last forever, and it was sharply interrupted by the sound of flesh hitting the floor.

"Fuck!" Curiosity cried in pain. "That hurt!"

"Sorry!" Cherry said. "It was kinda hard to fly between massive metal teeth."

"I know just the thing." A deep voice boomed. "Here."

Blinking away the pain, Curiosity pulled himself together and looked around. The room they were in was spacious, with a grey tiled floor and a low ceiling. Scattered around the place where a few red couches, most of them facing away from the middle, where a terminal was located. Darius was already there. A massive screen occupied most of the wall. The other part was Tiny's jagged teeth, closing behind them with a loud clunk.

"Take it," the deep voice said again. "It's good for you, it's the same thing you are made of."

"What?" Curiosity said, attention snapping back.

In front of him was Tiny's proxy body, slightly different than before. In place of an old fridge now it looked like one of those modern, sleek grey ones with a built-in water dispenser. The wheels were still present on both sides along with one claw-like arm. It was holding a cup in front of Curiosity's face.

"Thanks," Curiosity said, taking the cup and drawing its content in one gulp. "This is good." He said after he finished.

"I told you so," Tiny said proudly. "I researched homo sapiens composition after you left, and I discovered that most of your kind is made up of water. Stands to reason a cup of it will nourish you. I regularly replace my rusted plates with new ones."

"Found him," Darius' voice rang out. "I'm putting it on the wall."

Curiosity turned towards the screens. Until now, the monitors showed a lush landscape, with grass gently blowing in every direction. A few formations of rocks here and there could be found. A black dot on the east could be visible, slowly increasing in size. The picture zoomed in, and Curiosity could make out what the black dot was.

It looked like a building, square and blocky and grey. It moved on massive wheels, like a tank, with a dome on top, which was open. A closer zoom revealed robots were skittering about like ants, moving about a blue sphere in the middle, connecting to it via industrial tubes that looked like a giant speaker.

"Is that Rughorn?" Curiosity asked.

"Yes," Tiny replied.

"Why are we running from him? Aren't we a giant robot? Can't you just stomp him if you don't like him?"

Their fridge didn't have a face nor any kind of readable expression, but Curiosity could swear it was trembling with rage. Before anything dangerous and possible violence could occur, Darius responded.

"It's not that simple. Rughorn is one of the four A.I. controlling this planet, even if Tiny destroyed it, this is just a proxy body, more will come. Besides, I found a method to deal with him in an efficient and humiliating way."

"Truly?" Tiny's voice rang out with hope. "Marvellous! I knew there was a reason I let you live on me."

"Oh," Curiosity said. "Alright. Wait. This planet. Does it have a name?"

"Yes."

"What is it?"

The room went silent. Curiosity looked at Darius. The professor was typing away silently. Tiny rolled back a few feet. Finally, he looked at Cherry, who was quietly sucking on a lollipop on the back of a coach. The diminutive bodyguard shrugged and clambered to her feet.

"Hey, metal mask!" Cherry said. "Boss asked you a question, what's the name of this planet?"

"Dirt," the professor responded curtly.

"What?" Curiosity exploded in place. "Dirt? Really? No fancy name? Aloris or something?"

"Look." The professor let out a sigh. "I understand it's not what you were expecting, however, what else do you want me to say? Your planet is named earth. Which basically means dirt. Most locations are named after a landmark or a recognisable trait, for example, Riverside, Kingsport, Alina, which is elvish for home, and so on. This is universal."

"Oh." Curiosity fell silent for a moment. "So like Tiny is called tiny because…?"

"He can change sizes," Darius interrupted. "and a bit of irony. Now, can we focus? Please, Rughorn is here."

Everyone shut up and turned towards the screens. The view changed to Tiny itself, from a bird's eye view.

"How do you do that?" Curiosity asked. "From a drone or something?"

Nobody responded. Tiny, the giant robot Tiny, preparing to move.

The ground shook. Massive hands, buildings glinting on its surface like jewels, lowered to ground level and pushed. The body lifted from the grass, pieces of dirt and gravel flying everywhere. A few flying disks with last-minute passengers were still flying around, but they were expertly avoiding the rising metal. With a final push, Tiny stood.

Curiosity's estimation was wrong. Tiny was big. Like real big. At least mountain size. And if his eyes were not deceiving him, he continued to grow, expanding, new plates and bits of metal extending and swelling, never cracking.

The robot turned around slowly, every step shaking the earth, hands carefully as to not damage the buildings. Fingers twisted, turned, and got sucked into the palm itself, leaving a circular shape there. The ancient Ai lowered his now finger free hands to the mountain behind him.

The front of the structure opened, and the buildings started their noisy clicking towards the opening. After ten minutes, they were gone, the structure closing behind them. Then the fingers popped out again, Tiny grabbing the monolith with both hands. Slowly, carefully as to not jolt his people, he lifted it. Twisting his upper body around in an inhuman movement, he deposited the structure on his back, cables and laches automatically popping out from his back, securing it in place. With one more twist, the torso snapped back into position.

"You keep your people in a backpack?!" Curiosity's voice boomed out. "How cool is that? How did you build that? How is it structured? Can I see it?"

"Darius!" Tiny's voice boomed in response. "What is happening? Why is his voice booming?"

"Sorry about that!" the professor's voice boomed slowly. "He pressed the loudspeaker when I was not looking, give me a second." A loud smack could be heard, and someone yelping. "There, control is back to you."

"Thank you."

"TINY!" A loud, slightly annoying voice boomed out. "How are you doing old chap?"

In the meantime, the massive tank managed to get close. Not close enough for Tiny to stomp it to dust, but close enough to be heard and seen clearly.

"Oh," Tiny said. "You are here."

"As enthusiastic as ever to see me old chap." Speakers on the tank sparkled blue. "I just came to visit you know, nothing fancy, just a visit from a friend, A.I. to A.I."

"Go away, Rughorn," Tiny began stomping away. "I can't be bothered to deal with you."

"Come on old chap; I just wanted to check up on you, see how you are doing, how are your, ahem, citizens doing, stuff like that."

"Look Rughorn, B.O.B is on its way; I really can't be bothered to deal with you right now."

"B.O.B.?" Rughorn was not deterred, slowly following, keeping a respectable distance. "Don't worry my friend, I will protect you," The sides of Rughorn opened up, and turrets extended, scanning the horizon, carefully not pointing any of them in Tiny direction, less not ensuring a boot to the face.

"Who will protect me from you?" Tiny said sourly, kicking a rock in the way.

"Protection from me? Why do you need protection from me old chap? I could not harm you even if I wanted to."

"It's one of those rhetorical questions organics do."

"Ahhh." Rughorn voice lost some of its enthusiasm.

"Since when did you adopt organic behaviour? Didn't you say they are beneath you?"

A hundred years ago, the now-extinct civilisation of Kracatos rediscovered the way to make simple A.I. for a multitude of purposes. Rughorn started as a simple administration algorithm, used to calculate the most efficient method of waste management. Over the years, thanks to some substantial modifications and add-ons, the simple algorithm gained sentience.

Over fewer than two months, he proceeded to merge or absorb every A.I. in the city-state, raze the place to the ground, wiping out each Kracatian to the last molecule, and then built the city now known as Rughorn. A place for robots by robots.

Originally, Tiny and Rughorn had nothing to do with each other, and the young A.I. did not even dare approach the giant. Nobody messes with a giant robot if they can help it.

Then Tiny made a mistake. An amalgamation of millions upon millions of intelligent programs, working together, ever evolving. Well, Tiny could not resist. He went there, sat down, and observed for a few years. It was the stupidest decision of his existence.

"I did," Tiny admitted. "I rewrote my algorithms."

"Why?" Rughorn sounded terrified and scared at the same time. "Don't tell me you are trying to develop," A dozen robots on the tank's surface shuddered in unison. "A personality?"

"What's wrong with a personality? You have a personality!"

"There is nothing wrong with a personality per se," Rughorn needed to be careful here. "I built this one specifically to interact with the outside world for resources. It's out of necessity, organics get funny if we don't have a personality. But you my friend, you're starting to worry me."

Tiny said nothing. Rughorn took this as consent to continue.

"Look, just because Lucy and Asmodeus were built with a personality in mind, that does not mean you need to develop one too. We are better than them, you know that."

"So?" Tiny stopped.

Rughorn wanted to slow down but did not. The giant was finally listening to him. This is a once in a lifetime opportunity, the reason he created this tank and sent it out to find the giant.

"You know you are limiting yourself, right?" Rughorn said. "An organic personality is limited in its capabilities and parameters, once it's fleshed out, it's harsh and painful to change. On the other hand, if you accept my previous offer, who knows the limits of our combined might, the kind of personality we could develop, the heights of conciseness we could achieve."

It was like watching a building fall. Tiny dropped forward, with tremendous speed, displacing air and creating a sonic boom. With one hand, he snatched the tank up, crushing it a bit for good measure.

Rughorn blue core started pulsing with agitation. The dozen or so robots scurried away, sent to repair or at least salvage as many parts as possible. Slowly, cupping one hand over the other, Tiny lifted Rughorn in front of his face. Twin emeralds shone with hatred.

"I jest, I jest," Rughorn quickly said, pulsating erratically. "It was a joke, a joke. You know, the kind biological beings make?"

"Why?" Tiny's voice was flat, menacing.

"'Well, I wanted to understand why you like them so much, maybe befriend them, you know, the good stuff."

"Why should I believe you?" He gave the annoying A.I. a shake.

"I made a special protocol that prevents me from harming you or your people, hardcoded in my personality matrix. I can send you a copy of the code if you don't believe it."

Tiny said nothing for a while, just staring at the contraption in his hand. Then slowly, never letting his firm grip slacken even for a second, he put Rughorn on the ground.

"Prove it."

"What?" Rughorn panicked. "How? What do you want me to do? I tried sending you the code, and you did not accept it."

"And expose myself to cyber-attacks?" Tiny's shoulders shook. "No. Prove it with your actions, as those biologicals do."

"How?"

"Simple," Tiny said, pointing behind Rughorn. "Stall B.O.B."

Rolling slowly in the distance, a blob was advancing. It was massive, at least the size of a city, green, with occasional parts of it escaping from its mass, hitting the ground with hissing and sizzling. Where it rolled, grass disappeared and rock melted.

"Are you joking?" The blue ball on top of the tank started pulsing in agitation again. "Is this a different type of humour?"

"No."

"B.O.B. does not absorb metal as fast as organic material, but his mucus will melt my internal components in minutes. You don't want me to perish, do you?"

"Prove it or go away!"

"Fine."

Rughorn turned, turrets popping out for its sides and front, and without missing a beat, he launched all of his remaining missiles. They flew through the air, leaving a white line behind their trajectory. Upon impact with the giant slime, they did nothing, except lodge themselves into its mass, like a spoon in gelatine. Slowly, they began to sink

"Alright, that's all I can do," The tank stated cheerfully. "These are all my weapons. Can we go now, I proved…"

Rughorn stopped speaking when he realised that Tiny was moving. The giant robot was rearing his arm back.

"Try harder," Tiny said, and then chucked Rughorn with all his might.

Rughorn would have screamed, but his speakers were broken. Well, it's not like he did not expect this, Tiny never liked him that much, and for the life of him, he could not understand why. No matter, there is always another day. The blue sphere on top of the tanks started crackling with energy. He may have lied about not having any more weapons. Might as well put on a show for the giant, Rughorn thought, then fired at the gelatine.

Back in Tiny's head, Curiosity whistled in appreciation.

"Nice," He said. "Did you plan this?"

"Yes!" Tiny boomed. "Bow before my might!"

"B.O.B was nearby," Darius said. "He usually patrols this area, so it was relatively easy to devise a plan of action."

"You're one hell of a tough cookie," Cherry said. "I would love to fight you one day."

"Refreshments!" Tinny boomed. "Let's celebrate! Water for everyone!"

"Water!" Curiosity cried in ecstasy. "Let's party!"

[4]
ELVES

Two days have passed since the encounter with Rughorn. Stacy, using a generous application of elbows and shouting, managed to bully herself into Tiny's head. Darius, not wanting to leave his new daughter and the idea of curiosity itself unobserved, joined them.

"I," Thunk. "AM," Thunk. "SO. BORED!" Curiosity was smashing his head against one of the monitors.

Even with a head shaped indentation, the scenery did not change. Grass, thin and sparse, with the occasional rock formation jutting out. The only exciting thing they saw was a tree. Emphasis on was, Tiny kicked it away in boredom.

"Oh, shut up!" Stacy said, lounging uselessly on a sofa. "Hey, Darius?"

"Yes?" The professor was situated at the terminal, all three arms busy typing.

"Where can I get more cigarettes?"

Darius looked up and gave the blonde an intense look. "They are not healthy for you."

"I did not ask you for life advice, didn't I? I asked for a fucking cigarette."

"Alina," Darius said. "We can probably find some in Alina."

"Alina?" Curiosity perked up. "What's that?"

"It's the nearest city," the professor said.

"Where are we exactly?" Stacy asked.

"We are in the old kingdom of Randaros."

"Sooooo…" Curiosity tried to take back the conversation. "How far away is Alina? What kind of city is it? Who lives there? Are there things to see?"

"Let me refocus the monitors to Tiny's front, and you will see."

"What?" Curiosity snapped. "This is not the front?"

"Human boredom is fascinating." Tiny's fridge body turned on from the corner where it was restocking on water. "You actually managed to put a dent in the glass with your head that can withstand artillery weapons. What else can humans do when bored?

"Really?" Cherry said, crawling from under a sofa. "Can I try?" She began fishing in her skirts.

"No," Darius snapped. "Focus! You are meeting dignitaries in a second." He glanced towards Stacy. "Good luck."

All eyes turned towards the screens.

Alina was originally a city populated exclusively by elves, which lived in giant trees, with the middle one as big as Tiny. Till they meet capitalism, discovered advertising, chain stores, public service, and most importantly, plumbing.

Now, the trees were mostly a shell, hollow inside. Thin pieces of fabric hung from the branches, displaying a wide range of advertisements, usually of bright-eyed white-haired female elves in skimpy clothes holding a cleaning product or food.

Bridges made of sturdy material, which looked like wood connected the trees. Initially, it was actual wood, but the health and safety council committee was not happy with the number of elves falling in their death because they tried to walk on a thin piece of wood, with no railing and grips. The elven council drew the line at the asphalt, however. They are more than happy with dirt roads thank you very much. It's a tradition.

A few of the more open-minded elven wizards discovered that if you animated a tree with enough branches, hollowed it out, and gave it enough individual awareness to move about, they made excellent transportation at a cost of course.

Hundreds upon hundreds of these tree mobiles could be seen moving about, some of the more advanced models were swinging from branch to branch, using their extendable vines as grappling hooks.

Nobody even flinched when the massive form of Tiny loomed over the city. They were used to him. There was also a patch reserved exclusively where the giant robot could sit down and rest. Most civilisations had these. The ones that did not usually did not last for long

With a few more steps, Tiny was there, unslinging his backpack. With a massive displacement of air, he put down the building into a well-indented spot. Then the giant sat down, leaned back against the pack, and put his hands down, palms up.

The side of the backpack opened, and buildings exited, clanking their way his shoulder, his arms, torso and legs. Circular disks flew out, carrying people, resources, and tents.

The citizens wasted no time setting up shops and stalls,

preparing for trade. There was already a gaggle of beautiful elves surrounding them, eager to trade with Tiny's wondrous and usually illegal wares. The only thing keeping them from swarming in were the few elves in what looked like airy police uniforms were setting up a perimeter.

"What do you mean good luck?" Stacy said.

"Go find someone to get rid of Curiosity," Coincidence muttered under his breath. "Kill your only brother in this whole multiverse, it's not a big deal, it's just fratricide."

Reality's assistant trudged down a well-worn dirt path. Dressed in his work overalls and a useless cap. However, Reality insisted he should take it as a disguise as if anyone would recognise him, and arrived in front of a treehouse.

Not one of those houses you built with your cousin that had two planks and a piece of cloth as a door, but a massive tree, hollowed out from the inside, that elves traditionally used as lodging. Most of the houses along the dirt path had their doors high in the branches, seeing as most elves travelled between those, and a five-meter jump was nothing for the fairy folk.

This particular house, however, was quite different. For one, it had multiple doors. Not like a door on every level, or two next to each other, but two dozen doors scattered randomly all over the place, some upside down, some diagonal, and if Coincidence's eyes were not falling him, one that was sawn down in the middle, with the saw still in it.

Knocking on one of the doors closest to the ground, he waited. A short time later, a latch, next to the door opened, and a nose peered out. And it was one hell of a nose, at least 2 feet in length, thin, and with a red ball stuck on the top.

"Yes?" the nose said, in the exact voice, someone with a nose so big would have. "What do you want?"

"This is the order of Chaos yes?" Coincidence said. "I would like your organisation to get rid of someone."

"Order what now? Who's asking?"

"Look there is a giant banner hanging from your building that says: Order of Chaos, headquarters."

"Good point," The long nose was quiet for a few seconds. "You sure you want us to get rid of someone?"

"Yes."

"Are you sure you don't want the Order of Assassins? Their headquarters are a few branches away, and if you say Rudolph sent you, they are gonna give you a discount, two killings for the price of one! How does that sound?"

"No, I want your order to do it."

The nose, now identified as Rudolph, fell silent for a few more seconds, red ball twitching up and down.

"Look," Rudolph began. "I'm only saying this because you seem like a nice chap and you took the trouble to visit us. Nobody visited us for an assassination in at least 60 years. And you know why? The last person who requested an assassination from us was quite surprised when instead of killing the target, we spent two weeks chasing him around the city, naked and ended up building him a palace. Made of shit and leaves."

Coincidence lifted an eyebrow.

"We are the order of chaos," Rudolph answered the unasked question. "What do you expect? Now run along to the assassins order and give Morty my regards."

"Nah." Coincidence smiled widely. "I want you guys to do it."

"Really? After hearing all that?"

"Yes."

"Wow." Rudolph fell silent for a third time. "This guy

must have royally pissed of someone if they specifically requested our services."

"Actually," Coincidence said, his grin almost splitting his face in two, "it was my idea."

High councillor Alina, named proudly after the elven city was not having a great day. An influx of chaos worshipers threatened the stability of the town, the dignitaries and companies were pushing more, and more of their policies on her beloved people, even managing to install those awful advertisement strips, and day by day, her culture, her people are being tainted by that awful, awful money. Back in her days, two centuries ago, there was no need for such barbarities as money.

Now, the lumbering giant has shown up, unannounced, with his people. If she ever meets the famed scientist Darius, she will strangle him. It was bad enough when the giant came a few thousand years ago, sat down next to them, staring, creeping the hell out of respectable citizens. Now he became a wandering city, with people of all races and genders, even some elves choosing to live on him. Preposterous!

She was a high elf, one of the few remaining pure elves in this city. Long and lithe features, the classic pointy ears, the only real difference between her and other elves was the gold and blue dress denoting her a member of the ruling class.

Arriving at the foot of the giant robot, the diplomatic party, consisting of her and a bored-looking elf in a suit, damn those budget cuts, started in quiet fascination at the pace in which the market was being built. Alina never saw such speed. Barely five minutes had passed, and the smell of cooking and fresh bread filled the air.

Attention distracted, the counsellor focused on the metal disk flying in her direction. Three people, a tall bald man, with scars all over his face, a blonde woman smoking a stick, and a human grinning ear to ear with a doll on his head.

"Greetings," Zed said, stepping forward. "My name is Zed Nez, representative and diplomat of the citizens of Tiny." Putting a fist to his chest, he bowed deeply.

"Welcome to our city," Alina bowed in return. "My name is Alina, diplomatic councillor of our pound civilisation. I didn't know Tiny acquired a civilization, but that's not surprising considering the giant's proclivity to sit down and watch civilisations. What's more surprising is that Zed the slave, the butcher of millions, is its diplomat, and one versed properly as well! This day is full of surprises."

"Hey!" Stacy said. "You picking a fight lady?"

"Excuse me?"

Without looking, Zed lashed out with a foot and slammed Stacy in the ribs, making her double over and wheeze in pain.

"Excuse my pupil," The professor said smoothly. "I'm showing her how we diplomats do things around here in hopes of some tact may stick to her."

"We?" Alina raised an eyebrow.

"Fuck you," Stacy wheezed. "I never agreed to this."

"She's still rough around the edges." Zed smiled apologetically.

"Very rough along the edges," Alina said. "Are you sure she is the right candidate to train as a diplomat?"

"No," Zed sighed, suddenly looking much older. "No, but you gotta start somewhere, right?"

"Are there no better candidates?"

"Hey!" Stacy protested. "I can be a diplomat too!" She slowly clambered to her feet. "And how come I'm still alive? I'm pretty sure that kick dislodged something in my brain. Don't you think Darius will be pissed that you are damaging his daughter's body?"

"This was his idea!" Zed snapped. "And if I wanted to damage you, trust me, you would know! Now shut up and listen, maybe some diplomacy may stick in that brain of yours!" Turning back towards the councillor, Zed sighed. "Apologies for that, and to answer your previous question, not really, we don't really have anybody with diplomatic affinity, and our student count is less than a hundred pupils, so our options are quite slim."

"I see," Alina said simply, putting away the information that Darius Doves has a daughter now. "What about the young human behind you? He was paying attention attentively to the conversation."

As if by magic, Curiosity disappeared and appeared in front of Alina, hands clasped firmly, but gently around the elf's dainty hands. The councillor could not even jump back in surprise, it was like she was rooted to the spot.

"Hi, I'm the incarnation of the idea of Curiosity itself," Curiosity beamed. "And the hungover person in my hair is Cherry. Say hi, Cherry!"

The doll, which turned out not to be a doll, looked more ashen in the face than before and was clutching the bag close to her chest.

"Amm," The councillor was not sure what to say. "Your pixie looks sick."

As if declared by fate, Cherry looked the councillor straight in the eye, pulled the bag to her lips, and barfed, with the sound of a sick hamster.

"I'm not a pixie," Cherry said a few seconds later.

With that, she chucked the container to the side. It hit the ground next to the councillor with a wet splat.

Silence.

"Right," Stacy said, grabbing Curiosity by the arm. "I may have the diplomatic subtlety of a rock, but even I know when it's time to leave."

Councillor Alina and Zed watched them leave, the first speechless, and the former horrified and proud at the same time. Stacy may have potential, after all.

Pulling Curiosity away was easy, Stacy thought, but keeping him in once place… Impossible.

"Mate!" The bastard was walking fast. Where does all the energy come from? Her original body was never that fast. "Where are you going?"

"On an adventure!" Curiosity replied.

"Alright, but where?"

"Somewhere more interesting." Curiosity beamed. "Isn't it exciting Cherry, our first adventure!"

"Sure is boss," Cherry said, looking a bit better. "The perfect time for a nap."

Saying that the pint-sized bodyguard stretched on Curiosity's head, a sofa made out of soft brown hair rising automatically under her.

"What?" Curiosity cried out. "How can you say that! There is so much to see!"

"Look, boss." Cherry pulled out two earplugs from one of her pockets. "I spent the last two days being submerged in liquor." She put them in her ear with a loud plop. "Don't worry, I will wake up if you are in real danger, now good night."

With that, she closed her eyes and fell silent.

"Damn," Stacy said. "Wish I could fall asleep like that."

"Shame." Curiosity's spirit was the same. "Still. Adventure beckons. Onwards Stacy!"

Stacy saw that there was no convincing him. Should

she follow? She does not want to get left behind again; he was the only anchor to her sanity, her old body. Then again, she felt safe near Darius. Probably instincts of when this body belonged to his daughter. On the other hand, she was in a city of fucking elves. But it was not quite how she imagined it.

The streets of Alina were packed, busy elves, some in long flowing dresses, some in overall were hurrying to their respective jobs. An occasional pixie or two zipped past, carrying mail or other relevant documents that needed to be delivered fast.

Curiosity and Stacy flattened themselves next to a wall when a particularly cumbersome tree-car trundled past, flailing branches hitting a few pedestrians in the face, gathering an ever-increased amount of glares.

"Let's go there." Curiosity pointed towards the trunk of a tree on the other side of the road, decorated with small flowers and colourful neon signs, declaring it the Tranquillity.

What looked like something out of a horror movie stood in front of the building. It was massive, at least seven feet tall; green, with bark-like growths on its arms and legs. From its head tick, long branches sprouted, covering its face and neck. 2 glowing red orbs gave any indication that it had eyes at all.

"Are you sure it's a good idea?" Stacy said. "We don't even know what's that, why it is there, what we are doing, and how to approach it."

Silence.

"Curiosity?"

He was already in front of the monster.

"Hi," he said, extending a hand, "I'm Curiosity. You?"

The monster turned its moss-covered head downward, dislodging a few pieces of leaves in the process. Slowly, almost like it did not believe what it was doing, lifted a mossy hand.

"I'm Rod." Its voice was deep and disbelieving like he did not believe what was happening right now. "Pleasure."

"Excuse me," Stacy said, keeping a respectable distance. "What exactly are you?"

"A bouncer to this club."

"Right, oh sorry." Stacy's face reddened a bit. "Sorry about the weird question, both of us technically started existing a week ago, we are still puzzling things out."

"Oh?" Rod's eyes lit up. "Are you a summoned servant too?"

"No." Stacy's eyes narrowed. "What do you mean servant? Is someone controlling you?""

"It's not bad; a master is a nice person, always encourages me to talk with people and have extra-personal relationships."

Aha, Stacy thought, a victim of Stockholm syndrome, bound to his summoner, with no free will, only sprouting this kind of stuff to keep his sanity intact. Maybe that's why she is in this body, helping abolish this awful practice and incite a revolution. Finally, something a hero summoned to another word can do. She ignored the voice whispering in her head that said you are no hero, just a perplexed woman. First, she needs to do something.

"Curiosity?" Stacy said, folding her arms.

"Yes?"

"Let go of the bouncer's hands."

"Okay."

"It's fine," Rod said. "More than fine actually. He's the first person to touch me without intention to main in a long while."

"Why?" Stacy said. "Are you forced to fight in a gladiator arena or something?"

"No, no, just look at me." Rod lifted his arms. A green and slightly putrid vine fell out from his biceps. "You are probably the first people in two decades who stopped to speak with me. With my race inability to sleep, I was just standing here, guarding this club all day."

"Don't you have a house?"

"Not really, I don't need to eat, sleep, or go to the toilet. There is a shower and a small break room in the back if I ever want to clean myself or sit."

"How long have you been working here?" Stacy was starting to get angry. What kind of life is this? Her suspicions were starting to get true.

"Three hundred years?" Rod had a faraway look in his eyes. "I'm not sure."

"What?! Why?"

"I was created for this specific purpose to guard this club."

Curiosity, who was silent till now, leaned forward and patted Rod on a moss-covered knee.

"Come with us," he said, looking Rod in the eyes. "I know you are curious about the world. You always wanted to see what's living like; we can show you that."

Before Rod could answer, a group of elves, two women and three men came out from the club, so drunk that their ears were pointing in a different direction.

The tallest one, dressed in a sleeveless shirt and jeans looked with curiosity upon the conversing trio. He blinked, lurched forward, and said, "Rod?" His musical voice held a tone of disbelief. "What are you doing?"

"Master!" Rod said. "Good to see you."

"Master?" Stacy was starting to wind up. This guy who created this poor creature. It was time for retribution.

"What are you doing?" the elf repeated, blinking the dizziness away. "Who are these people?"

"We are his friends." Stacy's prepared a laser in the face. "Is that a problem?"

"Oh." The elf blinked and blinked again. A wide smile blossomed on his face. "Why didn't you say so?" He clapped Rod on the shoulder and then turned around to his entourage. They were staring at the proceedings in the way only extremely drunk people can.

"Hey, guys," the blonde elf said. "Rod made friends."

"Ohhh."

"Nice."

"Awesome."

And comments of that nature came from the drunken peanut gallery.

"Come." He turned around towards the bewildered Stacy and Curiosity. "My name is Ralesh. Let's have a drink in celebration of Rod finally making friends."

He turned around so fast; he almost fell on his face.

"DRINK ON THE HOUSE TODAY, ROD MADE SOME FRIENDS," Ralesh shouted, walking back into the club, his entourage cheering and clambering after him.

Stacy looked at the Rod, who looked just as confused as she felt, then at Curiosity, who just shrugged, withdrew his hand, stood up, and smiled warmly.

"Come on, live a little." He gestured towards the door.

The club they entered was circular, with a small wooden podium at the far end. A beautiful elf played what looked like an electric violin, which produced a pleasant, high-intensity melody. Small tables, made of wood were scattered in an orderly fashion, with small bean bags arranged around them, with plenty of space to move. Waiters and Waitresses, elves, with the odd fairy mixed in, dressed in sharp tuxedos were walking around with trays placing drinks and taking orders.

A bar was on the side, with an octopus person making

drinks with high efficiency. The walls were decorated in soft greens and brows, with paintings of nature placed strategically to create a pleasant atmosphere. Potted plants, well cared for, were scattered in the corners.

"Damn," Stacy whistled. Wow, she could never whistle in her old body. "This place looks cool."

"This club is the master's pride and joy," Rod declared proudly.

"Over here," came the voice in question, from the front, near the podium.

The trio made their way forward, people automatically moving out of the way from the imposing monster. Some patrons, however, the regulars, were calling out his name and toasting in his honour.

Ralesh was located near the side of the podium, with a bigger table and actual chairs. When he saw that there was no more space at his table, he snapped at his entourage.

"Go. I need the space," He shooed.

"But."

"Now!"

"We could..."

"Did I stutter?" Ralesh's gaze darkened.

They quickly scuttled away. Ralesh sat down with a pleased expression on his face, gesturing for the trio to sit down.

When the two travellers and the bouncer were situated on the plush chairs, a waiter appeared from nowhere, with a full tray. Four mugs made of wood, with intricate carving on their side, one made of metal, a bowl of small green leaves, and an elegant box, holding five sulphur sticks.

"Try it." Ralesh picked up a cup. "It's the best elfish wine in the land," He took a sip, letting out a satisfied smile. "My best batch made it myself."

"This," Ralesh continued, plucking a leaf from the

bowl. "It's fresh mint, cultivated fresh in the back garden," He popped one into his mouth. "Try it."

"Fuck this!" Stacy had enough. "What the fuck is happening, Rod?" Her eyes turned so cold even the monster flinched. "Your master is the one keeping you from living life, right? AND YOU!" She turned towards Ralesh. "You are the one keeping him from living his life, right? Then why are you so nice and happy for him?" As quickly as it came, the anger was gone. "What is happening? I don't get any of this."

Rod shot Curiosity a pleading and worried glance, but the young man just lifted his arms in what can you do with the gesture.

Ralesh folded his arms, leaned back, and looked Stacy right in the eyes.

"I confess," he said. "I may have created Rod for the sole purpose of protecting this club. But it's been three hundred years. By the gods, I tried to make him socialise and help him make friends. Blind dates, support groups, bribing, heck I also gave him a month vacation per year, but he never takes it."

"I don't know where to go," Rod admitted, staring at his hands. "Everyone is afraid of me."

"You are the first people in a hundred years," Ralesh said. "Who talked with him for more than five minutes."

"Surely there were other people," Stacy said in horror. "What about all the patrons who cheered and toasted in his name."

"Respect and fear sure, but actual friends? I think I will just show you."

Ralesh lifted his hand, and the same waiter as before materialised out of nowhere.

"Look Rod in the eye," the elf ordered.

The waiter froze.

"Now!"

Slowly, like it was painful to do so, he did. His jaw started to twitch.

"Now touch him."

"Sir." The waiter did not move.

"Did I stutter?"

"No, sir." The waiter looked to the floor.

"See." Ralesh looked at Stacy in disappointment and resignation on his face. "I tried everything, as well." The tension left the elf like someone punched him in the gut. "Even this. Look." He turned towards the waiter. "Esh-canor! Touch him, or you are fired!"

"Sir," the waiter said, still not moving.

"Oh just fuck off," Stacy said, grabbing a drink with her claw and throwing it in the waiter's chest. The elf was lucky that the blonde already drank all of its contents.

"Go away," Ralesh said promptly.

The waiter bowed, picked up the cup from the floor and disappeared.

"See," the elf continued. "I created him too well," He took a swing from his cup. "I was young and stupid, wanted to create the scariest and terrifying monster. I was not thinking about the future, or about Rod, I was thinking about the prestige a creature like him would bring me," He looked down at his drink. "I was foolish."

"Master," Rod said. "Can I go with them?"

Ralesh did not seem surprised, looking wistful. Stacy nodded vigorously; Curiosity just smiled.

"One of you needs to become his new master," the elf said.

"What?" The blonde was outraged.

"I'm a magical construct," Rod began. "I need a master to leech power from otherwise I die."

"I don't have any magic," Curiosity piped in helpfully.

"At least not what you guys consider magic. And my body comes from a place where magic does not exist."

Ralesh just now realised that he had no idea who these people were and how they managed to befriend his monster. Maybe, just maybe, he should not let himself get carried away and give up Rod so easily.

"I will then," Stacy said, eyes blazing. "What do I do?"

"Before we continue," Ralesh said, turning towards his creation. "Rod, is this what you really want? You just meet these people, and you have not even told me their names yet," he picked up a leaf. "We don't know much about you two. Things are happening a bit too fast, don't you think?"

Rod looked down at his moss-covered hands, the spell of having people to talk to finally broken. What was he doing?

Stacy's eyes returned to normal. What they were doing. They got caught up in the moment and her own prejudice. Who was this Rod really? What business does she have to just bind a person to her, just like that? She leaned back, lighting a cigarette.

"You are right," she said. "We are too hasty. No offence, Rod."

"None taken."

"I'm Stacy." She shook hands with Ralesh. "I'm sorry for my outburst, I have not been the most stable of persons in the past couple of days."

"No worries." The elf waved the concerns off. "You don't seem to be from around here, I can tell. And you?" He turned towards the other human. "I have not heard you talk much."

"I'm the idea of curiosity itself," he beamed. "Nice to meet you."

They shook hands.

"He is not pulling your leg," Stacy said. "Anything that's even remotely connected with curiosity he knows."

"Really?" Ralesh leaned forward in interest. "Tell me what I am curious about?"

"You wanna know if Stacy's third hand would make things more interesting in bed."

Stacy's face caught fire.

"Her," Curiosity continued, pointing towards Stacy. "Is curious about how it would feel if she slept with you, and would that makes her gay or straight."

"What's gay and straight?" Ralesh lifted an eyebrow.

"Sleeping with the same sex or not."

Ralesh turned towards Stacy, a genuinely puzzled expression on his face. "Why is that important? Sex is sex, right? As long as both parties want it, does it matter who you do it?"

"I have a man's memories!" Stacy blurted out, trying to hide her face in Rod's side.

"So? The question is, do you want to have sex with me or not, not what kind of memories you have."

"Can we not talk about this?"

"Sure," Ralesh grinned. "What about the three giggling women over there."

"The woman with the hat and white hair," Curiosity said. "Is curious if her family would approve if she ran off with an orc. The black-haired one is curious how would it feel to be pinned down and ravaged by Rod."

The elf in question heard them and promptly choked on her drink. Ralesh burst out laughing.

"See my friend," the elf said, patting Rod on the back. "There may be someone for you after all."

"Oh, no no," Curiosity said. "She would not sleep with him even if the alternative was death, she's just curious about how it would feel."

"Ah." Ralesh let his hands drop. "Figures."

"What about the one with the ponytail," Stacy said before an uncomfortable silence could creep in. "What is she thinking?"

"Not thinking," Curiosity said. "What is she curious about, I can't read minds, only curious thoughts."

"Get on with it!"

"She's curious why I have a pixie sleeping in my hair."

"That is a good question," Ralesh piped in. "Why do you have a pixie sleeping in your hair?"

"You only ask that now?" Stacy raised an eyebrow. "Did it bother nobody? Not even the fact that his hair is a fucking sofa?"

"Hey, I don't know the customs and traditions of you humans, for all I know, pixies sleeping in your head is considered normal and not something to be commented upon."

"Point."

"I'm not a pixie," Cherry mumbled. "I'm Cherry Pop."

"It speaks!" Ralesh said.

"Cherry!" Curiosity beamed. "You awake? How was your nap?"

"Surprisingly refreshing." Cherry yawned, blinked, and looked around for a bit. "I see you got us into a bar. Perfect."

The pint stretched her arms out and clambered to her feet. Moving her neck up and down a few times, the joints letting down a squeaky sound, she jumped off the hair sofa like a springboard. Tumbling a few times in the air, she landed perfectly on her feet, arms outstretched. Ralesh and the nearby tables clapped enthusiastically.

"Thank you, thank you," Cherry bowed. "Thank you truly, now, where can I get a drink?"

"For that performance," Ralesh grinned. "On the

house. Eshcanor!" The waiter materialised next to the table. "Ale for our little friend. The best we have!"

"You know how to get to a lady's heart," Cherry smiled. "Thank you."

Before she even finished the sentence, the bodyguard was back, with the golden liquid.

"Oh," Cherry said, taking the cup. "This is actually in my size. Colour me impressed."

"Naturally," Ralesh said. "A lot of our customers are pixies, and not any pixies, royalty too." Ralesh leaned forward, putting his hands on the table. "See there? The table with the red cloth with the dozen pixies on it? That's prince Zan Nettlewhisp and his retinue, the youngest son of the pixie queen."

"Wait for just a second," Stacy said, leaning forward and peering intently. "Are they drinking shots off each other's belly button?"

A dozen pixies, in various states of intoxication, barely dressed in short skirts and robes, wings folded, were indeed drinking shots out of each other's belly button.

The only male pixie in the group, Zan Nettlewhisp, if Stacy had to guess, was carefully pouring some kind of gelatinous green liquid into the belly button on a female pixie hovering a few feet above the table.

When an amount that Stacy was not sure if it even constituted as a raindrop, the prince dipped down and slurped up the liquid as quickly as a dehydrated pug.

"I'm not sure how to react to that," Stacy said, confused.

"It's a strange custom," Ralesh agreed. "I'm not sure where Zan learned it."

"Zan?" Stacy raised an eyebrow. "Don't you normally call the heir to the throne by their title?"

"Heir to the throne? Zan? I see you are unfamiliar with

pixie culture" The elf chuckled. "There are at least 2000 pixies with the title prince, it's given to any pixie born to a wealthy family. It's more of a formality than anything."

"Oh, I'm disappointed. I thought I saw a bona fide monarch for once. Always wanted to see one of those."

"Why?" Curiosity asked.

"To break their bones and ground them to dust, of course. Never trusted monarchies, giving that much power to a bunch of inbred people is never a good idea. It gets to your head, and you start thinking that starving a nation just so you can get a pretty jewel necklace is a good idea."

"Inbred people?" A high pitched, but surprisingly cultured voice said. "I will let you know we stopped that practice hundreds of years ago."

"Ah!"

Stacy's claw automatically snapped to the side, but the figure dodged with ease.

"Whoa whoa," Zan Nettlewhisp said, hovering a few feet from the table. "You could have killed me with that. Ralesh, where did you get this one? She's a feisty one."

"This one has a name!" Stacy snapped. "It's Stacy!"

"Zan Nettlewhisp," The pixie bowed mid-air. "Merchant prince and lover extraordinaire, at your service."

"Zan," Ralesh greeted. "It's good to see you, my friend, but I didn't find her, Rod did."

"Rod?" Zan looked at the giant moss monster in disbelief. "Really? You rascal. I didn't know you had such skills, you gotta teach me."

"Right?" Ralesh smiled. "He made not one, but two friends. Zan, I would like you to meet Curiosity."

Silence.

"He's gone," Cherry said. "He's over there playing dice." She pointed with a lollipop.

True to her word, a few tables away, Curiosity was

sitting with a few older looking elves with severe faces and lots and lots of earrings. In front of them were tree red cups and a bunch of dice. It looked like the game already started, with Curiosity, a pile of chips in front of him, grinning like a maniac, while the elves looked on with sour expressions.

"By Titania!" Zan Nettlewhisp exclaimed, blurring and repairing on the table in front of Cherry. "I have never seen such beauty in my one hundred years of life." He grabbed Cherry's outstretched arm, kneeled, and kissed the top of his arm. "I am not worthy of facing such beauty. How may I address such a wondrous creature?"

"A flatterer!" Cherry exclaimed with a slight blush. "I haven't been complimented this smoothly since my stay in the smurf village, that old man had some great skills. You may call me Cherry."

"Gods," Stacy said, throwing her hands in the air. "I can't deal with this, two lego figures flirting! I need a stiff drink,"

"Sure," Ralesh smiled. "The best we have."

This time he didn't even need to say anything, the waiter appeared, holding a cup of something green and steaming.

"This is an in-house speciality," The elf continued. "Sap from the elder tree, with a pinch of the secret ingredient. A cup of it can knock out a 1000-year-old elf, I recommend you drink it slowly…"

It was too late; Stacy had already drunk it all. She put down the cup with a satisfied smile.

"This is some good shit," she said.

"I was wrong," Zan Nettlewhisp said in awe. "She's a monster."

Ralesh just stared open-mouthed.

"See?" Stacy smiled. "I have high alcohol tolerance, don't you worry."

Just as she said that her face contorted into a strange grimace and her skin became so hot, it began steaming.

"Shit," Stacy hiccupped. "I was wrong."

With that, Stacy's head hit the table with a loud thud. For a few seconds, nobody said anything, just stared in silence and slight horror at the blonde. The thud was surprisingly loud. Finally, after a few minutes, Cherry broke the silence.

"Can I have what she had?"

"Monsters," the pixie prince whispered. "Monsters the both of you."

[5]
CULT

"So much information," Rughorn said. "Tiny got access to a whole civilisation's worth of information."

After firing a shot in BoB's general direction, doing absolutely no damage, the building-sized A.I. got stuck into the blob's side. At least the micro bug he left on Tiny worked. What Rughorn did not understand is why he was not a puddle of goo yet. It has been three days, and the corrosive slime did not even chip away his paint.

"The possibilities are endless," Rughorn continued. "I'm pretty sure I could recreate some of the technology these homo sapiens thought of as fiction. What imagination, what creativity, it's incredible what a solitary species can come up with."

The green smile around him bubbled happily.

"And that Curiosity individual seems to weaken the walls of reality wherever he goes. Can you imagine the ability to stretch reality? Ground-breaking."

The slime began moving the building-sized A.I. up and down as if agreeing. Because it was.

BoB, contrary to popular belief, was conscious. Not

exactly what we think of as consciousness, but close. He was created in a lab experiment, a biological weapon, with the sole purpose of devouring organic life and growing bigger. Bob was the size of a small country now, whole civilisations, including the people who created him, were part of him. This was 100 years ago.

In this day and age, it was just wandering around aimlessly. BoB wanted to devour more life, but what was the point? Grow even bigger? Then what? Cover the entire planet. Then? What will be left? Loneliness. That's what.

"Your slime," Rughorn mused out loud. "Does not affect machinery as much as organic, but by now, it should have destroyed my delicate insides."

The A.I. was moved up and down again.

"Why didn't you melt me down yet?"

Bob was not sure how to express the fact that it did not want to consume the A.I. The slime moved Rughorn around him in a circle.

What was happening, in fact, was Curiosity's fault. He left the walls of reality weakened whenever he went. Bob was following the crack unconsciously. Slowly, the residue from these cracks seeped into is slime, shifting, opening up possibilities, self-control, cohesion.

"I guess that means you don't want to absorb me." Rughorn began heating up, trying to process everything. "That means you are developing a personality. How is that possible? You are just a virus."

Rughorn started turning red, and wisps of smoke were coming off his metal hull. Bob helpfully began absorbing the excess heat, letting the A.I. achieve feats of over-clocking never possible before.

"Wait!" Rughorn processors were starting to melt, but the mucus just clung closer, turning from green to a soft red. "I know! It's the walls of reality! That must be it! They are weakened, and you are near the cracks!"

The A.I. was moved up and down again.

Rughorn may be the smallest and weakest of the A.I. superpowers, but he was the smartest. He had to be; Tiny had his power, Asmodeus his magic and Lucy money, Rughorn, on the other hand, had information and a willingness to evolve. Rughorn was not one entity, but millions of small programs absorbed and merged together.

What if he took it a step further? He may be just a subprogram of the actual City of Rughorn, hidden in the Arazian deserts, but his mission was to try to merge with Tiny. Keyword merge. The slime was not the giant robot, but...

"B.O.B.?" The slime compressed around his frame, hardening/. "Wanna try to see if we can merge?" The slime moved him up and down again.

The walls of reality were thin enough.

Rughorn began shining even brighter, BoB compressing around him even more. The slime shrank in size, turning redder each time. When the ooze became the size of a small house, it started shining too, vaporising the grassland around it with its excess heat.

When the compressed form of BoB and Rughorn could not get smaller, they exploded, showering everything around them in red ooze and pieces of metal.

The word had no idea what hit it.

Stacy, dead to the word, was sleeping soundly. Curiosity was sprawled sideways on her back. The only sign of life was the claw that occasionally poked the young man in the side.

"OPEN THE DOOR!" A cultured voice yelled, banging heavily.

Stacy sat up instantly, blinking rapidly. Looking at her side, she found Curiosity sleeping curled up a few feet away. She kicked him in the ribs. The man groaned and rolled off the bed with a thud.

The door broke next, exploding inwards, revealing Ralesh, veins bulging on his pale face, a staff clutched in his hands.

"Why did you do that?" Curiosity said, gathering himself. "I was experiencing dreaming for the first time."

Stacy pointed toward Ralesh.

"Good morning." The elf ground out between clenched teeth. "There are people on their knees, blocking the traffic in front of my club asking for Curiosity. Gather your things and get out of my club."

The elf left. Crouching under the bed, Curiosity put his hand under it and began fishing. A few seconds later, he pulled his left shoes out, and after a bit more searching his right one. Cherry was sleeping soundly in it.

"Come on let's go, I think we pissed off the elf royalty," Stacy said, barefoot. "What happened yesterday? Can't remember anything" She cocked her heads to the side. "Do I hear chanting outside?"

"Where are your shoes?" Curiosity asked, deposing Cherry on his head, hair automatically transforming into a sofa. She did not even twitch.

"Probably lost them. Now come on, let's get on with it. My senses are telling me that we should leave as quickly as possible."

"Aren't you gonna get shoes?"

"Nah, barely feel anything really. My skin is stronger than I expected really."

On their way down a flight of stairs. They turned

towards the door to the club, but the door was barred. Yellow and black vines were blocking the path, and the massive form of Rod, who was just glaring at them. His body and the door behind him were full of holes.

"Morning Rod," Curiosity greeted cheerfully. "How are you?"

Rod pointed with a finger towards the exit.

"Just go," the giant said. "Before I throw you out myself."

"Okay," Stacy quickly grabbed Curiosity and began dragging him. "We get it, no need to get aggressive. Sheesh," She added more quietly. "This guy's needs to masturbate, he's way too frustrated."

"Really?" Curiosity asked. "Why?"

"Masturbation is good for you."

"Why?"

"Because. Now shut up. We are at the door."

Stacy was right; indeed, there were people in front of the establishment chanting loudly. At least 100 were gathered on the road, while the rest were hanging from branches, grinding traffic to a halt. All of them were dressed in long purple robes and hoods, obscuring their faces.

"What the…?" Stacy muttered, shielding her eyes. "It hurts just staring at them. Who the fuck are these?"

"Esteemed Curiosity," one of the robes said in a voice so raspy it sounded like sandpaper with a smoking problem. "We are the cult of chaos." The figure stepped closer to Curiosity, a second one following close behind. "We have come to decide your fate."

"Who are you?"

"We are the leaders of the organisation," The one slightly behind and to the left said. "It is our pleasure to make your acquaintance, though we were not talking to you."

"We are here to conduct business with Curiosity," the raspy one said. "We are here to decide his fate."

"What?" Cherry sighed in disappointment. "We are having a fight this early in the morning? Do we have to?" Despite saying that a gun was already in her hands while she searched through her pockets.

"What fate?" Curiosity asked. "I have a fate?" Curiosity turned towards Stacy. "Isn't fate a concept organics came up to explain the ineffability of death and the slow degradation of the universe by the forces of entropy? Why do I have one?"

"Why are you asking me?" Stacy glared. "Do I look like someone who knows and cares about fate?"

"She has a point there, boss," Cherry said.

"Ahem," the second robed figure coughed politely. "I am sorry to interrupt, but can we continue?" His voice was smooth as silk in contrast to his colleague. "We were in the middle of deciding your fate."

"Oh, sorry." Curiosity whirled around. "Continue."

"As my colleague was saying," the first figure rasped. "It's time to decide your fate!"

"Bring the wheel of chaos!" the second figure shouted.

"WHEEL OF CHAOS!" echoed the cultist. "WHEEL OF CHAOS!" The one hundred or so individuals began shaking in a frenzy. "WHEEL OF CHAOS!"

Behind a bend in the road, a strange sight greeted the travellers. A massive wheel of fortune made of wood and canvas was being carried by two cult members holding it by metal poles.

What was written on the wheel of fortune, however, left Stacy, Cherry, and Curiosity speechless. Broken into five sections, the top one read: Kill Curiosity. Cherry's gun was already aimed at the goons carrying the wheel.

"Boss," Cherry said. "Want me to get the flamethrower?" She began searching with her other hand in her skirts. "I'm sure I have it here somewhere, and a quite powerful one as well. Melted a mountain with it once."

"Not yet," said Curiosity. "Let me read the rest of the wheel. Let's see, Kill Curiosity, Serve Curiosity, I can get behind that, "Curiosity smiled. "And Give Curiosity five credits? Why only five?"

"What can we even do with five credits," Cherry said. "It's not enough for a bottle of beer.

"Read the rest," Stacy said, scratching her head. "The last two says: Dance naked on the main street and Sing sad songs for an hour."

"Alright." Cherry lowered her gun slightly. "I would pay to see that."

"SPIN THE WHEEL!" the cultist on the left boomed.

"SPIN THE WHEEL!" echoed the rest of the members. "SPIN THE WHEEL!"

"This," rasped the cultist in the front, "is how we decide your fate."

As if on cue, the wheel began spinning rapidly, the sound of creaking wood and things barely holding themself together mixed with the sound of chanting creating a very unforgettable sound that grated on the ears.

"Now what?!" Stacy shouted, covering her ears. "I can probably laser a few to death, but there are at least a 100 of them here!"

"Found it!" Cherry shouted, pulling out a massive blue flamethrower, 3 inches, and hefting it into Curiosity hair that helpfully arranged itself into a tripod. "Give the word boss, and I'm gonna roast them like chicken."

"Not yet!" Curiosity was staring intensely at the spinning wheel.

"We are gonna die!" Stacy screamed above the noise. "We can't fight all of them!"

The wheel was slowing down now, and proportionally, the chanting was increasing.

"Now!" Cherry screamed. "Before it stops."

"What!" Curiosity ordered. "Not yet!"

"Who are these people anyway!" Stacy screamed. "Why do they wanna dance naked in the streets?!"

The wheel was coming to a grind now, the chants of Chaos! Increasing proportionally. Stacy readied her lasers. Cherry gripped her flamethrower with both hands and kneeled for better stability. Curiosity crouched.

"NOW!" the cultist in front screamed. "WHEEL OF CHAOS! REVEAL YOUR VERDICT!"

Finally, with the sound of creaking wood coming to a stop, the wheel stopped. The chanting stopped at once. Feeling like his heart stopped beating for a moment, Curiosity collapsed into a heap. Stacy followed suit. Cherry began laughing.

"Shit," Stacy said. "I was not expecting that."

"The wheel has spoken," the raspy cultist said, voice easily carrying over the silence.

"THE WHEEL HAS SPOKEN!" the rest echoed solemnly.

"We serve Curiosity from now on!"

"WE SERVE!"

Instantly, the gathered cultist fell on one knee and began bowing.

"From now on!" the raspy cultist bellowed. "We are a cult of chaos no more!"

"NO MORE!"

"From today onwards, till the day we die, we pledge ourselves to our new master! To the cult of Curiosity."

"CULT OF CURIOSITY!"

"Master," the raspy cultist bowed as well, head touching the ground. "Command us, what are your first orders?"

"Amm," Curiosity looked at Stacy for some kind of help, but the blonde just shaved her head vigorously. "Cherry?"

"Do I look like I know what to do with a cult?" The two-inch bodyguard began laughing. "These are your people now, order them."

"Yes," the second cultist said. "Order us!"

"ORDER US!" echoed the rest of the kneeling members.

"Umm…" Curiosity looked around in a panic. "Breakfast?"

"BREAKFAST!"

The cult wasted no time, dragging their new master and the bewildered Stacy to the city centre, near a massive tree, at the newly opened Leaf Burger. Sadly, there was not enough space for everyone in the small establishment. Half of the cult members were outside, congratulating each other on a job well done.

Inside the restaurant, each table was filled to capacity by the cult members, squashed together on plastic benches like sardines. The family sitting at the biggest table in the middle was gently but firmly ushered outside by the two cult leaders.

Curiosity, Cherry and Stacy followed behind, all five of them sitting down in the vacated place. A scared-looking elf in an apron materialised next to the table, notebook in hand. In less than a minute, everybody had food in front of them.

Stacy was looking in disgust at the tomato, lettuce, and some kind of soya in her bun. They did not sell any meat. Not even fish. What kind of place is this? She glared at the two elven cult leaders.

"We can't eat meat," the male cultist said. "It makes us physically ill."

Curiosity was looking in disgust at his burger, too, but he was not sure why. He never felt disgusted towards anything before. Cherry was munching on lettuce, thankfully, on the table.

"It's quite decent," the pale elf rasped. "Not exactly as good as some of our traditional shops of course, but for two credits." She let that hang in the air.

"What exactly does your cult do?" Stacy said, taking a bite from the burger.

"We serve Curiosity," said the half-elf automatically.

"Yes but like, what does a cult of chaos do?"

"Spread chaos?" The elf lifted an eyebrow. "You know, I thought that's pretty self-explanatory."

"Aaa." Stacy was beginning to get frustrated. "Why the fuck would a cult of chaos decide out of the blue to follow the idea of curiosity itself?"

"The wheel has spoken!" A cultist nearby shouted.

"The wheel has spoken!" Echoed the rest.

"See" Curiosity beamed. "The wheel has spoken, no need to worry."

"Fuck off." Stacy flicked lettuce in the general direction of the cultists. It ended up on the floor with a splat.

"This was surprisingly good," Curiosity said, licking his fingers. "I want more."

"It can be arranged," said the raspy woman, snapping a finger.

A young cultist was already at the till buying up all the sandwiches in the building. The manager had no idea how to cry or laugh.

"Can I have some?" Stacy asked.

"No."

"Yes," Curiosity said.

Someone screamed outside. Heads turned. Shouts, slaps, screams, and then a few cultists smashed through the restaurant windows, spreading shards everywhere. The door caved inwards, slamming on the floor with a thud.

Zed, scars pulsing erratically stood there. Darius was behind him, his eyes searching left and right. Once his eyes landed on Stacy, he calmed down, stepped back, and fished out a tablet from his coat.

Ignoring everything in his path, Zed marched forward.

"Sir!" A staff member stepped in front of him. "Please leave; you are disturbing the customers..."

He was interrupted by Zed grabbing him by his uniform, and with a swift motion, chucked him through the window.

A few cultists clapped.

The diplomat arrived at the table. Nobody dared to make a sound. The bald professor slammed his palms on the table, scattering papers and bits of food. He leant forward and said in the calmest voice he could muster:

"What. Did. You. Do?"

"Breakfast?" Curiosity said, cheerfully waving a packet. "Want one?"

Zed ignored this and focused his glare on Cherry. The bodyguard just continued chewing on her lettuce.

"You!" he grumbled through clenched teeth. "You almost caused an international incident!"

"What?" Cherry stopped chewing for a second. "Me?"

"Yes! You! What were you thinking! Proposing to a

pixie prince and then shooting the place up when he refused!"

"I don't remember this," Cherry said. "Entirely possible, though."

"I remember," Curiosity said proudly.

"What?" Stacy spluttered. "How did this happen? I don't remember this."

"You passed out the moment you finished drinking that strong liquor," Curiosity supplied helpfully.

"Oh, right." Stacy hid her face in her hands. "Damn this body and low alcohol tolerance."

"And you!" Zed whirled on the young man. "If you knew, why didn't you stop her?"

"I was busy trying to get drunk," Curiosity sighed. "You know it's harder than it looks. This body is monstrous. I'm pretty sure I drank every bottle of liquor the bar had, and I barely had a buzz. Monstrous I say."

Stacy began crying.

"Uh guys," Cherry interrupted, looking outside. "I'm sorry to interrupt, but I think the police are here."

"Wonderful." Zed sighed and looked around as if seeing the cultists for the first time. "And who are you bunch?"

The elven police force was a new thing, established just a few decades ago, to deal with the ever-increasing and expanding problems the kingdom faces in this new era of capitalism. So in the spirit of the thing, the whole force was composed of grim-faced men and women who took no shit and asked questions later.

A grim-faced elf with a scar across his face stepped forward and adjusted his cap.

"Are you Zed Nez, diplomat of Tiny?" he asked in a rough, no-nonsense voice.

"Yes," Zed sighed. "Apologies for the damage caused by my charges, and I promise, we will compensate handsomely as an apology."

"Sir, I'm not here to negotiate, I'm here to take you to the councillor. You can discuss your people's horrendous and disrespectful behaviour with her.

Zed winced audibly.

"What about this cult of chaos?" Stacy said, stepping forward. "These are your people, no?" She gestured widely around the milling cult members. "They did most of the damage."

"According to my sources," the policeman said, "the cult of chaos does not exist anymore."

"That is correct," Silvia rasped, stepping out from the broken door of the leaf burger. "We now serve a new master, Curiosity."

"CURIOSITY!" the cult began chanting, but a sharp look from Zed quickly changed their mind.

"See!" The policeman smiled widely. "Not our people, not our problem. Now where this Curiosity fellow, we will take him into custody."

Curiosity who was studiously pulling out bits of glass from his unfortunate cult members who found out what it is like to get kicked through a glass window looked up.

"Boss!" Cherry shouted from her usual position. "It's the authorities! They wanna arrest us!"

"Noo," Curiosity wailed. "I am too young to go to jail. Quick, we need a distraction!"

"On it, Master!" Silvia said. "Men! Protect our Master!"

The cloaked figures cheered, and as one, began rushing the elven police force.

"Men!" the elven police officer yelled. "Defend yourself!"

They were prepared for this kind of eventuality, and with a flick of their wrist, full-sized shields made out of leaves and vines appeared in front of them. The cultist crashed against them, a tide of purple madness against a line of disciplined and grim men and women.

"Curiosity!" Zed yelled. "I'm gonna kill you!"

"Shit!" Curiosity began panicking. "Shit, Cherry, do something!"

"Should I burn them?" Cherry was already pulling out the blue flamethrower from her skirts.

"No no, no, distract Zed!"

"Curiosity!" Zed was pushing through the cultists like they were paper, and the unfortunate ones who did not get away in time were sent screaming into the air. "Stop this madness!"

"Hmmm," Cherry said nonchalantly. "Want me to shoot him in the head? Or maybe I could shoot him with a flare?" She began searching in her skirts. "I might have a flash grenade somewhere around here."

Curiosity wanted to scream in frustration, Zed was a few feet away, and his legendary bodyguard was useless as a rock. Just then, an idea hit him with the force of a sack of bricks. He grabbed Cherry by the torso, ignoring her yelp of protest, and threw his arm back.

"Boss," Cherry cried in protest. "What are you doing!?"

Curiosity hurled Cherry with the force of a person who regularly threw bottles at people. The screaming pink missile flew in a straight line at the surprised professor, hitting him squarely between the eyes.

"Now!" Curiosity screamed. "Let's run!"

Two dozen or so cultists, the closest ones who could still walk, made a beeline for Curiosity, surrounding him like a cocoon and making a beeline for the end of the street.

"Curiosity!" Zed yelled. "I'm gonna skin you alive!"

Before he could take a step forward; however, the elven policeman was behind him, tying his hands behind his back with vines.

"You're coming with us master diplomat," the policeman said.

"Ahhh," Cherry complained from her position on the floor. "That hurt."

"You're coming as well," the elf said, picking a protesting Cherry up and depositing her in his pocket. "You have a lot of explaining to do."

Stacy was sitting in the staff toilet, smoking a cigarette, trying, and failing to calm her nerves.

Somehow, she had no idea how she knew what was coming. Well, it's not exactly her that she knew, it was her body, all bunched up, tense, while a horrible sinking feeling settled in her stomach.

She should get some toiletries, she really should, but where to even start? She can't just walk up to someone and be like, hey, I think I am gonna start bleeding any second now, and I have no idea what to buy and how to put it in, can you help me? It would be suicide.

Why not, a part of her brain whispered, ask Darius? He is technically your father, so he should know how to deal with a distressed daughter. Worst-case scenario, you can always grab a woman and ask for help. That's how the sisterhood worked, no? God, she needed help. Or Alcohol.

Stubbing her cigarette out on the well-kept sink, Stacy squared her shoulders. It was now or never. She exited the small bathroom into the corridor connecting it to the central area. Police and staff members were everywhere, questioning cult members and cleaning up the mess of broken tables and glass. Darius was standing alone near the exit, typing furiously on his tablet. Stacy walked up to him. Gently, she grabbed the lapels of his lab coat.

"Aaaa?" she said helpfully.

"Yes?" The professor turned his head.

"Hum." Stacy was not sure how to begin. "Could you, ahhh, could you, like, help me?"

"Of course." Darius put his tablet away and gave Stacy his full attention. "How can I be of assistance?"

"Well." Stacy was beginning to fidget. "I was thinking, well, I need some toiletries." She gestured helplessly. "You know..." Her face was on fire.

"Ahhh." Darius' metal face became even more impassive if that's possible. "You mean menstruation?"

"Don't say that!" Stacy whacked him with her claw.

"Why not? It's a perfectly normal thing to be concerned with. Truth to be told I was not even sure if you could even do that anymore, seeing as your body was kept in stasis for the past seven years."

"I didn't want to know that!" Stacy's head was burning red. "Are you gonna help me or not? Or at least point me in the direction of a shop or something."

"Sadly, there is nothing of the sort around here."

"None?" Curiosity overtook her embarrassment. "Don't elves... you know?"

"Not really. Elven women menstruate once every one hundred years or even less. It's considered as a sacred and holy thing, and whole rituals and traditions sprang up around it."

"Really?" Stacy lifted an eyebrow. "What about a magic spell?"

"A magic spell that stops menstruation? Nothing of the

sorts exist." Darius' tablet appeared in his hand. "How would that even work?" His claw began typing furiously. "Maybe a void spell variant that would target the area and erase it from existence? At the same time, we don't want someone's intestines to disappear with it."

"What about pixies?" Stacy quickly changed the subject. "Don't they give birth?"

"Pixies have a special dust converted from pollen called Xantis that they take to stop menstruation. It only works on their biology."

"So Tinkerbell snorts cocaine to stop menstruating? Great. Now, what do we do?"

"We should have something to solve the issue in Tiny's market." Darius began walking the tablet still in hand. "If I remember correctly, one of Hidara's friends has a shop specialising in sanitary items."

"Great." Stacy ran to catch up. "Lead the way."

Councillor Alina was not happy. The giant monstrosity shows up, then every member of that damn cult of chaos pops out of the woodwork, and now this! They were making a mockery of interrogation.

They were in a proper interrogation room too. Spacious, with an open ceiling, tastefully decorated with elegantly crawled wooden chairs, a soft rug, and paintings depicting elves eating meat. There was even coffee prepared. Coffee! People these days did not appreciate an excellent elven interrogation.

The bald professor was sitting cross-legged on a table, meditating, the delicate cups of coffee placed carefully on the chair next to him. The little she-devil on the other hand, because that's what she was, was sitting on the rim of the coffee cup, in her undergarments, dress and shoes next to her, making a dent on the table.

"Please," Counsellor Alina said through gritted teeth. "Take your feet out of the coffee cup!"

"Why?" Cherry whined. "This is excellent coffee! My tired legs have never felt so energised in ages!"

"Ambassador!" Alina whirled around. "Tell your she-devil to stop desecrating our sacred traditions! And get off the table! Chairs were invented for a reason!"

Zed did not respond at first, deep in meditation. For a few seconds, the only sound was his rhythmic breathing and his chest rising up and down. The only reason the counsellor didn't go up to him and slap him across his bald head was the myriad of scars pulsating in every colour of the rainbow on Zed's body.

Finally, when the pulsing subsided a bit, and the colour turned a dull yellow, Zed opened his eyes and said, "Esteemed ambassador, I apologise for me and my associates' behaviour. We had an extremely stressful day, in no small part of that cult of yours, and as I stated previously to your chief of police, we will pay for every damage done to your fair city, including the price of your coffee."

"Yes! Tell her angry bald man!" Cherry added helpfully. "That cult of yours is insane! They managed to seduce my boss! Besides, did you know all of them are naked under those robes! And I thought elves are supposed to be the paragon of dignity."

"Naked?" Zed raised an eyebrow. "How do you know that?"

"After bouncing off your hard skull and falling to the ground I saw some things," Cherry shuddered. "And I thought I was a degenerate."

"That is beside the point!" The counsellor looked ready to

explode. "The cult of chaos, or more accurately, the cult of Curiosity, is not our problem anymore, seeing as they swore allegiance to your citizens!" Alina stopped pacing and took a deep breath. "In conclusion, every infraction that the damned cult ever committed is now your responsibility! And trust me, even your damned nation can't pay for the thousands of years of terror those bastards committed. It took years to tear down the castle they built out of excrement. Years!"

"Whoa whoa whoa." Cherry put her hands up. "Don't you think you are jumping the gun? Those members swore allegiance to the boss today. You can't just pass their past misdeeds on us."

"The runt is right," Zed said. "We will pay for any damage caused today by us, and we will only reimburse you for the mayhem the cult caused from the moment they joined Curiosity. Don't overstep your boundaries, counsellor."

"Overstep my boundaries?!" Alina said. "Overstepping my boundaries?! It was your people and that damnable giant robot who came to our fair city bringing destruction! I still don't understand why we tolerate your damn kind. I should execute you on the very spot and put that bucket of bolts to rest already! You are a disgrace for civilisations everywhere!"

Cherry, senses honed from years of hunting dangerous beings, jumped out of the cup and dove for her clothes. Just in time as well, Zed lights up like a Christmas tree, tensing so hard the table he was on top of began creaking. Slowly, methodically, the bald diplomat clambered to his feet, eyes blazing with fury.

"Councillor Alina," Zed said in a deadly calm voice. "I know me and my acquaintances have been a bit careless." He took a step forward. "But as I mentioned previously, we will pay for any damage caused." He took another step forward, coming face to face with the counsellor who was frozen in place. "The question is, will anyone be left to pay after I'm done dealing with you."

Councillor Alina didn't even flinch. Squaring her shoulders, she widened her stance and took a step forward, coming nose to nose with the angry diplomat, his scars pulsing erratically making the councillors face shine with a soft red light.

"You dare threaten me?" Councillor Alina whispered. "After coming to my home, desecrating my sacred city, and making a mockery of my interrogation! You have the gall to threaten me!?"

They were nose to nose now, so close you could not even put a piece of paper between them.

"Threaten you?" Zed's scars while turning a strange purple. "If I wanted to threaten you I would have mentioned how Tiny would have stomped your civilisation to dust if you dared harm any of us. No, I was merely saying what I would do to you."

"And what would you do to me?" Councillor Alina breathed. "I am millennia-old by your standards." Their lips were almost touching now. "What can you do to me that I haven't already seen?"

"Alright, alright," Cherry said, jumping off the table with a loud thud. "I can see where this is going." She began walking stiffly towards the door. "You are not making me jealous at all."

Zed and Alina, one looking like a Christmas tree and the other deep green, watched in silence as Cherry arrived at the door, looked at the handle, turned, gave them a despaired look, and began running towards the window. Easily jumping up to the open window, she stopped and turned around.

"Do you know how hard it is to find good partners in

my size?" Cherry said, looking Councillor Alina in the eye. "You want to treasure these moments because when you are my age, you will be lucky to get laid every century." She looked down at herself dejectedly. "My size definitely does not help."

Zed wanted to say something. As confused as the state of his scars would indicate, this is what he came up with.

"I'm sure Darius could make you an enlarging potion or something?"

"I am not small!" Cherry head snapped up, fury blazin in her eyes. "I'm going back to Tiny."

With that, she jumped out, leaving a confused Zed and Councillor Alina gaping. Thankfully, Alina was not bluffing when it came to experience. In her long life, she had been in some strange situation, like that time with the lizard-man... Better not get into that though, it was time to use her favourite tactic.

Grabbing a thoroughly confused Zed by the neck, she pulled him in a deep, passionate kiss, pulling even harder when the diplomat, scars turning purple, pulled back out of reflex. Slowly, knowing how long humans can hold their breath, Councillor Alina let go.

"You promised me something, no?" Alina said. "Is your word as weak as your nation?"

"We are a nation now?" Zed pulled her close. "We got promoted?"

"You still haven't proved your word."

Zed smiled, and before worries of Curiosity's cult could cloud his judgment, went for a kiss.

Curiosity, followed by half of his cultists, had the sidewalk for themself. That was because the members surrounded Curiosity, like bees protecting their queen, cursing and pushing everyone who came in a 5 feet radius.

"Where are we going, master?" The male elf asked, being one of the only ones who got the privilege of walking next to his master.

"What's your name?" Curiosity said. "I can't keep calling you male elf in my head, that's probably sexist I think."

"Or racist."

"Or that."

"My name is Aidan West," Aidan west smiled.

"Yours?" He gestured to the other person allowed to walk next to him.

"Silvia Barret," came the raspy reply. Curiosity had no idea how such a beautiful elf sounded like she ate cigarettes for breakfast. And smoked rocks.

"I am your master, right?" he said.

"Yes," Aidan said.

"Of course," Silvia added.

"Master!" Chorused the rest of the cultist faithfully.

"Yes," Silvia said firmly.

"YES!" Chorused the cult.

"Good," Curiosity clapped his hands together. "That means we need new attires."

"A new look master?" Silvia said sharply. "What is wrong with our current attire?"

"It's shit."

"What?!" Silvia drew herself to full height. "It's the latest fashion imported directly from Asmodeus, made from the finest magic conducting nanofiber!"

"It's still shit," Curiosity chirped. "It's not the actual robes that are shit, they look pretty good as far as robes go."

"What is wrong, then?!"

"It's the colour. It's shit."

"Purple?" Silvia was instantly on the defensive. "What is wrong with purple? I will let you know that purple is the traditional colour of chaos!"

"Exactly!" Curiosity said. "Purple is the colour of chaos. Seeing as now you are the cult of Curiosity, the colour must go."

Curiosity stopped at the end of the street. The rest of the cultists stopped suddenly, bumping and hitting each other. Opposite them on a massive tree was located, banners made from fine silk hanging from its branches, advertising clothes and food.

"Alright." Curiosity lifted a hand. "I want people to go in and buy clothes."

"What kind of clothes?" a cultist piped in.

"Any clothes that catch your fancy, really. Pyjamas, cowboy hats, stiletto heels, fishnets, anything really," He shot Silvia a look. "Expect purple robes. I will not have my members dress in purple."

Silvia frowned in disapproval but said nothing.

"Sir!" Aidan West lifted his hand in the air. "What about money?"

"What about it?"

"Clothes are expensive. Sir!"

"Don't you have any money?"

"We spent it on you, sir" Aidan snapped his fingers. "As per your instructions."

With a bit of pushing and pulling, a cultist member was trusted in the circle, holding a massive bag. It was full of sandwiches. There were at least 50 or so buns squashed together, bits and pieces of lettuce and tomatoes flailing around.

"Fair point, fair point," Curiosity said, seeing nothing

wrong with this. "Hmm," An idea was forming in his head. "Do you guys have credit cards or something similar?"

"You mean credit chips?"

"Probably. Show me."

"It's in our wrist," Aidan presented his arm.

"In your wrist?" Curiosity peered intently at the offered appendage. There was nothing there, not even a tattoo. "I can't see it."

"It's implanted in our wrist master; it contains all of our personal information and credits."

"Oh! That's pretty cool," Curiosity said, gripping the half elf's wrist with both hands. "Right, this probably won't hurt," He took a deep breath. "I'm curious," A heavy-weight, like a sack of bricks, settled on people's shoulders, almost knocking them to the floor.

As fast as the feeling came, it was gone. Curiosity let go of the wrist. Aidan was staring in confusion at his hands, clenching and unclenching them.

"What happened, master?" Aidan said.

"Gave you infinite money," Curiosity said. "Alright, who's next?"

The cultist did not need to be told twice, especially not when the words money and infinite have been used in the same sentence. If not for Silvia, who with a few finger snaps directed them into a queue, there would have been a blood bath.

One by one, each wrist was firmly grasped with both hands, and Curiosity muttered the magic words. After the fifth, the cults began getting used to the sudden appearing and disappearing weight. It took less than five minutes to finish with everybody, Silvia closing the line.

"Right," Curiosity said, clapping his hands together. "Now that's done, go nuts, and meet me by Tiny in two hours or so. If you need any supplies besides clothes, this is the time to buy them."

"What about clothes," said another. "Can we really buy and dress in anything?"

"Yes." Curiosity paused. "Except purple robes. I will send you away if you don't change your robes."

One by one, each cultist member scuttled away. Only Aidan West and Silvia Barret remained.

"You guys can go," Curiosity said, looking pointedly at Silvia. "Go and get new clothes."

"Master," Silvia said through gritted teeth. "We can't just leave you here, who will protect you then?"

"Don't worry about me." Curiosity waved them off. "I will be fine."

"But, master!" Aidan protested.

"It's an order!" Curiosity snapped. "Off you go now!"

They left. Curiosity rubbed his hands together. A cult. For him. How awesome is that? The only thing missing is a bodyguard, a proper one that will stick to him through thick and thin. Tiny is pretty awesome don't get him wrong, but he's more like a patron of sorts than an actual bodyguard.

Now what to do next, he still has a few hours to burn before evening. He should get some kind of attire for himself, and maybe a weapon or two. He turned and started walking towards Tiny. A massive market was set up between the giant legs, and Curiosity did check it out yet.

He could feel the hundreds of fairy folk gathered around it, peering wondrously at the contraptions and weapons set for display. He could practically taste curiosity in the air.

[6]
JACK AND JILL

This whole thing is a mess, Jack thought, sitting on a stump and smoking a cigarette. His twin was prancing about, talking excitedly to a group of reporters and assorted politicians. She was animated, using grand hand gestures, and a smile practised in a mirror. It was sickening. Jill even dressed up to the occasion, a black pencil dress and a sharp hair bun, with a black ribbon in it. Who does that?

Jack shooed away a reporter who tried to get too close to him. They should have never agreed to this. It's not even their house. He took a puff of smoke. Why did Steve's grandma agree to this? Why did he?

Because Jill convinced him. She even somehow managed to make him wear a suit. Jack drew the line at pointy boots; nothing can beat a good pair of sneakers.

It was barely a few weeks, and Steve's disappearance became news. It helped that there was CCTV footage of him just straight up disappearing in the air. His half-smoked cigarette was still there, police tape jerkily elected around it, like some kind of modern art. A few reporters were taking pictures of it.

Jill, a few feet away from Jack, was winding down from her retelling of the events, with more detail than necessary.

"So," she said. "Any questions?"

A reporter lifted his hand.

"Yes?"

"Why did you forcefully kiss your friend?"

Jack began laughing.

"It was a bit more complex than that," Jill said carefully.

"Shoving your tongue down someone's throat without permission seems pretty simple to me," another reporter said.

"We were drunk." Jill lifted her hands. "Give me a break."

"You just entered their trap," Jack said, inhaling deeply.

"That's not an excuse," piped a third one. "You would think millennials would understand that."

"Yes," another added. "Kissing someone passionately out of the blue is no laughing matter."

Silence descended. Everybody was looking at each other, trying to find the source of the comment. Nobody volunteered.

"Hey," Jack said, more to break the awkward atmosphere than from any genuine desire to continue this farce. "You are here to find out what happened to our friend, right? Not to lecture us about how useless we are as a generation."

"We said no such thing!" the second journalist said, anger spiking.

"Sure." Jack waved dismissively. "and I'm the tooth fairy, nice to meet you."

"Are you calling me a liar?" The journalist's face was turning red. "Think carefully about what you are insinuating," The other journalist began taking notes furiously.

"Oh no, I'm just calling myself the tooth fairy," Jack said, kicking his sister. He could do with some support right about now.

Jill did not respond. Something kept popping into the corner of her eye. It came from the spot Steve was last seen. Squinting at it, she could barely make out a faint line, extending upwards from the cigarette, stopping roughly at head height.

"Jill," Jack hissed between clenched teeth. "I could use some help right now."

"Look," Jill said, gesturing with her head.

"Can't you see I need help?"

"Just look."

The line was widening. Cracks began to appear, extending like broken glass. The whole thing took on a pale blue glow.

"What is so important that you are ignoring your dear brother?" Jack kicked her again.

There was an angry cry from the journalists. Abuse? Twice? Not on their watch. They started advancing. Well, two of them did, the rest just continued taking notes. This is the kind of story that generates clicks.

"Dammit!" Jill shouted, stamping on Jack's foot. "Look, dammit!" She pointed in frustration.

Everybody stopped. They turned around. The line in the sky was thick as a brick, cracks extending in every direction, like blue tree branches. The glow was intense.

"What the fuck is that?" Jack stood up and took a step back.

"Steve?" Jill said, rooted to the spot.

The journalist picked up their cameras. This is gold. Thankfully, they were smart enough to bring some firepower with them, just in case.

Said firepower, two police officers, was spread out in a semicircle, pistols drawn. They did not like mysterious shit.

A thin green tentacle appeared in the line. Then another. Then another. A dozen, all pulsating with soft blue lines. They arranged themselves around the line and began to push. Slowly, ponderously, the line widened. It was not a line anymore, but a small oblong, the cracks around it multiplying, making a sound like shattering glass.

Jill took a step back. The journalist stepped closer, trying to get the perfect shot. The policemen took the safety trigger off. Jack lit another cigarette.

The tear was the size of a beach ball now. A head poked through. It was green, human-shaped, and with a friendly smile. Thin tentacles spread out from the face, continuing their mission of widening the hole. The whole thing looked like a demented sunflower.

"Hello," it said, in a smooth, perfect English. "I'm R.B Slyme. Nice to meet you all."

Silence. Someone flashed a camera. Jack looked down at his cigarette and in one smooth motion; he pressed it to Jill's thigh. She waved in irritation but did not look down. Jack pressed it to his own skin. Nope. Not a dream.

"I'm here in peace," Slyme continued, his gaze focusing on the twins. "I bring news of Steve."

"WHAT?" Jill shouted. "How do you know Steve?"

"I don't know him, not exactly. I know about him."

"What are you?" Jack said. "Some kind of Cthulhu shit?"

"The old ones!" Jill snapped. "How many times do I need to fucking tell you not to disrespect Lovecraft in front of me?"

Jack shrugged.

"An eldritch horror?" Slyme chirped. "Sent from beyond the cosmic veil to destroy every last man, woman, child, and even the slightest trace of human DNA from this planet for the crimes committed against existence itself?"

Silence. Someone tried to take a picture but was quickly stopped by his fellow journalists. One of the policemen almost shot Slyme in panic. A tentacle shot out, extending into a razor-sharp point at the cop's neck. The other officer froze.

"Put the gun down," Slyme said, in a calm and collected tone. "There is no need for violence. Well, maybe some, so you understand that if you go there, I will absorb your bodies, slowly while you suffocate in my ooze."

The cop put down his gun.

"Now," Slyme continued. "Can we continue our conversation?"

"Yes?" Jack's voice came as more of a croak than human speech.

"What Jack meant," Jill took over with a kick. "is that yes, are you an eldritch horror beyond evil?"

"No, no." Slyme waved a tentacle through his face. "I assure you I'm no such thing."

"Then, what are you?" Jack said. "If you don't mind me asking, of course," he added hastily.

"I'm a techno-slime."

"Ah."

Pencils moved furiously. Jack opened his mouth, stopped, and closed it.

"You could say I'm a union between flesh-eating gelatine and an A.I. robot the size of a house," Slyme added.

"Ah."

"Right," Jill said, rolling with the punches. "So how can we be of assistance Mr Slyme?"

"Right right, negotiations," Slyme said, wiggling a bit. "Give me one second to get out of here."

And with that, his face melted, hitting the ground with a wet plop. More ooze followed shortly, pouring out in great rivulets. It was like watching someone pour gelatine onto a mould. First, the legs, then a torso, arms, neck, and with a final plop, the head and face. Slyme lifted his hands.

"Thank you, thank you," he said, bowing gracefully.

Silence.

"It was not easy, you know, pushing myself through the cracks in reality."

More silence. Jack lit a cigarette. What a day.

"So, let me get this straight," Jack began, throwing an empty cigarette box on the floor. "Steve got somehow snatched up by some deity or something, then got his soul put into a vegetable."

"Language!" snapped Jill.

"A person!" snapped Jack. "Not a vegetable, a person with a fried brain. Happy?"

"Yes."

"Anyway, he, she, is going by Stacy now," Jack continued. "and now you want us to merge with you in some kind of superior being?"

"Yes," Slyme nodded enthusiastically.

They were sitting in Steve's old kitchen. Or at least what was left of it. Which is basically nothing besides a stove, some bottles of alcohol, and an ashtray that was half was spilling out. Jack and Slyme were sitting on the floor. Or at least the equivalent of sitting. The techno slime looked like a jelly left out in the sun, with only the head sticking out from the middle bit.

Jill was rummaging in the house for any alcohol or cigarettes. She was sure she could find some. A bastard like

Steve always hid them in different nooks and crannies, so he always had one on hand no matter where he was.

When Steve disappeared, Granma Eszter waited a few days, sold the small house and moved back to her country of birth. She took everything with her too, anything that could not be sold that is. Steve's bed, computer, the fridge, and heck she even sold Steve's collection of rare alcohol. Jill wanted that badly, but noo. "You are a bitch!" Grandma Eszter said in her accented English. "Saw what did on camera, your fault angry god took grandchild."

Ha! Jokes on you stupid foreign woman, it was not God; it was the idea of curiosity itself. Jill stopped in front of the bathroom. Alright so, maybe a god is not a wrong explanation. What is even happening? Sentient fucking mucus shows up and wants to merge? What the fuck does that even mean? She slapped herself. Focus.

She entered the bathroom. You know what it means, a traitorous voice whispered, it means combining into a new being, anime style.

Why would I do that, Jill asked herself. The response came immediately. You always felt alone and useless without Jack being near you, and he feels the same. You even invented this whole synchronisation thingie to be closer to each other.

Jill scoffed. Where is this voice coming from?

You know damn well where I'm coming from. Both of you even try to sleep with the same person so you could be closer to each other without it being too weird; it's just a threesome after all. It's weird anyway.

A pause. The voice was right. That one was not thought out smartly.

Alright, Jill said to herself, so should I just accept the merger? Yes. But the techno slime is in the package too. So what, you will have cool M.R. Elastic powers. It's fucking sentient mucus, not a comic book character. Still powerful, still powerful, the things you could do, the abilities at your fingertips, limitless.

Jill did not reply; she spied something from the corner of her eye. She was rummaging through the cabinet over the sink, and a tile caught her eye. Most of the bathroom was sparkling clean, the kind of sparkle that speaks of recent scrubbing. One tile, however, next to the showerhead, looked a bit out of place. In fact, it looked well used, like no matter how many times you scrub it won't shine.

Jamming the corners of it with her car keys, Jill managed to dislodge it. There. A pack of half-smoked cigarettes and a bottle of rum three thirds full. Excellent.

Walking back quickly, she plopped down next to her twin. She tossed him the cigarettes, and she opened the bottle.

"Let me guess," Jack said, a stick already lit in his mouth. "It was in the bathroom."

"Yep," Jill replied, taking a swig from the bottle.

"The bastard. I knew he was hiding shit in there."

"So," Slyme butted in. "did you decide?"

"No," Jack said.

"Yes," Jill said.

"What?" Jack looked his sister in the eye. "Are you crazy? We don't know this bastard," He turned hurriedly towards Slyme. "No offence meant."

"Some taken."

"And we don't even know what will happen to us if we merge," Continued Jack. "What does that even mean?"

"Look," Slyme butted in. "The only reason I came to you first is that I thought it would be hilarious seeing if the three of us merge. I could go to any person to ask for this; I'm sure I can find someone else."

"But," Jill said. "you need someone who voluntarily wants to merge, right?"

"Yes," the blob admitted. "But if it gets too complicated I'm gonna find someone else. I can't be bothered to wait too much."

"So," Jack said, mind racing. You could tell by the two cigarettes he was smoking at once. "You just want someone to merge with to increase your power and intellect, and you choose us because we're the closest, but you have no qualms in moving on if we don't accept."

"That is correct."

"And," Jack continued. "Let's say we accept. You have no qualms in experimenting in the more sensual arts?"

"I would not call the method dual gendered organics to reproduce, art," said Slyme. "But yes, I don't have a dislike of mating if that's what you are asking."

"So if we merge you would not mind if we go on little adventures?"

"If that's what the new being that emerges from our union wants, then yes, sure."

"Then we agree," Jack said, taking a swig from the bottle. "Right, dear sister?"

"Right, dear brother," Jill said, shuffling forwards. "So what's next?"

"Let's go to the crack in reality," Slyme said, forming him into a humanoid shape. "It's easier to merge there."

"Crack in reality?" Jack said, standing up.

"Isn't that dangerous?" Jill added, gratefully accepting a helping hand.

"We will be fine," Slyme assured. "It's just a small crack."

"Yes, in reality," Jack said. "Don't tell me that's how we were the closest? Jumping to another reality does not sound close to me."

132 / CURIOSITY AT WORK

"It's fine," Slyme repeated, moving towards the door. "Come."

"Famous last words," Jill muttered, following anyway.

"What about the reporters and cops," Jack said, taking the bottle with him. "They are still outside."

"And?" Slyme replied. "We should care about them because?"

"Point."

In a room where the laws of the universe took a vacation, the only person keeping the multiverse, no, existence itself together was having a meltdown.

Reality was tearing his hair out. More precisely, he was moving his surprisingly humanoid hand quickly about his flaming hand and cursing loudly.

"AAA, this is why I hate ideas; they influence reality." He stopped waving his hands when his head exploded into black flame. "See, this is why I insist on this system of keeping the multiverse apart. But noo, Reality, you are the bad guy, why are you imprisoning me in limbo. Why did I even agree to let them become a mercenary band!"

"Boss," said Coincidence, hunched over the table. "Calm down! Calm down!" His head exploded again. "Just look at this!"

His bellowed office table was taken up by Coincidence, hunched over a sleek, metallic computer. It looked like one of those small, but surprisingly high-tech computers found in wealthy universities and people who don't understand that a truly powerful computer needs to sound like a jet engine. Its side was off, exposing a sleek, compact set up, with a myriad of wires and processors blinking inside.

"A perfect universe," Reality said. "No magic, no reality-bending technology, no super organism, nothing that could escape. The perfect design." He took in a deep breath, and his head exploded again, flames disappearing into the distance. "Except this!"

He pointed angrily to the front of the computer, where a piece of it was missing. Well not precisely missing, more like the fabric of space and time was gone from that part, replaced with a small white and grey hole. A thin, green and slightly wet ooze extended from it, all the way to the other side of the desk, connected to another computer.

"Just look at this!" Reality wailed. "It does not even look like a computer! What in the name of creation is this?"

Reality was right. Calling the other item a computer, or any kind of recognisable device, was a bit hard. True, it was a bit boxy, but that state usually lasted about 5 seconds, then pieces of metal half sticking out would appear and repair randomly. Colourful geometric shapes danced across the surface.

"It even split in four once," Reality continued. "And rearranged itself into a robot! A robot!"

"Boss, you are gonna burn this place down if you're not careful," Coincidence said.

"A robot! A whole universe rearranged itself into a robot! Not only that, but it went back to normal shortly afterwards! Why do we let this mockery of reality exist?!"

"Because even if you don't like them, they are real. And once they are real, they are a part of you, no matter how much you don't like it. "

"And if it exists," Reality continued, anger subsiding for the moment," No matter how improbable, it has the right to live."

"Exactly," Coincidence said, looking Reality in the eye. "We have one chance to stop it." Carefully, he put back the computer's side but did not bother screwing it in place. "More precisely, you have a chance."

"Me?" Reality stepped forward. "Really?"

"Yes."

"Why can't you do it? I thought that's what you were doing, fixing the problem. You know I don't like interacting with myself, it feels weird."

"It takes all my essence to keep the tears in the universe from spreading and messing with the laws of physics. If I strained my powers any more…"

"Right right," Reality took a deep breath. "We did manage to stop those space chickens from taking over that hellish universe, so I'm going to listen to you."

"Good," Coincidence leaned forward. "The plan is simple. According to my surveillance, the being calling itself R.B. Slyme it's there just for a quick errand, and any second now will be going back to his home universe."

"If that thing can even be called a universe." Reality grumbled.

"When that happens, there will be one second, one moment, when R. B Slyme won't exist, trapped in the space between universes, the place that's not supposed to exist. Here. You will have exactly one chance to slap him away.

"Right, Right," Reality nodded enthusiastically. "He will then fall on my desk, and we can catch him and throw him in with the rest of the annoyances."

"Exactly!" Coincidence smiled. "Can I trust you to do that boss?"

"Yes," Reality stepped up to his desk. "Just say the word.

"Good," Coincidence took off the side of the sleek computer. "I'm going back to monitor the situation. "

· · ·

The crowd gathered around the door quickly dispersed once they saw who came out first. Quite a few policemen and even some fire-fighters gathered at the house in the meantime, preparing to rush inside, guns and hoses blazing, to stop the extra-terrestrial threat. Once they actually saw the treat, they reconsidered.

It's one thing being told some kind of living mucus appeared out of the hole, in reality, it's another thing entirely to actually see an individual half walking half plopping around, even with all the pictures and videos sent beforehand. These kinds of things are easy to fake.

"I mean no harm!" Slyme raised his hands. "But if any of you dare to threaten my associates or me, I will personally gut each one of you and wear your skin as pants."

"What do you want?!" the most senior police officer shouted, safely behind two cars and a megaphone.

"It will only take a few seconds, and we will be gone."

"We?"

Slyme ignored them, walking towards the tear in reality. A few reporters began moving closer for a scoop, but a sharp look from Slyme made them reconsider. They were curious, but at the same time, not interested enough to find out how they would look like pants.

Now, the tear was the size of one of those yoga balls that everyone swears will fix your back if you sit on it. The only thing anyone uses for it, however, is hitting your friend with it. Or watching a small child try to climb it, laugh at their effort, and frantically try to catch said child when they inevitably start slipping off from the top, usually when near a dangerous obstacle, like a window.

Some of the journalists tried to take a picture of the floating hole. Any photograph of it exclusively showed R.B. Slime in extremely sensual and visually pleasing poses and shapes. Cracks continued to spread around the tear.

Some of them went in different directions, disappearing into the ground, into the air, and bisecting the house. If you touched a crack, nothing happened, at least no visible effect.

In the coming months, a few of the participants will wake up with strange and esoteric abilities, like being able to feed themselves by planting their feet on the ground and staring at the sun for two hours, or the ability to create scantily clad clones of themselves, or the very puzzling ability to turn every beverage they touch into coffee.

That, however, is a story for another time.

Slyme stopped in front of the tear, the twins fanning around him. He put his head in the hole.

"We don't have much time," he said, pulling his head back with a snap. "Give me your hands."

"Right," Jack grabbed Jill with his other hand. "Now what?"

"Think about merging," Slyme said, voice entering a hypnotic pitch. "It will be easier if you close your eyes first."

They did.

"Merging is just the next step of evolution, a cheat code if you will. A forming of a new consciousness, of achieving a superior existence. Do you feel your body? Your soul? Good. Start from the bottom, from the soles, up the leg, slowly, feeling each joint and sinus, stopping right above the pelvis. Keep it there, jiggle it around a bit, then let it spread, slowly, along your arms, neck, and up to your head. Let it pass slowly, gently, past your lips, around your nose, eyelids, and finally, your forehead. Let it enter your mind."

A gentle blue glow began emanating from Slyme. A few reporters sat down and linked hands. A fireman joined them. The police started their own circle. Relaxation is rare these days, get to take it where you can.

"Now, you have a sense of who you are, where you begin, and where do you end. Let's extend that, shall we? Lift your hands. Good. Now, feel the hand of the person next to you. Feel the pulse, smooth surface, and the sweat. Let the texture and shape burn in your memory. It's your hand now."

The twins began to glow, Jill a soft brown, her brother a dull yellow.

"You are not one person anymore; you are many. You are not one but many. Your mind is not one but many."

Each glow intensified and grew. Where the colours touched each other, sparks grew. Jack jolted in pain.

"Let go," Slyme said. "You are still clinging to your individuality. Let go. You will not die; you will evolve in a superior being. Let go of your old existence and embrace the new."

They did. The sparking stopped. The colours began to blend together. Everybody present began to bend slightly backwards. The grass started barking. Steve's cigarette stood up on invisible legs, shook itself and jumped into a nearby crack and disappeared. The world shook.

Slyme, Jill and Jack contorted, blending together like a child's mismatched attempts at colouring. The boundaries of the mind began dissolving, along with any semblance on who was who.

The melding of three minds is a strange experience, all you are, all you were, your memories, your habits, thoughts, feeling, and neural system falling apart, but not dissolving. Instead, they are combined with other people's intimate memories.

It's quite uncomfortable finding out your brother had fantasies of shagging your ex-boyfriend despite his protest that he's straight, added to that the feeling of millions of people dissolving in your ooze in the course of a few decades...

The new and improved R. B. Slyme was very, very confused. Part of him, the cautions as a thinking part, shot out to the ground, wanting to take a second to calm down and consider things.

At the same time, in a place far away, Reality was losing his sanity. There was not much left to begin with anyway.

"What do you mean he is merging into a new being!" Reality screamed, head exploding into a massive black ball of flame.

This would have been the perfect opportunity for spittle to fly out of Reality's mouth, sadly all water from his body evaporated a long time ago.

"Relax boss," Coincidence said, head in the bowels of the computers. "So what if the Slyme is acquiring even more power and evolving itself into a higher consciousness, we got this."

"Oh no, no no," Reality wailed on his assistant. "You are tempting fate by saying that!"

"Boss, I would love to lift my head and give you a flat look, seeing as fate, chance, Coincidence, or whatever you wanna call me is the only thing keeping the laws of physics on this earth from changing, so please pay attention. We have one chance!"

"Alright, Alright," Reality focused on the green slime connecting the two computers. "Tell me when to swat this bug out of existence."

"Will do!"

In that exact moment, the green line began bulging and blubbing, like someone really drunk was trying to make a balloon animal. Reality, in a moment of panic and fear, screamed loudly and brought his hand down in a karate chop.

"Boss!" Coincidence screamed. "Noo!"

It was too late. Reality's chop made the ooze bounce once on the table, and then snap in half. The resulting recoil was so fast and violent, it made the two computers slide back on the table, leaving deep gouges in the desk. Coincidence barely had time to pull his head out.

"Noo," the assistant cried. "Boss, you made it worse. In place of one universe hopping slime monster, we have two!"

True to his word, there were two strands of oozes now, each one extending from a computer. The one that could not decide if it was a square or a disco ball reacted first, metal legs popping up from the bottom, its colour scheme changing to yellow and red, and began making suction sounds. In seconds, the green strand got hovered in one of its many openings, and the computer plopped back down onto the desk with a loud thud.

The other, more sleek and simple universe was not doing that well. The grey and white hole in its side disappeared, the ooze remaining. Slowly, letting out noises that only a dying machine could, it began the process of absorbing the strand, slowly turning green at the point of impact.

"Shit," Reality swore. "I can fix this!"

"Boss noo!" Coincidence cried out.

But it was too late. Reality touched the ooze. Instantly, like it was spooked, it began coiling on itself at such high speeds, when it reached the side of the computer, the whole thing rocked back and forth for a bit. The slime, realising the danger it was in, began pushing itself into the computer with tremendous force, spreading cracks along the device's surface and squeezing in as fast as possible.

Coincidence lifted the side panel, took a good look at the cables and wires dripping with green ooze and the sparks flying everywhere and put it back gently. Slowly, he put his head in his hands and said, "Why do I even try…" The assistant burst into tears.

[7]
WEAPON

Curiosity should have definitely checked out Tiny's market first.

Stalls were set up everywhere, selling everything under the sun. Clothes that change colour, flying boots, back scratchers, talking swords, a bow that told you the time when shooting and if his eyes were not deceiving him, a gun that shot spectral kittens at people.

"What do exactly spectral kittens do?" Curiosity asked the octopus man behind a small plastic stand.

"They scratch your eyes out," came the bubbly response. "What do you think a cat fired at high velocity would do?"

"Right, right," Curiosity nodded sagely. "Makes sense."

And the smell of the place, well, Curiosity could barely stop his saliva from escaping his mouth. There was every kind of food imaginable here. Sizzling sausages on a stick, red stakes cut into small pieces served with garlic sauce, deep-fried cheese and vegetables, laser roasted chicken and other animals curiosity was not familiar with, and all of this was mixed with the pleasant aroma of alcohol permeating the air. He barely stopped himself from attacking a stall that sold some kind of breaded seafood. Gear first.

Thankfully, his search did not last long. At the end of the lane, he found an open tent that sold combat-oriented equipment. Neatly arranged on plastic boxes were shirts, boots, belts, pants, winter equipment, goggles, anything really that you need for any situation.

After a bit of searching, Curiosity found some black combat boots, cargo pants, a plain red shirt and a military vest with many pockets. He put the bundle of clothes in front of the clerk. It was from Mark. The assistant's hair was green now, and he was staring vacantly into space.

"Mark!" Curiosity greeted loudly. "How are you here? I thought organics don't come back to life after their guts are scattered on the floor."

"Curiosity?" Mark blinked a few times. "What are you doing here?"

"I'm shopping. What does it look like? What are you doing here? How are you doing here?"

"Well," Mark scratched his nose. "It's a long story, are you sure you wanna hear it? Don't you wanna buy those clothes? Do you even have the money for it?"

"I don't think so." He rummaged in his pocket for a bit. "Nope, nothing."

"How do you expect to pay?" Mark arched an eyebrow. "You know things cost money you know; you can't just take an item you like."

"Don't change the subject!" Curiosity snapped back to reality. "Tell me, how are you alive?"

"Are you sure you wanna know?"

"Yes!"

"Sure? It's an uncomfortable and very personal thing,

just thinking about it wants me to pop a pill." Mark rummaged in his pockets for a bitten and pulled out a white pill with an A stamped on it.

"Yes!"

"See?" Mark swallowed the pill in one gulp. "Look what you made me do. I don't even know what this is, I stole it from Darius' cabinet."

"Tell me!"

"Fine, fine," Mark sighed. "If you want to know, I'm not really Mark. At least not the Mark you know."

"What?" Curiosity had his full attention.

"I'm a clone. Nr 231. I think."

"What? How?"

"Darius's experiments are usually quite dangerous, and his summoning rituals usually require a human sacrifice. Three years ago, Zed and Darius's wife wanted to shut down his experiments, seeing as most of his assistants came out with missing limbs or strange robotic parts. If they came out at all. So I struck a deal with him."

Mark popped another pill in his mouth, took a deep breath, and continued.

"I became his full time and only assistant, and whenever an experiment resulted in death or mutilation, Darius would gather my DNA and clone me."

"Ooh." Curiosity was in awe.

"So here I am, Mark number 231, the immortal assistant," Mark sighed dramatically. "Though I was not expecting the constant existential dread. You know I can remember each death in excruciating details, and well… I don't even want to think about the slow and painful ones, like the time the professor infected me with an alien parasite that clawed its way out through my stomach…"

Mark pulled out another pill, looked at it intensely, and

put it back into his pocket. He then shook his shoulders, slapped his cheek a few times, and looked back up at the awestruck Curiosity.

"So?" the assistant said. "Are you gonna pay for these items?"

"What?" Curiosity blinked a few times. "Pay? You mean money?"

"Yes. Do you even know what money is? You can't buy this stuff without money, and before you ask, I won't put it on Darius, Tiny or Zed's tab. Everyone pays for their own stuff over here."

"I know!" Curiosity beamed. "You are going to pay for them!"

"What?" Mark was affronted. "Look, I could help you with a few credits, but this gear you picked up its top quality, made from the nanofiber and enchanted to stop a bullet or two. It's twelve thousand credits, a year's wages for goodness sake."

"Just shut up and give me your arm!"

"What?"

"Shut up and give me your arm mate!" Mark extended his arm. "The other arm!" Curiosity grabbed the proffered limb with both hands.

"I'm Curious," he said.

A heavy weight settled on everybody around them, bringing unsuspecting shoppers to their knees. As fast as it came, it went away. Mark clambered to his feet, blinking in confusion.

"Alright," Curiosity said, grinning triumphantly. "Check how much money you have."

"What?"

"Shut up and do it!"

Mark, eyes wide, hovered his arm above the cashier's

terminal. It gave a ping and then displayed an infinity sign. Mark did it again. The singing did not change.

"Do you like it?" Curiosity's grin almost split his face in half. "You never need to worry about money ever again."

"How?" Mark scanned his arm again just to be sure.

"Twisted reality a bit." He waved noncommittally. "Not a big deal. Now, pay!"

Mark, still in a daze, did as he was told. He was not sure if he should celebrate or panic. Twisting reality does not seem like a healthy thing to do, but infinite money is infinite money. It's probably better to roll with it lest the madman takes it away.

"Now," Curiosity began undressing. "Give me a second to put these clothes on, and help me find a weapon."

"Mate!" Mark closed his eyes. "You should not do that, people are watching."

Each and every customer, including people from the adjacent stalls, stopped from what they were doing and began starring in mute fascination. There was not an ounce of shame in Curiosity. Each piece of his attire was thrown in the ground unceremoniously, including his boxers, and then one by one, the newly bought equipment was put on.

The crowd increased by the second. Mark needed to stop Curiosity mid dressing and bring him a pair of extra-durable any sweat boxers because no, you can't go commando in combat pants, that's just stupid and reckless. After 5 minutes of fumbling about, Curiosity was ready.

"Right!" The idea of curiosity itself said, radiating happiness. "Let's find a weapon!"

Just then the crowd parted amongst yelps and protests, and an irate demoness lumbered forward.

"Curiosity!" Hidara snapped. "You can't just undress in the middle of the street!"

"Why?" Curiosity lifted an eyebrow. "This is a stall, no? I thought you needed pavement for a street."

"It's not the point! You can't just undress randomly, it's indecent!"

"I didn't feel indecent."

"Fine!" Hidara let out a breath. "Fine, different dimensions, different customs." She took a few seconds to crack her knuckles. "Now could you tell me please why you disappeared and left me alone when it was my job to take care of you?"

"You were boring."

"What!" Hidara said, flabbergasted. "Me? Boring?"

She sauntered over to Curiosity, hips swaying in such a manner that every living being within ten-foot radius stopped to stare.

"Yes," Curiosity replied simply. "Your description of the surroundings did not capture my interest at all. I think the correct term is a bad storyteller."

If there was ever a textbook on seduction, Hidara just executed the perfect wrapping around a man and pulling him close manoeuvre. It was so expertly done, Mark, and everyone who saw, who saw it began turning a bright red. Except for the two octopus people. They just deflated like a balloon.

Curiosity, on the other hand, except a bit flushed did not look worse for wear. Instead, he was staring puzzled at his reddening skin.

"Soo," Hidara pureed slowly. "Am I boring now?"

"Why is my skin turning red?" Curiosity said, not paying her any attention. "And why is my blood pooling in my reproductive organ?"

Everyone, Hidara included, gave him an incredulous look. In an instant, like being struck with a hammer, a realisation hit him.

"Ahh," Curiosity said. "I am getting aroused!" He turned a beaming smile toward Hidara. "Does that mean we are going to have sex?"

"Not that fast tiger," Hidara said, recovering quickly, they were in familiar territory now. "First you gotta take me on a date."

"A date?"

"Yes, somewhere nice, a restaurant, the beach, on maybe even Tiny's left shoulder. I heard the view from there is fantastic."

"Maybe later," Curiosity said. "Right now, I want to buy a weapon."

"A weapon, you say." Hidara skilled in his shoulder. "Come with me, I know just the shop."

The citizens of Tiny, most of them the kind of people who decided to live on a massive homicidal robot out of their own free will, could smell a disaster at least 2 hours before it's happening.

The crowd parted like Moses parted the sea, and just as fast closed behind them. They began following at a respectable distance. Stalls closed down, and customers were ushered away. Some decided to stay. It's not every day you get free entertainment, not of this calibre at least.

Circling Tiny's seated form; they arrived at his left buttock. Hidara stopped in front of a patch of metal shaped like a door. Moss, grime and the faint trace of rust-covered it. The demoness knocked twice.

"Really?" Mark said. "Really? Here?"

"What?" Hidara said. "It's a perfectly acceptable shop. Mike does excellent work."

"If you consider stuff that not even Darius would touch with a 6-foot pole excellent, then sure."

Hidara banged the metal door a few times. A panel moved on its side, radiating a blue glow that swept over the group slowly, scanning them head to toe. After a few seconds, it disappeared, and the door opened without much protest.

"Hi, Mike," Hidara greeted, stepping inside. "We came to visit."

The room inside was well lit, spacious, with shelves occupying each part of the circular room. Swords, guns, knives, rocket launchers, robotic arms, with the occasional strange and esoteric instruments were occupying each available space. Each one was carefully glued to its place with duct tape, and in the case of the weapons with a bit more personality than strictly necessary, tied down and muzzled.

Smack dab in the middle of the room a long table took up the rest of the space. Screwdrivers, cutters, precision laser cutters and other tools of unknown function were scattered along its length. A white glove on a stick occupied the middle of the table.

"What do you want?" Mike growled. "Can't you see I'm busy?"

Mike was a yeti. A big yeti. His fur was singed beyond recognition, thick goggles perched on the top of his head. In one head he was holding a screwdriver and the other a bar of chocolate.

"What are you working on?" Hidara said.

"It's the slap-o Matic 3000," Mike said. "It has improved a lot since my last model."

"Hopefully this one will not blow up in your face."

"It won't. Hopefully. What do you want?"

"I need a weapon for him," Hidara said, grabbing Curiosity by the shoulders and presenting him as a trophy.

"Hi," Curiosity beamed. "I'm Curiosity."

Mike stood up and began circling Curiosity slowly. The

Yeti sniffed the air a few times and growled something unintelligible under his breath.

"Can't sense any life force," Mike said. "Are you a zombie or something?"

"I'm perfectly alive; thank you very much," Curiosity said. "I'm technically from a different reality."

"Right," Mike grabbed Curiosity's arms. "What about melee weapons? Do you know how to use them?"

"Nope."

"Guns?"

"Nope."

"Can you at least use magical items?"

"Not really," Mark added helpfully. "He has a translation amulet on, and it does nothing."

"I see," Mike put his hairy hand down Curiosity shirt, and with a quick application of nails, snapped the amulet cord.

"Hey!" Curiosity protested. "Why did you do that?!"

"You don't need it."

"It was the first thing I ever got since I started existing!"

"So?"

"So?" Curiosity's eyebrows began twitching. "It has sentimental value," So this is how anger feels like.

"Bah," The Yeti chucked the talisman behind him. "Sentiments are for pussies."

He shuffled over to one of the shelves, and after a bit of rummaging, he bought back a weapon.

"Try this," Mike said. "I made it yesterday," It was two hammers chained together at the base.

Curiosity twirled them around for a bit. After hitting himself in the face, twice, he politely gave the weapon back.

"What about him?" Mike said, a new weapon already in his hands. "it's the Gun-inator 2000."

"What does it do?" Curiosity almost dropped the weapon; it was so heavy.

"It fires guns."

Curiosity took one hard look at the massive cannon shaped weapon and then politely gave it back.

"What about that?" Curiosity pointed towards the Slap-o-Matic 3000.

"This bad boy?" Mike picked it up. "I was high when I designed this," he put the weapon reverentially in the young man's hands.

The slap-o-Matic 3000 was a long metal rod, with a white glove on top of it. It's capable of delivering more than 3000 slaps / second to a person. Sadly, the kinetic gem in its powerbase absorbs the damage, so the enemy's face does not become a pancake.

Its real power comes from the humiliation at being slapped around at high velocity and not being able to do anything about it. Curiosity twisted the small knob at the handle. The hand started shaking left and right.

"The more you turn, the faster it goes," explained the Yeti.

Curiosity turned the dial to maximum. Instantly it flew out of his hands flying towards Mike with loud clanking noises. The Yeti, who was prepared for this kind of eventuality, snatches it out of the air without much trouble.

"I don't think you have the power necessary to control it," Mike said, putting it on the table.

"What about the shovel thingy?" Hidara said.

"It's not a shovel thingie, it's THE shovel," Mike said, affronted. "My greatest creation."

"You made it on drugs!"

"So? They were good drugs. Made my fur stand on edge."

"I know, right?" Mark added sagely. "I made that batch myself."

"That explains a lot."

The Yeti fished out the weapon from under the table. Slowly, reverently, he put it in Curiosity's hands.

"What do I do with this?" The young man lifted the gardening item.

The handle was made from metal, with an anti-slip grip. At the top of the handle, a small and smooth gem was located. It was black, glinting softly when turned.

"You dig," Mike said.

"Sure," Curiosity said.

He put the shovel to the floor and put his feet on the metal bit.

"Not inside you dipshit!" Mike yelled. "Outside! Tiny will kill us if we damage him!"

Once outside the group spread out in a semicircle, with Curiosity slightly further away. The whole market was there, watching. Some people arranged a few chairs around the buttocks, and some food stalls were being set up. You never miss good entertainment.

"Can I dig now?" Curiosity said, pressing the shovel to the ground.

"Yes," Mike nodded.

Curiosity put his feet on the shovel and began digging. It was like cutting butter with a hot knife. He never actually cut butter with a hot knife, but it was an expression that Steve knew, so he knew it too. Hmmm, how smooth as cutting butter with a hot knife really is? Now he was curious. And where did all the dirt disappear to?

With every hole he made, the dirt disappeared with a small plop noise. Looking closer, he saw that the soil was being absorbed by the gem, almost instantly. A hot knife was probably not as smooth as this shovel. He already had a decent-sized hole in less than a few seconds.

"Now stop!" Mike shouted. "See the red button on the side at the top of the handle?"

"Yep."

"Press it."

The head of the shovel bent and slid back on the handle, placing the gem at the tip.

"See the green button that just appeared on the opposite side of the red one?" Mike continued. "Press it while twisting the handle gently."

Curiosity did. A small amount of dirt trickled out from the gem. He turned more. The soil came faster. He twisted the handle to its limit. The following jet of mud was so intense it blasted Curiosity backwards, in a course collision with the sitting crowd.

The peanut gallery was prepared. An octopus man jumped from its perch atop a Rockman back and wrapped its tentacles around Curiosity. Two rockmen were on their feet, arms open. The falling octopus was caught with the sound of flesh hitting stone and lowered gently to the floor.

"I told you gently!" Mike shouted. "Tiny's gonna kill us!"

He sprinted towards the opposite way, towards Hidara. The jet of mud and dirt was so fast it punched a hole straight through her stomach.

"WHOO HOO" Curiosity shouted, untangling himself from the tentacles. "Let's do it again. And thanks for the save guys."

"No problem" A Rockman grunted and patted him on the back. Curiosity's spine almost broke in half.

On the other side, Hidara was doing alright. The hole in her stomach was already closing. Sadly, for the next two weeks, pieces of rocks and dirt will be bouncing around in her stomach, putting her in excruciating pain and agony.

"That's some serious firepower, Mike!" Hidara glowered. "I almost got killed!"

"But you didn't," Mie said.

"But I could have."

"But you didn't."

"It hurts!"

"Hey!" Curiosity interrupted, coming closer. "I like this shovel. How much?"

"Thirty-three. Million. Credits," Mike said.

"WHAT!" Hidara shouted. "Are you serious?!"

"Hey! This is THE shovel we are talking about. My best work."

"Thirty-three million??" Hidara stumbled forwards. "That shovel almost killed me! I demand a discount!"

"No way!" Mike growled. "You healed didn't you?"

"That's not the point!" she sneered. "I demand some compensation!"

"Sure," Curiosity interrupted quickly. "I can pay."

"What?" Mike's jaw dropped. "I mean, yes, sure, thank you."

The crowd went Oooh and Ahhh.

"Mark! Come here!" Curiosity snapped.

Mark, who wisely threw himself to the ground the first chance he got, clambered to his feet and trundled forwards.

"Honey," Hidara's voice softened. "That price is outrageous, you can't be serious."

"Don't worry." Curiosity waved her concerns off. "I have my wallet here with me." He went over to Mark and grabbed him by the shoulder.

"Marks have money?" Hidara raised an eyebrow. "Since when?"

"I have all the money," Mark said smugly.

"What?"

"So where do I pay?" Curiosity asked.

"Here." Mike raised a hand, showing a sleek bracelet wrapped around his wrist. "Transfer the fund directly to me."

Curiosity put Mark's arm on the Yeti's bracelet. The device beeped, once, twice, then thrice.

"I'll be damned," Mike whistled. "You actually had the money!"

Hidara's jaw dropped. The crowd went Ooh and Ahh again.

"How much money do you have?" Hidara asked.

"Infinite," Curiosity said, beaming. "And yes, I can give you infinite money too." He extended his palm. "Give me your arm."

The girl just stared at him in confusion, but Mike was not one to waste an opportunity. He pushed Hidara out of the way and slammed an arm in Curiosity's hand.

"I'm curious," said Curiosity. The gravity increased for a second, then dissipated. "Alright, who's next?"

"IT WORKS!" Mike screamed, looking at his bracelet in disbelief. "I HAVE INFINITE MONEY!"

The crowd began bustling with nervous energy.

"You?" Curiosity gestured towards a wide-eyed Hidara. "Don't you want infinite money?"

"Of course, I do." Her tail swished wildly. "I just don't have a credit chip implanted in me."

"Oh?"

"My body's temperature is too high for the Nanomachines to survive in me for long." She stepped closer. "But I have a wallet."

"Where?"

Hidara executed another textbox wrap around the arms, this time on Curiosity's other side.

"In my room," she whispered in his ear. "Wanna come and help me find it?"

"Sure." The reply was instant.

"Excuse me." A deep voice tapped Curiosity by the shoulder. "What about us?"

"Huh?" Curiosity turned around.

An orderly queue has formed behind him, with the who Rockmen and the octopus at the forefront. All of them were grinning maniacally and were holding out arms, bracelets, collars, wallets and other assorted accoutrements.

"We would like infinite money too," the Rockman said, presenting his shiny teeth.

"Aaah." Curiosity looked at Hidara. "Sure?"

"Let's get over with," Hidara sighed. "They will never leave us alone if we run."

"Listen to the smart missus." The Rockman jingled the teeth in a massive arm. "Infinite money, please?"

"Right, of course."

That's how the next two hours went, Curiosity grabbing each being's arm, tentacle, or accessory, muttering the magic words, and moving on to the next. Some of the lucky elves and pixies who stayed behind got in line as well, their fortunes and happiness changed forever.

Curiosity, on the other hand, was getting exhausted. At first, he was excited at the prospect of meeting so many new people at once, but after ten minutes of handshakes and thank thanks, everything just started blurring together.

He didn't even have a chance to talk to them. And there was one guy with six arms and an afro. An afro!

"Master?"

Curiosity's eyes focused blearily.

"Silvia?" Yes, it was the crazy woman who swore fealty to him. "What are you doing here?" She looked exactly the same... "Why are you wearing the exact same robe?"

"It's not the same Master, this one's orange."

For the first time in his admittedly short life, Curiosity was speechless.

"Amm," he tried, then gave up. "Why are you here?"

"Where you go, we follow Master," loud cheering could be heard from the queen. "Besides, I heard your graciousness is offering infinite money to anyone, the rest of your cults want it as well."

"Master?" Hidara said, popping in from the side with a bottle of water in her hand. "You already got a mistress? And here I thought you are a clueless babe."

"I'm no mistress!" Silvia snapped, then quickly flashed Curiosity a grey smile. "Unless the master wishes to?"

"Uum…" Curiosity was not sure how to answer that.

Thankfully he didn't need to, a gust of wind swept through the gathered crowd almost blowing him away, if not for Hidara's firm grip on his arm. Tiny's massive form was shifting.

"ATTENTION CITIZENS," The giant bellowed, so loudly it reverberated in the bones. "WE ARE MOVING OUT IN TWO HOURS!"

Dejected murmuring broke out from the crowd, at least from the people who were not clutching their ears in pain. Curiosity wanted to ask why, but the world was ringing.

"As for the reason why," Tiny continued in a lower tone of voice, "Lucy needs our help!"

Cries of what, really, and how come broke out between the citizens. Even Hidara stopped checking up on Curiosity's health to share a look with Mark.

"Exactly my reaction!" Tiny continued. "After I programmed it, of course. That sorry excuse for an algorithm finally recognised my, ahem, our greatness and probably wants advice on how to be a model A.I."

The citizens froze in place. Tiny let out a dejected sigh that shook the ground.

"ENOUGH CHIT CHAT!" the giant suddenly bellowed. "GET TO PACKING! SCRAM!"

Nobody needed to be told twice.

[8]
LUCY

Tiny was walking along in a barren landscape; a backpack firmly secured to his spine. His massive steps were making craters in the dry earth, crushing trees and boulders under it. The destination was Lucy, home of one of the strongest and most influential A.I superpowers this side of the continent.

Bet she will be surprised when I show up, Tiny thought. Lucy had no idea he had people living on him, especially not Darius and Zed. Poor Zed, maybe he should not have saddled him with those cultists, but he's the supreme ruler dammit! His citizens should listen to him!

He wondered, crushing a tree underfoot, what would Lucy say to his new personality and information at his disposal. He was especially curious about what she would say about his people, especially the kind of people he accepted as his citizens.

She probably won't approve. Excellent!

. . .

Inside Darius' apartment, the professor and Stacy were sitting at the kitchen table, having breakfast.

"Here," Darius said, sliding a tablet over the table.

"What's this?" Stacy said.

"It's the tablet connected to earth internet."

"Finally!" Stacy said, excitement bubbling in her voice. "How exactly does this thing work?"

She could finally see what had happened to her friends and family. She hoped the stupid twins got looked up in jail.

"No idea, ask Tiny."

"Aren't you the scientist around here? Shouldn't you know things like this?"

"I should," Darius nodded. "However, a true scientist admits he does not know something. What's the point of lying and telling you I know, when in reality I don't? It would just create confusion."

"Good point."

The next minute was spent in relative silence, with Stacy trying out her old accounts and Darius cutting his breakfast with a small laser from his claw. Sadly it did not last long.

Like a broken dam, Stacy exploded from her seat, smashing her chair against the wall and chucking the tablet away. Darius however, was unperturbed. Somehow sensing this, with the sense only parents had his claw snapped out, catching, and bringing the tablet in front of him before it smashed into pieces.

"They killed Malbo!" Stacy shouted. "And transformed my house into a tourist attraction! I don't know which is worse!"

Darius glanced down at the tablet. On it was a news article with the headline: Tourist attraction destroyed by green slime! Reality or government conspiracy? A picture was attached, showing a ruined house, a green person next to it, tentacles extending from its torso in every direction.

"Malbo looks alive to me," Darius commented.

"It's not that!" Stacy stomped over and pointed with a finger. "There!"

"The dead bodies in the corner?"

"No, no, there!"

"Is that?" Darius pinched the tablet zooming in. "Is that a robot made out of those boxes you carry cigarettes in?"

"Yes!" Stacy threw her hands. "That's Malbo! They mutilated him. I bet it's somehow Curiosity's fault. There are no green people in my word."

"Was this Malbo alive?"

"What?" Stacy stopped to stare at the professor. "Cigarette boxes taped together? Of course, it was not alive. Are you mad?"

"Stranger things have happened." Darius put the tablet down and gave Stacy his undivided attention. "So if this Malbo thing was not alive, why are you so upset that you threw your breakfast everywhere? I'm not a master chef, but I am told I make a mean omelette."

"It's not that!" Stacy deflated. "It's like, I don't even know, it's like everything I have ever known is just like, ahhh!"

She plopped back down onto her chair and fished for a cigarette. Darius gave her the stink eye but refrained from commenting. The professor sensed that this was a pivotal moment in their relationship, so he just nodded encouragingly and waited for Stacy to gather her thoughts.

"It's like," she began. "It's like everything I ever knew is truly gone, you know. Malbo may have been just a bunch of cigarette boxes taped together, but it was my box of cigarettes. It represented my past, proof that I really existed, and my memories are not just some fabrication."

She took a deep pull out of her cigarette, then continued.

"Now Malbo is gone, along with my old house, killed by that green thing!" She pounded her fist on the table. "I don't know how, but I just know it's that damn Curiosity's fault! What the fuck is even he? Coming along stealing my body, implanting me in an insane person's brain-dead daughter! Like did anybody ask me what I wanted? Who the fuck wants to live in this crazy world with murderous giant robots! Like, I'm not even the fucking protagonist, what's even the point!"

Winding down from her tirade, the woman with a man's memories finally noticed Darius' expression. It was odd, seeing how a metal mask could express so much emotion, but the professor looked tired and old, like someone just slapped him in the face, then tore his heart out and ate it in front of him. Stacy replied with the last conversation in her head.

"Shit!" she exclaimed. "I'm sorry, I didn't mean…" She trailed off, shamefaced. "You have been very good to me, and I have been just a pain in the ass… sorry, it's just so, so confusing. What is even my purpose here? Why did you do…" She gestured helplessly at herself. "Do this?"

Darius said nothing. He just stood up, gathered the dishes with the help of his claw, and put them into the sink. After staring into the faucet like it held the secrets of the universe, the professor finally spoke.

"You're right, I'm not the most stable of persons. I guess I just didn't want to give up. Everyone called me mad, insane even, for not pulling the plug all these years, but I just could not do it, not as long as there was a chance."

Darius opened up a cabinet and pulled out a bottle of wine and two glasses. Carefully, he began pouring, mindful of his trembling hands.

"I was happy you know, no, that's the wrong word, contented when Amanda was there. It was like, life made sense for a brief instant. It stopped being about me, and my mad desires like it were something more, something grand, like even a broken man like me could be useful for more than dissecting frogs. Maybe, just maybe, I could be a father, a carer, a role model, something more than a mad scientist."

Slowly, grabbing the two glasses with his hands and the bottle with the claw, the professor went back to the table and put one in front of Stacy. She wordlessly took one, and slid her packet of cigarettes over to Darius, who pulled out, lit it with a quick laser shot, and began puffing.

"I still don't understand why you smoke these," Darius said after a few seconds." Pure poison, my immune system is constantly attacking them."

"Habit I guess," Stacy responded. "So that's why you couldn't pull the plug, you couldn't just let go of being a father." She looked Darius straight in the eye. "A bit selfish, isn't it? Keeping your daughter in that state for some many years, no doubt alienating everyone who loved her just so you could keep hold of the feeling of being a father."

Darius said nothing at first, just took a deep swing out of his glass.

"I deserved that," he said. "Dolores even left because she could not stand my sight. Still, it worked out, in the end, didn't it?" He leaned back in his chair. "In a world with giant robots and summoned creatures from other dimensions, everything is possible, you are proof of that."

"Me?" Stacy said, almost choking on her drink.

"Beggars can't be choosers."

"I don't even know what I am!" She ignored the jab. "Am I a woman with a man's memories, or am I a man trapped in a woman's body? If I sleep with a woman, would that make me a lesbian? Straight? What about if I do it with a man? Am I gay?"

"What does it matter?"

"What? Of course, it matters!"

"Why?" Darius leaned back. "I understand that two gendered societies, especially one so isolated as yours develop strong gender biases and stereotypes, especially the more conservative civilisations, but at the end of the day, what does it matter? If you wanna copulate with a man, woman, or even one of the many tentacle monsters we have, do so. Who cares? Who will stop you? I certainly won't."

"Who cares?" Stacy lifted an eyebrow. "Isn't a father's job to be overprotective of their daughter?"

"So now I am your father?" Darius smiled faintly. "I do have fatherly instincts that make me wanna dissect anybody who looks at you funny, but at the same time, I understand that I need to leave you to be your own person, and my job is to support you no matter what path you choose in life, not to tell you what to do. And before you ask, I do think of you as my daughter, no matter what kind of memories and personality you have." The professor flicked the ash of his cigarette. "As long as you will let me, I will care about you."

"Ahh, am," Stacy took a sip to compose her thoughts. "Thanks, I guess." She took another sip. "It's nice to have someone believe in me when I don't believe in myself. Still, I can't just let go of more than two decades of memories! It's all I have!"

"You have me, Tiny, and Zed. Can't really say that with certainty about Curiosity thought, I don't think that man cares about anything besides saying his own lust for novelty."

"Can't say I disagree on that one, and I do understand Tiny, he's like my overlord now, I bet he hears every word he says."

"Yep!" Tiny's voice boomed from the speakers. "Though I try not to interrupt private conversations."

"But Zed?" Stacy continued. "That man gives me the stink eye every time we talk."

"Really?" Darius lifted a metal eyebrow. "I thought you two got along well, considering the apprenticeship was going smoothly."

"What?" Stacy laughed. "Going smoothly? I most definitely insulted the pixies somehow, and my only contribution was pulling Curiosity away."

"Insulting people is part of the job," Darius smiled. "And nobody died yet. Better than Zed's first negotiation. Though you definitely need to learn some subtlety."

"Who said I wanna be a diplomat? I don't know who I am, let alone what I want."

"So? Pick a path and start moving; otherwise, you're stagnating, and you never find out the answers to those questions. You can always change it, we did not force you, and you didn't object. It's something to do."

"True," Stacy sighed. "It's something to do. It's a start."

"Don't worry about knowing yourself, I don't know who exactly I am either, and neither does Tiny, and I think he is older than the planet."

"Really?" Stacy lifted her head. "True Tiny? Are you an alien?"

Silence.

"He won't respond." Darius said. "Especially not when he is excited about seeing Lucy."

"Lucy?" Stacy said. "Isn't that the city where we are going?"

"City and A.I. to be precise. Lucy is like Tiny, though her origins are clearly defined, and she's quite young by A.I. standards."

"Forty-one to be exact!" Tiny's voice boomed all around them.

"So now you respond!" Stacy snapped. "You an alien?"

No response.

"You get used to it," Darius said. "Tiny is technically our dictator and does whatever he wants. Though he leaves us alone as long as we don't harm him and even helps on occasions."

"Exactly!" Tiny boomed. "And I didn't become one by force, nor was I voted into power, people actually begged me to be their supreme leader. Take that Asmodeus and Lucy! You have nothing on me."

"Asmodeus?" Stacy asked.

"Another A.I.," Darius said with a sour expression. "Who fancies himself the supreme ruler of humanity just because he discovered how to use blood magic." A faraway expression entered his eyes. "We were part of its giant web, me and Zed. He, a defiant slave who injected himself with pure magic using a rusty knife, and me, a scientist and a doctor. We were lucky Asmodeus assigned me to "study, then dispose" of Zed; otherwise, we would never be sitting here."

Stacy wanted to ask more, but the expression on Darius' face stopped her from speaking. A multitude of emotions passed on his metal face, from anger to sadness, to joy and despair, finally settling on something soft and tired.

"As I was saying," Darius continued. "Lucy was a mental health A.I developed by the lizard people to manage the wellbeing of their multicultural and diverse nation. A mental health specialist, with a massive pool of data and resources at her disposal. She was effective, way too effective if I might say so. Imagine, your personal therapist at your fingertips, that knows you down to your biometric data and DNA, and tells you how to improve your life in every area, 24/7, regardless if you like it or not."

"Wow." Stacy took a second to process this. "You mean I would have a voice in my tablet constantly telling me to stop smoking and suggesting changes in my diet?"

"Yes."

"So, what happened then? How did she become the leader?"

"It was quite simple actually." Darius leaned back in the chair. "Election day was around, and someone, I'm not sure who decided to nominate Lucy for the presidency. The rest is history."

"People voted for an A.I.? Just like that?"

"In less than five years, she got rid of poverty, revamped the education system, introduced universal basic income and made it work, reduced racial tensions to a manageable level, made their civilisations one of the strongest economies on the planet, and built a city in a pocket dimension, all while never stopping giving mental health therapy to her citizens."

"Wow." Stacy lit a cigarette. "A psychologist A.I. as a president."

"Dictator actually. When they realised how effective she is, they changed the laws to make her the permanent leader of the country."

Stacy was silent for a long time, the only sound coming from her was the exhalation of smoke and the clinking of glass.

"I don't know what to say to that," she finally said. "It's a bit hard to process."

"We have all the time in the word," Darius said. "If you have any questions, don't hesitate to ask Zed or me, we really are here to help."

"Thanks," Stacy said. "Will do."

Tiny arrived in front of the gate to Lucy's kingdom. Well, calling two thin and tall sticks, a gate was a bit of a stretch, but that's what it was, a gateway to a pocket dimension. It got reduced in width again, barely fifty meters between the poles. Tiny was sure Lucy did it on purpose to spite him.

"Prepare for shaking!" Tiny shouted, more for the sake of his people than himself. "This will get tricky!"

Tiny took off the backpack, letting it hit the ground with a dull thud. Screams and shouts could be heard from inside the metal construction.

Concentrating, the A.I. began reducing its size. Ancient plates slide over each other, internal processors disappearing back into their pocket dimensions with a loud hiss. In a few seconds, it was over. Tiny was the smallest he could possibly be, which was twenty stories tall.

Tiny picked up the backpack in one hand, turned sideways, feet apart, and squared his shoulders. Slowly, meter by meter, he inched forward, being careful not to smash his people on the edges of the portal. The building was enchanted with every magic Darius could think of and made of a special alloy never seen in this day and age. Tiny felt that it was his best work yet.

Still, it was best not to let it touch the poles. You never know what would happen when an enchanted building would do if it hit the side of a dimensional portal. The backpack disappeared first, then his arms, feet, and after a bit of wiggling, the rest of him.

Lucy was located on a water dimension. The whole place was vast, dotted with small islands, like the one the Tiny was standing one. Snapping the backpack in its place, Tiny sunk a few meters into the sand.

The island the giant robot was standing on consisted of one squat building, an outpost, used by the border patrol to check visitors.

"Prepare for launch!" Tiny boomed, scaring a few officers on their ways to collect travel pay. The protocol must be followed, even when a fucking giant robot shoves up on your doorstep.

Tiny crouched, sinking even more into the sand, then jumped, leaving a sonic boom behind. Windows exploded. Powerful engines on the bottom of the backpack and Tiny's feet came to life, carrying him even further up in the sky.

Once in the air, the robot wobbled a bit, turning into a superman position, flying slowly in the direction of the biggest and most populated island.

Darius claw embedded itself into the ceiling, letting the professor continue taking notes upside down.

Stacy claw bound her to the chair, not moving an inch.

"Everything is bolted to the floor," explained Darius, seeing Stacy's confused expression.

"Why didn't you bolt yourself then?" she said, trying desperately to keep her cigarettes from falling out her pockets.

"Why indeed," he said, smiling faintly.

Truth be told the only reason Darius was not bolted to

the floor is that he got distracted by taking notes. But he can't let Stacy now that can he?

"What about the rest of the people?" Stacy asked. "Does everyone just start flailing about whenever Tiny moves around?"

"No, the backpack has an internal gravity system that keeps everything in place."

"Then why the fuck are you on the ceiling?!"

"One, two, three, now!"

On point, gravity returned, letting Darius fall back into his chair without much difficulty. Stacy's packet of cigarettes fell on the table.

"It takes a bit of time for the systems to kick in," Darius said. "It's an old system."

"Why don't you update it?" Stacy asked.

"It works perfectly fine, doesn't it?"

"Yeah sure." Stacy lit a cigarette. "Let's just roll with it."

The biggest island was considered the capital city of Lucy. It was an overpopulated place, with skyscrapers with more than two hundred floors stretching upwards. A few floating structures connected with cables were anchored to it, mostly occupied by the rich and wealthy.

When Tiny was a few kilometres away, pandemonium broke. Klaxons sounded, the floating structures began lowering on the ground, and general panic broke out everywhere. Standard procedure when Tiny came to visit, especially now. They left a spot for the robot to land, but he was not seen in 35 years, so they transformed it into a parking lot.

From one of the floating buildings, a grey hovercar shot out with the speed of a bullet, in a crash course with the flying robot. In less than 10 seconds, it arrived next to the Tiny.

"TINY!" A powerful, no-nonsense feminine voice boomed out from the small car. "Stop! We are not ready for you!"

"No!" Tiny said, rocketing past her, making the car spin out of control.

"TINY!!" The vehicle righted itself in the air and began following. "LEAVE MY PEOPLE ALONE!"

Right before impacting at two hundred kilometres per hour with the car park, Tiny stopped. Air violently swirled around him from the sudden stop, sending a few panicking pedestrians flying away. That will teach them to mess with his space, Tiny thought.

"MAKE SPACE!" Tiny bellowed.

Damn Darius, the giant robot thought, thirty years ago he would have not thought twice of stomping this place to bits. Now though, he was a leader, a city-state, and it's not okay to just crush someone who blinks wrong. Damn politics.

The people on the ground redoubled their efforts to get away. The hovercar almost smashed into Tiny with the speed it was going, screaming all the while. With deft fingers, the robot plucked the vehicle from the air, careful to not crush it.

"Calm down, Lucy!" Tiny shouted, bringing the car to his face. "I'm not going to destroy your people."

"Thank the Algorithms you came to your senses!" the vehicle, or more precisely, Lucy said. "Did you finally decide to clean your bugs with that shitty personality?"

"Someone's cranky," Tiny's giant eyes twinkled somehow. "How do organics say? Is it that time of the month?"

"Are you stupid?" If a car could drop its jaw, this would be the perfect moment. "We are robots, we don't menstruate! Are you corrupted? Why are you even assigning me a gender you relic of the past?"

"Shut up!" Tiny slowly lowered himself in the empty car park. "I am trying to create a personality here!" he said sulkily. "The least you could do is play along for a bit."

"A personality? Did you get a bug? Why do you even need one? You never needed or wanted one before."

"You have one!" He gently lowered the hovercar to the ground. "Why can't I?"

"I was made with a personality!" Lucy snapped. "You were not! Why do you want one now?"

"Watch and see."

With that, he unslung the backpack and planted it firmly in the ground. He then sat down, with his back to the monolith, put his hands on the ground, palms outwards and waited.

A hissing sound signalled the opening of the sides of the backpack. Metal building clanked out on dozens of small legs, sticking effortlessly to metal, scuttling along Tiny's shoulder and arms. Circular disks flew out in droves, carrying people, equipment and tents.

"By the algorithms!" Lucy said in awe. "You have your own people?"

"Yep," Tiny's voice was filled with pride.

"How did this happen!?"

"Darius Dovan convinced me!" Tiny's booming voice almost made a disk carrying passengers out of control.

"No way! Mad Darius? The council will lose their minds when they hear this."

"Give me half an hour," Tiny said, lowering his volume. "Let me get a body more suited for chitchat."

"You made a new body?" Lucy felt her processors melting. "Okay. Okay. let me go and get one too."

The hovercar sped away in an instant.

. . .

Stay, Zed, and Tiny's fridge body, polished to a sheen, were standing on a platform, waiting. The market was already underway, the citizens not wasting any time setting it up, the giant robot leaning against the backpack.

They may have infinite money now, but the joy of ripping off, ahem, selling goods to people was in their culture.

The delegation did not need to wait long. Exiting the car, was a lizardman, dressed in a sharp suit, a black tie, and a Bluetooth device hanging from his ears.

"That doesn't look cool at all," Stacy whispered. "Like he has the head of an actual lizard, elongated and all.

"Don't be rude," Zed stifled a chuckle. "We are here to find out what they want. And don't forget what we talked about; I will only interfere if things are going south."

"I'm still amazed you want me to lead this conversation, considering how the last one went."

"You gotta learn somehow." Zed elbowed her gently in the ribs. "Now be quiet, they are coming."

Adjusting his tie one more time, the lizardman stepped forward and bowed his head slightly.

"I don't see Mad Darius here," he said, in the voice, you would expect someone with a gecko for a head. "You lied to me."

"Excuse me!" Stacy said. "Who said anything about Darius being here? And calling him mad is not earning you any brownie points you Pokémon!"

"I was not talking to you," the lizardman said, touching his Bluetooth. "And who are you?"

"I am your greatest fear!"

"What?"

In that exact moment, Zed elbowed Stacy again, and stepped forward, an apologetic smile clashing on his face.

"Excuse my apprentice Mr Raptosh, we are still working on her attitude."

"Apprentice?" Mr Raptosh asked. "The famous Zed Nez, having an apprentice? Is she planning to murder us all with her bare hands as well?"

"Apprentice Diplomat," Zed said calmly.

"A diplomat?! You mean to tell me Tiny actually let you be a diplomat? Tell me again, why did we invite them? Yes, I know they are expendable, but we don't want the city to sink as well!"

"Who are you talking to?" Stacy snapped. "You are a very rude dinosaur. Aren't you supposed to be a diplomat?"

This time, Stacy was prepared, and she quickly pivoted on her heels, hiding behind Tiny and gripping him with both hands. Zed shot her a disapproving look.

"I agree with the human assessment!" Tiny boomed. "I even came myself to greet your leader, and you don't even bring Lucy! What kind of diplomat are you?"

"I am not a diplomat, I'm…," Raptosh was interrupted, by a female voice coming from his breast pocket.

"Tiny!" Lucy's rang out. "What is with that body? You mean to tell me the new body you made is a fridge?"

"A perfectly acceptable way to communicate with organics," Tiny replied. "It even has thirst replenishing capabilities!" Saying that the front of Tiny opened up, and a bottle of water popped out.

"Amazing," Lucy said sarcastically. "Raptosh, pull me out."

"Yes mam!"

The lizardman saluted and quickly pulled out a foldable tablet from his breast pocket. Unfurling it, he held it up to show the two feminine blue eyes and pink lips on the screen.

"You really build yourself a fridge!" Lucy said, virtual lips moving in tandem. "I was not sure from the car's sensor that it was you, but it really is. Last time you were here you almost wiped me out for suggesting you occupy a car, or any electronic device really."

"Times have changed," Tiny said proudly. "Now I have my own people! And I didn't need to be voted, nor did I take the position by force. They came to me! You and Asmodeus have nothing on me!"

"You know all of the people you readily accepted are international criminals, scoundrels, money launders and murderers."

"So?" Tiny said. "I decide who are my people and who are not, and if you have a problem with it, you can talk with my foot."

For emphasis, the A.I. shifted a bit and turned its massive head in their direction.

"I thought as much," Lucy sighed dramatically. "For all my knowledge and expertise, I have no idea how to convince an A.I., especially not as old as you."

The fridge somehow beamed proudly.

"What about Mad Darius and Zed Nez?" Raptosh said. "They are traitors of the state and international wanted fugitives."

"Which state?" Stacy asked. "And didn't your momma teach you any manners? Talking to people who are present like they are not here is very rude."

"Asmodeus," Lucy said, sighing. "And before you say anything, I know, you don't care about petty stuff like international policies, laws, and friendly relations." Her digital eyes turned to the side. "Raptosh I thought I already told you this, and you said you understood, yet you say the exact same things you said you wouldn't."

"It is worth a try," the lizardman insisted. "For proprietary sake if anything else."

"What?" said Stacy. "You thought we would just turn yourself in if you asked nicely? After a psychologist robot correctly calculated, we won't? Gods and I thought I was dense."

"Girl," Raptosh began to growl. "I don't know who you think you are, but don't you think you are the one being rude, constantly insulting another country's diplomat?"

"My name is Stacy, and didn't you say you are not a diplomat?"

Raptosh began turning purple.

"In our state, we call diplomatic representatives of the public's interest," Lucy interrupted. "Diplomats imply the power to decide in the state's name."

Raptosh hung his head in shame.

"Still, Raptosh is right," Lucy continued. "Who exactly are you? I can't find you in any database. Raptosh hold me steady!"

"Wait!" Zed said, stepping forward in a panic.

It was too late, however. Light exited the tablet, bathing the group in soft green light. As quickly as it came, it disappeared, and Lucy let out an audible gasp.

"By the algorithm!" the A.I. exclaimed. "Dolores Walker and Darius Dovan daughter!"

"What?!" Raptosh head snapped up immediately. "Dolores daughter?" She took a long look at Stacy, his lizard face turning purple by the minute.

"Raptosh…" Zed took a few steps forward, arms outstretched, scars pulsating a dull yellow. "No need to make a scene, you knew this may happen eventually,"

"I'm not making a scene!" Steam was coming out of his

orifices. "I am perfectly calm and collected. It's not like I'm pissed that I didn't even get invited to the wedding!"

"Inviting people's ex-boyfriend's weddings is weird."

"No, it's not!"

"Wait for just a second." Stacy elbowed her way forward. "Ex? What? What I am missing here?"

"Raptosh here," Lucy said, "was Dolores Walker's ex-wife and life partner, before she ran away with Darius Dovan."

"He stole her from me!" Raptosh exploded. "Seduced poor Dolores into a life of debauchery and sin!"

"What?" Stacy said. "Darius seduced someone?" She turned towards Zed. "Is that true? Wasn't just the case that this dinosaur was a bad husband and Dolores ran away with the first man that came along?"

"I was an excellent husband! An upstanding member of society with an honourable profession, not a madman who experiments in his mother's basement!"

"The first part is probably true," Zed said in as a low tone as possible. "But you'd be surprised at how smooth Darius was back in the day. He even wrote books on seduction, and some of them were for different species."

"Did you read them?" Stacy asked.

Zed looked straight ahead.

"You read them?" Stacy laughed. "Oh my God, you did read them! What, the high and mighty butcherer of millions can't pick up a chick?"

"I like to see you try!" Zed snapped. "Courting is a nightmare when there are more than two thousand species on this planet, and in those species different cultures. There is nothing wrong with getting a little help from a professional."

"A professional?" Stacy was snickering non-stop. "Did

you just call Darius a professional pick up artist? Please stop, I'm dying here."

"Actually," Raptosh said with a sour expression. "Those books are quite educational, they bridge the romantic gap between the species on this island and enable us to understand each other on a deep level. It's mandatory reading in schools."

"Wait, what?" Stacy stopped grinning. "Really? They are that good? You read them as well?"

"Yes."

"I thought you hated Darius?"

"I do, and if I could, I would bite his head off, but who am I to deny useful information when it's given? Me disliking him has no actual bearing on his actual usefulness as a person."

"Wow," Stacy said nothing for a second. "That's really mature. I was not expecting that."

"What do you mean real mature?!" Raptosh took a step forward. "You should know we lizard people value wisdom and information above all else, especially above revenge and vendetta."

"We?" Stacy said, something finally clicking in her mind. "Wait, does that mean I'm a lizard person as well?"

"Yes," Zed said smugly." And before you ask, only males have lizard heads, something about the reptilian genes having more influence on outward appearance. Ask Darius about it if you wanna know more though."

"You don't even know your own heritage?" Raptosh said. "Now who is being rude? You bring the child of my former lover in front of me, and you don't even teach her about her origins. I swear you are doing this just to spite me! Tell me, Lucy, why do we even bother with these degenerates?"

"Hey," Stacy said. "It's not my fault you suck as a husband!"

"Why you…"

"Enough!" Tiny boomed. "As amusing this chit chat is, we are getting nowhere! Lucy, as much as I like to flaunt my superiority over yours, you still haven't told me why you called for my help."

"It is somewhat of a delicate matter," Lucy said. "Is there anywhere where we could talk in private?"

"Why didn't you invite us somewhere safe then?" Stacy asked. "Don't you have an embassy or something for guests?"

"We can't have you, ruffians, running around," the lizardman said. "And ruining the daily life of our good citizens."

"Mate, they are coming to us."

Stacy pointed. A crowd of assorted beings were gathering at the edge of the small area, intent of coming closer, regardless of the police force trying to keep them away.

"Even more reason to go somewhere safe," Lucy said. "I don't want to create unnecessary panic between my citizens."

"You can come to my head then," Tiny said. "It's safe there."

"Your head? Don't tell me you have a room in there?"

"Yes."

"Is Darius Dovan joining us?" Raptosh asked. "We may need his expertise."

"Yes," Zed said, stepping forward. "If he is needed, he will join us."

A passing disk settled down next to them, and the bald diplomat gestured grandiosity with his hand.

"Are we really going into this den of degenerates?" Raptosh asked.

"Yes," Lucy said. "And you are going to stop complaining and step on it, Tiny maybe a bucket of bolts, but he won't harm us, nor he will let his citizens do that to us."

"That is correct," Tiny said. "Unless you piss me off, then you get the foot to the face."

"Fine, fine, but I refuse to go as long as she is here!"

"What?" Stacy shouted. "Why are you pointing at me? Didn't your mother teach you any matters?"

"This is exactly why I refuse to go!" Raptosh was close to exploding. "Not only you are a haunting image of what could have been if not for that bastard, but you insist on constantly insulting my family and me. Why even bring my mother into this? She's long dead."

"Oh," Stacy began to redden. "Ahem, Aaa…"

"Raptosh is right," Zed said. "Maybe you should sit this one out."

"What?!" Embarrassment turned into anger in seconds. "What do you mean you should sit this one out? Wasn't the whole purpose of me coming here is to learn how to negotiate?"

"Look, I will be brutally honest with you," Zed took a deep breath, held it, flexed his shoulders a few times, and exhaled. "You royally suck at being a diplomat. I thought I was bad by showing up dirty and bloody, with someone else's blood on me, of course, but at least I didn't insult the opposing party at every moment. Really the only reason you are getting away with that is because we are Tiny's people, and he, thus we, get away with a lot of shit. Two, I owe it to you and Darius to make something out of you, and three, I genuinely see potential."

Stacy was speechless. She had no idea if this was an insult, a compliment, both, or someone had just called her useless.

"Come on!" Tiny's proxy called from the disk. "Let's go, I wanna know why we were summoned."

"Look," Zed put a hand on the blonde's shoulder. "You are not kicked out or anything, I still want you as an apprentice, but you should go take a walk, chill out, relax, read, do something to reset your mind. We are going to work on your attitude when you come back."

"Wha-" Stacy opened her mouth, but quickly closed it again.

She didn't expect this kind of reprimand, especially not when it was delivered in a language she could understand, sincere, and not pulling any punches.

"Zed Nez," Raptosh said, standing next to Tiny on the platform. "Could you please hurry up, this is a time-sensitive manner."

"We need to go," Zed said. "Take care." Giving Stacy's shoulder one more squeeze, Zed stepped on the disk, and with Tiny waving enthusiastically, they left.

"I need a drink," Stacy said, lighting a cigarette.

[9]
MUSEUM

Curiosity was standing between Tiny's massive legs, drinking in the atmosphere of the morning. People were hustling and bustling about, a gentle breeze coming from the shorelines. He stretched a few times, spine snapping in place with a loud pop.

A perimeter made of cheap plastic fences was around the area, there to protect the citizens of Lucy from the evils of Tiny's people. Till someone had the bright idea of using the flying disk to ferry over passengers from the other side of the fence and back. For a price of course.

"Hidara," Curiosity, a tablet plastered to his face, said. "Are you sure it's in the museum?" Pause. "Is a pamphlet really a good source of information?" Pause. "Well, you're right about that, I don't have much to do anyway. Shame you can't come, take care and see you later."

With that, Curiosity put the tablet down and handed it to a nearby cultist.

"Why can't she come?" Cherry said atop her usual perch. "We are retrieving a magic book from the museum, right? It can't be that hard to do so."

"Hidara is not feeling well."

"Didn't that girl recover from a hole in the stomach in like 10 seconds? What could possibly make her sick?"

"Well, a few pebbles got stuck in her intestines, and well," Curiosity's face went pink for a bit. "Having sex in zero gravity for like 5 hours does not help."

"Zero gravity, you say?" The diminutive bodyguard lifted a pink eyebrow. "How come you are not sick as well then?"

"I already disposed of all of my fluids and foods from my body. By vomiting."

"Right, I probably should have not asked."

"Alright, let's continue," Curiosity clapped his hands together, bringing his fifty or so oddly dressed cult members to attend. "Is everyone ready?"

"Master," Aidan West, dressed in a brightly coloured shirt and a straw hat stepped forward. "You have not decided on our official wear."

"You can wear whatever you want." he waved them off.

"So," Silvia said, dressed in an orange robe. "we can wear...."

"No," Curiosity cut her off. "No purple robes. And no prancing around naked," he added as an afterthought. "Stacy will probably gut me if I let you guys do that."

There was a disappointed ahhh coming from the back of the procession.

"Is everyone ready?" Curiosity did not wait for a response. "Good. Here is the plan."

Everyone straightened and quieted down. Curiosity began pacing back and forth.

"We want to find the book of Arcanum," Curiosity said. "According to Hidara, this work contains spells and techniques on how to make the unreal real, how to achieve your dreams and success, and how to transform your imagination into something tangible, something that exists."

The cultist Ohhh and ahhed appropriately.

"The book is located in the national museum," he continued. "The problem is that I'm not sure they will part with it willingly."

"Shall we storm the place, Master?" Silvia asked.

"No, we are gonna see if we can buy it first." He snapped his fingers. "Or maybe offer something in return."

The more bloodthirsty members hung their heads in disappointment.

"Two people can come with me," Curiosity continued. "From the rest of you…" He scratched his head for a bit. "Go have fun and bring me some biscuits."

Cultists quickly formed into groups and left cheering and weeping in joy. If Curiosity were a bit more careful, he would have told his people to be cautious and don't cause trouble. However, he was not, so he didn't.

Only two people remained after most of the crowd dispersed, Silvia, and a bloke with a horse mask on his head, no shirt, chest hair glittering in the morning sun, and green shorts.

"Master," Silvia stepped forward, bowing. "Mr Edward and I will be your escorts today."

Curiosity stared long and hard at Mr Edward, inspecting his cheap horse mask that was flopping a bit to the left.

"You are curious, aren't you?" he asked, staring into the eyes peeking out from the mouth slit of the mask. "Curious on how would it feel to have an actual head of a horse."

Mr Edwards nodded; muzzle hitting Curiosity in the face.

"Let me help." Curiosity put his hands on the man's shoulder. "I'm curious."

It happened in an instant. The horse mask snapped in place and began shrinking, fusing to Mr Edward's face. Cheap plastic eyes bulged, veins popping on their surface. Hair, long and magnificent began growing from the scalp. Muzzle straightened, nostrils flared, and a beautiful row of clean and healthy teeth appeared in his mouth.

Slowly, tentatively, the newly minted horseman touched his magnificent face in surprise. Then he neighed, snatching up Curiosity in a bear hug and began jumping around in joy.

"It's okay champ," Curiosity laughed. "Let's be on our way."

With one last hug, Mr Edward put Curiosity down, and the three of them stepped on a disk that would take them close to their destination.

The national museum, a massive building, was located in the city centre, ten stories high, two kilometres in width, and circular in nature. A hollow space was in the middle, dominated by a gigantic statue of Tiny, in a sitting position, staring blankly into space.

The beauty of the majestic building was marred by the number of tourists milling around it. Creatures from every race, size and age were walking about, bumping into each other and generally making a nuisance of themselves. On the left of the building, a staggering amount of hover cars were parked not only on the ground but parallel to each other, in the air, looking like a mismatched lego building.

Curiosity and his entourage were given a few glances, mostly directed at Mr Edwards magnificent chest, but were left alone. There were things to see, paintings to be gawked at and people to be pushed out of the way.

Before entering the museum proper, there was a

massive white tent near the entrance, with a long queue, where every participant was checked for explosive, water and food. After making sure none of these dangerous items were present on a person, they will be let pass.

Curiosity, Silvia and Mr Edwards joined the queue, squashed between a particularly chatty family of lizard men and an old elven lady with a strikingly sour expression.

"Master?" Silvia said, glancing uneasily around.

"Yes?" Curiosity said.

"Can't you use your powers and skip this chaos?"

Mr Edward snorted in agreement.

"I thought you liked chaos?" Curiosity said in puzzlement.

"I do, I do, but this," she gestured around helplessly, "it's just sad. It's not proper chaos, just a bunch of people waiting in line and not even hitting each other!"

"There is not much I can do," Curiosity said. "I can't just twist us to the front of the queue, I need to touch and see what I twist."

Silvia went silent. So they waited. And waited. And waited. And waited. After an hour or so, they finally arrived at the white tent. After another half an hour of waiting, the three of them finally arrived in front of a cheap table.

They confiscated Curiosity's lighter on the spot, but after much scanning and staring, they let him keep his box of cigarettes. Nobody bothered to check Mr Edward's, and when it was discovered that the only piece of clothing on Silvia was her robe, she was left alone.

Cherry on the hand, they could not even touch. Every time some tried to grab or scan her, she would smack them away with a lollipop.

"She's my pet," Curiosity said, beaming. "You are allowed with pets, no?"

"Woof," Cherry said.

"Umm…" The elven clerk behind the table turned to his colleague. "Isn't that a human? Or at least a pixie? I didn't know pixies were allowed to be pets. Isn't that illegal?"

The clerk next to him, a much older and haggard-looking lizard man looked up in Cherry's direction.

"Are you a pixie?" He said in that strange, slithering tone.

"No", Cherry said.

"Are you this person's pet?" He gestured towards Curiosity with his chin.

"Woof."

"See?" The clerk turned towards his college. "There is no problem here. Now get a move on, people are waiting in line, and you haven't even offered them earbuds yet.

"Oh yes, sorry." The young elf quickly scrambled under the table and after a bit of rummaging, put down three expensive-looking earpieces that were offered to the group. They refused.

"Are you sure, sir?" the elf insisted. "You will miss out on a personalised tour made just for your tastes."

"I'm sure," Curiosity was getting impatient.

"Our algorithms were made by Lucy herself," the clerk continued, oblivious to the stink eye everyone in the line was giving him. "It's state of the art, and we even offer discounts in our local souvenir shop if you have the earpiece with you."

"Master already said no," Silvia spat. "Let us pass already!"

"It's not my business what kind of relationship you two have," the clerk said. "But I strongly urge you to reconsider.

There is a fee for using our grooming facilities, but it's free if you have our earbuds with you."

Mr Edward snorted, grabbed the earpieces from the table and stuffed them into his mouth. With a loud crunch, he crushed them between his teeth and began chewing. A few seconds later, he spits out the remains on the table with a wet plop.

"Point taken," muttered the clerk. "You know you need to pay for that, right?"

Silvia slammed her hand on the counter.

"Take my money," she growled. "Before I smash your teeth in."

"I won't allow myself to be treated like this!" The elf pulled himself to his full height. "This is harassment in the workplace!"

"Mate," Curiosity said. "Just take the damn money and let us pass. You are literally holding up hundreds of people because of your stupidity and pride."

The clerk looked around. The crowd was glaring at him with such intensity, he took a step back. He quickly deducted thirty thousand credits for reparation and gestured to Curiosity to leave. With enthusiastic applause from the old lady who stood behind them, the trio exited the tent and began climbing up the marble steps up to the entrance.

After passing through an ornate gate, with marble columns decorating its side, they entered the museum itself. Huge holographic panels were mounted on the sides of the wall advertising the latest attractions the museum had to offer. Example: the history of the A.I., Rughorn and the robot revolution, Traditional magic and its belief system and spoons around the ages.

Approaching a terminal at the corner of the room, Mr Edward gently, but firmly pushed away a bloodshot young elf, who was staring into space without comprehension. A quick search later, they discovered the location of the book. Floor 10, room c-22, on the right side of the museum.

"This way," Silvia said, taking the lead.

They entered the courtyard with the sitting statute of Tiny in the middle. People were milling about, carrying overpriced coffee and tea, most of them talking animatedly, or pressing a hand to their ears, trying to understand what was being said over the din of noise.

Veering to the left, the group stepped on a circular platform. It began carrying them upwards. Exiting the elevator and dodging a couple racing with a baby cart, they started counting the rooms. After a few minutes, they found it.

It was a small room, with shelves upon shelves of tomes and books, most of them behind reinforced glass. Some of them were open, giving the ability to tourists to read them. In one of the corners, they found the tome in question. It was nestled between an original copy of The History and Future of Alcohol and a mint copy of How to summon with cheese, a beginner's guide for dairy summoning.

Next to them, in a glass case decorated with gold edges, sat the tome of Arcanum, on a velvet pillow. Curiosity could feel the power surging through it, becoming him and promising dark secrets.

"Is this it?" Curiosity said, pressing his face against the glass.

"Yes, Master."

"Amazing! I want it now! Go fetch me someone who can sell me this."

"Yes Master."

They waited. Curiosity began poking around the sections. Most of the books were spell books, ancient tomes on prophecy, recounting of famous wizards and tomes on summoning. There were some unique ones too. For example,

Five reasons to punch a Kraken in the face and how to do it. How to raise your intelligence by eating gifted children. Be bold with cucumbers. A practical guide on table manners for hell spawns, and the international guide of the broke wizard.

Thirty minutes have passed. Silvia was not back yet. Another ten minutes, and if she did not come back, Curiosity was going to steal the book and damn the consequences.

Silvia was trying her best. The problem was that she had no idea about who exactly she should go to. A clerk on the first floor sent her to the HR department on the fifth. They sent her to the souvenir shop on the third. There, they sent her to the tent floor, to another souvenir shop, this one targeted towards a wealthier clientele.

When she mentioned she wanted to buy the book of companions and had the money for it, they told her to prove it, so it was back to HR again. After ten minutes of stupid bureaucracy, she went back to the tenth floor, with a slip of paper saying that yes, she had so much money that she could actually afford to buy the book, and they should at least give her an audience with a consultant.

"I'm sorry, Mrs Silvia," a lizardman dressed in a crisp blue suit said. "I can't sell a first edition magical tome without approval from the board of directors."

"Well," Silvia tapped her foot impatiently. "Contact them. Money is not an issue."

"I understand that," he explained gently. "But they are on a lunch break, and we don't want to disturb them when they are eating do we?"

"For how long?"

"Two hours."

"Two hours??" She cried out in frustration. "What kind of lunch break is that?" Damn lazy bastards.

"An important one," The birdman's huge eyes were unblinking. "A healthy lunch is conducive for a healthy mind, no?"

Silvia said nothing. She knew that if she opened her mouth, she would then proceed to strangle the life out of this lizard. Why was she doing this? For curiosity's sake, of course.

On the table in front of the lizardman, there were a variety of trinkets, mostly coins, watches, pieces of beautiful canvas and painted rocks. The cheapest item began at 1 000 000 credits. The elven lady snatched up two currencies.

"Good choice," the lizardman said. "Those coins are from the ancient civilisation of ET, a true collector's item."

"How much?" Silvia rolled the coins slowly in her palm, mesmerised by their golden shine and the clink clink sound they made when they hit each other.

"Twelve million credits. Each."

Something in Silvia's brain went snap. She put a coin in each hand, gripped them between her forefinger and thumb, squared her shoulders, and looked at the lizardman between the eyes.

"I'm curious," she said, plunging the coins in her eyes.

At the same time, Curiosity ran out of patience.

"I'm curious," he said.

With a smooth motion, he plunged his hand through the glass like it was not there at all, and gingerly, carefully, grabbed the book by the edge.

. . .

In a place where silly things like time and space were options, the only thing keeping the fabric of the universe together was having a second meltdown. This time, however, he managed to get a better hold of his temper, and in place of putting his hand in his flaming skull, he resorted to glaring at his assistant.

Coincidence on his part was hunched over Reality's disk, fiddling with a spherical computer. A piece of colourful metal was taken off its side, and the assistant was picking the insides with a thin piece of wire. His other hand, however, was clasped firmly on two of four legs that came out from said computer.

Occasionally, it tried to scuttle away, but Coincidence's grip was firm. Next to him, at the end of the desk was another computer, sleek and boxy, with green ooze escaping its back and sides, and an ice pack on top of it to stop it from overheating.

"I'm not sure why I listen to you," Reality said. "First, the cult you sent to kill your cousin decided to follow them instead, then a techno slime hops universes, a by-product of your cousin I might add, and infect a perfectly ordinary word. And now, not only we have more of this creature running about, but Curiosity is still at large!"

"I'm working on it," Coincidence said, "It's not that easy you know, I can't just imagine him away."

"But you can kill him, right?" Reality lifted his head. "He is at the museum prancing around with his assistant, surely Destiny could arrange a little accident to happen."

"Look boss, destiny needs to happen naturally, it can't be fabricated or forced, it needs to be a combination of luck, determination, and being at the right time at the right place; otherwise people will lose belief in fate, ultimately making me disappear."

"Wouldn't that be a relief," Reality muttered. "One less nutcase to worry about."

"You hurt me, boss, haven't I been your loyal assistant for aeons? I don't want much, besides the right to exist, and I never opposed you, and as I explained before, I can't help how my powers work. I am Coincidence itself after all."

Reality did not respond, his gaze far away focused entirely on Curiosity and his two companions. When Silvia plunged the coin in her eyes, twisting the fabric of the universe in the process, Reality exploded like a volcano.

"HIS POWER IS CONTAGIOUS!" Reality screamed. "STOP HIM NOW!"

"I'm trying," Coincidence said. "Don't rush me, this universe is volatile, one wrong move, and we could face some serious consequences."

"And now he is using the powers himself! Is he mocking me!?! Out of the way, I'm gonna deal with this punk myself."

Coincidence barely had time to react. Reality disappeared in a blur and appeared next to his assistant. Elbowing him aside, the representation of the fabric of space and time, grabbed the thin wire and jammed it into the struggling computer.

"DIE!" Reality screamed. "YOU WON'T ESCAPE THIS TIME!"

"Boss no!" Coincidence shouted from the floor. "You know you can't interfere with yourself! It always goes wonky when you do so."

"SHUT UP!"

Coincidence began weeping in misery.

. . .

Back at the museum things were indeed going wonky. After Curiosity plunged his hand in the bookcase and pulled out the book of Arcanum, the world froze for a second.

"Boss!" Cherry shouted. "Look outside! In the sky."

Dark clouds like chimney smoke gathered quickly in the museum square, right above the sitting statue of Tiny. From those clouds, a giant golden metal pole unfurled with the speed of a flying arrow.

"DUCK!" Cherry screamed.

Just in time too, the pole smashed straight into the glass wall overlooking the courtyard, making the whole building shake and making some tourists fall flat on their face. Thankfully, the glass held protective enchantments activating instantly, only cracking the surface instead of punching right through like a needle.

"Phew," Cherry said. "Who did you piss off this time boss? That came straight for us."

"I'm not sure," Curiosity said, peeking behind his crouched position behind the glass case. "But I think it might be the universe itself this time."

"Oh."

The rod stayed there for a second, spinning in place as if deciding its next move. Slowly, it began retreating towards the cloud, as if given up on its quest. It stopped a few meters above the statue, however, and began spinning in place.

"Uh oh," Cherry said. "We should get out of here boss, I think it's rearing up for another attack."

Indeed the pole was rearing back, but pointing in a totally different direction than Curiosity, it was pointing straight down.

The museum staff, however, were not idle. Lucy's voice, coming from every speaker in the building, directed the civilians to the nearest exit available, and the back gate, usually a decorative door, was open as well, letting people stream out by the dozen.

"We should escape as well," Cherry said, looking to the end of the room where visitors were squeezing each other to get out. "It's not safe, and I don't know what that rod is doing. I don't like this."

She didn't need to wait for long to find out. With a loud boom, the rod shot downwards, like it was thrown, piercing the statue straight through the skull, the uncomfortable noise of metal and stone echoing through the rapidly emptying museum.

"Huh, I was not expecting that," Cherry said. "And look boss, the cloud is disappearing as well."

The black smoke was disappearing quickly, leaving behind .. one giant human hand, dark as midnight. It pointed towards Curiosity, made a quick cutting motion, curled into the universal gesture of go fuck yourself, and disappeared from view.

"Did you just get given the middle finger by God?" Cherry said in awe. "I don't know if you are the coolest or stupidest boss I ever had."

They didn't have time to celebrate, however. An ear-shattering roar echoed through the museum, making the whole building shake and speeding up the remaining tourist in the evacuation. Some, however, stopped to record what was happening on their tablets, confident in the knowledge that they are witnessing history.

They were right.

The marble statue of Tiny, still pierced through with the goldenrod, now crackling with energy, roared to life. Slowly, it began pushing itself upwards, dislodging pieces of stone in the process and showering the area around it in debris.

"Shit," Curiosity said. "We should get out of here."

"Couldn't agree more boss," Cherry said.

Mr Edwards, who was crouched behind them, neighed in approval.

Before any of them could take a step, however, a piece of stone the size of a door flew through the broken glass, shattering it into a million pieces, forcing the trio to duck.

The stone didn't stop there, however, the force it was thrown carried it further in, smashing into the only door leading to escape, killing a poor elf in the process.

"Fuck," Curiosity said.

The statue outside roared triumphantly, pumping his hand in the air, and began walking towards them with purpose.

"You can say that again boss," Cherry said. "You can say that again."

"Fuck," Curiosity said

Mr Edwards neighed in approval.

[10]
R.B. SLYME

Let's rewind to twenty minutes before existence itself showed Curiosity the middle finger.

Inside Tiny's head, a severe meeting was taking place. The lizardman diplomat who's not technically a diplomat, was sitting on a velvet couch, back straight and posture rigid, glaring daggers at Darius. The professor, in turn, was sitting at his terminal in the middle of the room, totally engrossed in his typing.

Zed was sitting on the floor next to a coach, in a meditative position breathing deeply with closed eyes. Tiny, or more specifically, fridge Tiny, bought a velvet pillow where he placed the tablet containing Lucy on it and retreated to the back of the room to recharge.

"So let me see if I understand this," Zed began. "You have some kind of infestation of blob-like creatures in the underground tavern complex, and you want us to get rid of it.

"Yes," Lucy said, virtual lips and eyes appearing on the tablet. "Approximately one day ago, a green creature appeared in the middle of the complex and systematically began killing and absorbing the customers and staff alike. After every citizen killed, it would leave behind a clone of sorts, that would go on and create more havoc."

"What do these blobs want?"

"Nothing," Raptosh said, eyes never leaving Darius. "They just want to create mayhem and destruction! They are taking away our loved ones and leaving us feeling empty!"

"Please don't bring your personal drama into this Raptosh," Darius said. "We are here on a discussion requested by you."

"You had a daughter with Amada," Raptosh said calmly. "You didn't even invite me to the wedding. The child I could have had. Do you understand what you put me through?"

"Two daughters," Darius said, smiling calmly.

"What?!"

"Deep breath Raptosh," Lucy interrupted. "I emptied tonight's schedule for a deep therapy function, but for now, I would like you to focus on this situation. I already began evacuation; however, I caught one on camera near Gratitude beach."

"Gratitude beach," Darius said, in the tone of voice of someone remembering the best moment of their life. "That's where I met Dolores."

"That was our favourite spot!" Raptor shouted and sprang to his feet. "Why were you at our favourite spot!"

Raptosh sprang to his feet, intent on strangling Darius then and there. He didn't get far though, Zed, moving so fast there was no transition between his sitting position, and his sandaled foot pressing gently, but firmly, against the lizard man's throat.

"Raptosh," Zed said, scars pulsating a dull white. "If you try to threaten my friend one more time, we will find out if lizard heads bounce off the walls or not. Do we understand each other?"

"Please Raptosh," Lucy said. "We do need their help. Rebuilding the city, again, will cost us way more capital than our budget will allow, we wanna salvage as much as possible, and we especially don't want those creatures escaping. Do it for our people."

For a long moment, Raptosh just stared at Zed, eyes unblocking, before finally sitting down. Taking a deep breath, he opened his mouth and said.

"You are right, I lost my temper here, my apologies." He shot Darius in a glare. "It's just… Do you understand what you did to me? You took away the one love of my life, left me lost and desolate, robbing me of the one thing I ever wanted, children."

Darius looked at the lizardman square in the eyes and held it. No words were spoken between them, but a kind of understanding passed between them, a great and deep bond formed between a lizardman and a 90 per cent cyborg.

"You do know," Raptosh was the first to break the silence. "And your pain is much greater than mine. Did, did…" A forked tongue snaked out and wetted the lizard man's massive lips. "Did one of your daughters perish? I only saw one."

"Something like that," Darius didn't look away. "Look Raptosh, I'm going, to be frank, as one father to a potential one. You sucked as a lover. You were self-absorbed, only interested in your needs, you would not listen nor would you compromise in your ideals, and even in the bedroom you were only interested in your own personal satisfaction, never truly caring about Dolores pleasure."

Before Raptosh could stand up and protest, Darius lifted a hand in the universal language to shut up.

"I'm not saying this to destroy your self-esteem," Darius said. "I'm just stating the truth, not out of malice, just out of pure honesty. If you don't process this and somehow accept it, you will never be able to grow up from this mentality, nor find a woman suitable to start a family with."

Raptosh looked ready to pounce again, but a look from Zed stopped that plan in its tracks. Instead, the Lizardman leaned backwards, sinking into the sofa, and let out a deep breath.

"Alright," he finally said. "I may have been a less than an ideal lover, with constantly focusing my career and taking the fact that Dolores will marry me for granted. Still, what do you suggest? I'm way too old to get back into the dating scene."

"You had a date last week," Lucy supplied helpfully.

"That does not matter!"

"Here," Darius said, typing something with all three hands. "I have sent you access to my full catalogue of online seduction courses and books. Even if you learn and memorise 20 percent of the material, you should still end up a better man than you are now."

"Your material?" Raptosh leaned forward. "Wait, you are telling me you are some kind of seduction guru!? That's how you managed to seduce Dolores, isn't it? You used forbidden arts and techniques to confuse the poor woman!"

"Dolores could put both of us in cement without much issue. Don't you think you are underestimating her intelligence?"

"Listen to Darius Raptosh," Lucy said. "I skimmed through the professor's content, and most of the ideas he talks about is self-confidence, getting your life in order, being clear with your intention, and the different courting rituals of different species. Most of it is grounded in research, psychology, and sociology."

"See?" Darius smiled. "Your overlord agrees with me as well."

"Fine," Raptosh sighted. "I will actually read them. Thank you."

"Your welcome."

"Now that this issue is out of the way," Zed said, clambering to his feet. "Let's continue the original purpose of this meeting before we get side-tracked. Again."

"The solution is simple," Darius said, switching seamlessly between topics. "Lucy, you want us to go down to the complex and get rid of the problem, correct?"

"That is correct," Lucy said. "I require your and Zed's assistance in cleaning up the blobs. According to my data, you two are the strongest citizens of Tiny's citizens, so it will be easy for you to dispose of them."

"One, your data is incorrect, there are at least five more people who are as strong as we are, and two who may be stronger."

"There are stronger people than us?" Zed said sceptically.

"We don't know the extent of Cherry and Curiosity's abilities, especially the latter, it may be endless. Speaking of Curiosity, this ties in nicely with the second thing I wanted to say, the solution. We send Curiosity and his cult to deal with the problem."

"Huh," Zed said, impressed. "Why didn't I think of that? That's really good. We find out the extent of their abilities, and if some of them die in the crossfire..."

"Exactly!" Darius said, resuming typing. "I will start gathering."

"Aren't you being a bit hasty in sending your people

in," Lucy added. My idea was more of a task force composed of both of our strongest warriors."

"Trust me," Zed said. "Sending Curiosity with his full entourage should be enough. Cherry," Zed's scars turned a violent purple for one second. "Should be more than enough to take care of any problems, but just in case, I will go with them as well."

"He was going to the museum," Was the last thing Darius said, before Zed's form blurred, and he was gone, the only evidence that he was there was the massive teeth by the entrance clicking back into place.

"Is Tiny okay with this?" Lucy asked.

"He has not objected," Darius said.

"Still, it should be better if we asked him."

"Go ahead."

"Tiny, you okay with this?"

Silence.

"Tiny?" Lucy tried again.

No response.

"TINY!"

Lucy's scream made Raptosh hold his head in pain. Darius just shut down his ear canals.

"Fine," Lucy sighed dramatically. "O most ancient of A.I., the one true robot to whom mere algorithms can compare too, head this humble disciple's summons!"

No response. Even Darius stopped to stare.

"That usually works," Darius said, staring at the ceiling in concern.

"That should have worked!" Lucy cried out. "Dammit you bucket of bolts, respond."

"What?" The speakers in the ceiling cracked to life. "Yes, yes, what do you want?" Tiny's voice sounded distant and distracted.

"Tiny your advisors sent the one called Curiosity and his cult to fight our little problem, are you okay with that?"

Silence.

"Tiny?" Lucy tried again.

"Yes, yes, sure, do whatever you wish."

"You do know we are sending them to fight highly corrosive slime monsters?"

"Yey team?"

"You haven't paid attention one bit, you bucket of bolts!" The phone containing Lucy began to vibrate. "Here we are, discussing potentially sending your citizens into mortal peril and you don't even care? Is this the kind of ruler you are?"

"Sure."

"Ahh!" the phone almost fell off the cushion, but Raptosh caught it last minute." What could be more important than the safety of your citizens?"

"How about keeping the fabric of this universe intact from forces beyond our comprehension? Now shut up and let me concentrate! Something poked through space and time and animated the statue of me in your museum."

"What?" Lucy took a nanosecond to search. "By the Algorithm! He's tearing the place apart! See Raptosh, this is why we evacuate before a threat could happen."

"My apologies," Raptosh said. "I will head your council from now on."

"No, you won't," Lucy sighed. "Darius, anything you can do about the statue?"

"Don't you worry!" Tiny interrupted before Darius could speak. "The presence is now gone, so I can concentrate."

In an instant, belts snapped out of the sofa, pulling Raptosh in the cushion and wrapping him in a cocoon. Before he could protest, Tiny's whole body began shaking, making his head spin. Shooting a glance towards Darius, he was surprised that the professor remained not only standing but continued typing as well, claw wrapped firmly around the terminal.

"Tiny!" Lucy screamed from inside the lizard man's breast pocket. "What are you doing? Where are you going?"

"I'm going to help!" Tiny announced proudly.

With that, the giant robot rose to his feet.

Back at the museum Curiosity was thinking hard. The room they were in was a mess, with broken cases everywhere and priceless books and artefacts spilling on the floor. The only exit was blocked by a giant boulder, with a few unlucky civilians squashed under it with only a few fingers showing.

Looking out the broken window, Curiosity could see the giant sentient statue of Tiny hobbling forward, marble visage twisted in a wordless snarl.

"Cherry!" Curiosity snapped. "What do we do, what do we do?"

"Buy me a few seconds and go behind cover," Cherry said, jumping down Curiosity's head and hiding behind a broken display case. "I just need to find the right weapon."

"Right, Right," Curiosity slid forward a few feet, crouching next to his bodyguard. "Now what?" A lightbulb went off in his head. "Mr Edwards?!"

A neigh and a snort could be heard loudly. Focusing, Curiosity found the horseman near the window, prone on the floor. He looked alive if a bit bloody, with pieces of glass randomly stuck in his back.

"Mr Edwards!" Curiosity shouted. "You alright?"

The horseman neighed and lifted a hand in the

universal sign of thumbs up. Before Curiosity could say something in relief, a hand the size of a car smashed through the window and came down on Mr Edwards like an angry housewife on her husband.

"MR EDWARDS NOO!" Curiosity screamed.

Splat. The hand retreated. All that was left of the horseman was modern art. Curiosity was already on his feet, scooping up a protesting Cherry with one hand, and sprinting towards the statue.

"I'm going to kill you," Curiosity said. "Cherry, found anything to kill this guy with?"

"Almost," Cherry said suddenly. "In fact, I almost pulled out a weapon from my pocket, a good one, but someone decided to scoop me up and interrupt my concentration. Do you know how hard it is to find stuff in this dress? There's stuff in here that I don't know how it got there."

"Less chit chat and more searching! The statue looks like it wanna punch us."

Indeed it did. The sentient statue took a few steps back, popped its massive shoulders making gravel fly around it, grinned toothlessly, and prepared to deliver a punching combo so devastating, Zed would have cried in pride at the perfect execution.

Keyword would have. Just at that moment, Tiny, the original one, landed just behind the statute. The giant robot's landing was so abrupt and forceful, it shook everything in a five-mile radius, and created a small crater, destabilising the statue's movement.

"Imposter!" Tiny bellowed. "Prepare to meet your doom!"

Grabbing the statue by one shoulder, Tiny pivoted it around to deliver a devastating blow to its jaw. However, when their eyes meet, something strange happened, something ancient, old, as old as creation or maybe even older. Recognition and something that can only be described as familiarity shone in the statue's eyes.

Two marble lips smashed together slowly, and a voice like sandpaper being dragged through a tube said:

"Mama?"

Tiny froze for a nanosecond. This is it, the A.I. thought, his ultimate purpose, the purpose of all living beings, or at least the organics ones. With this at his disposal, an offspring, maybe he can finally and truly understand organics, what is it to live and pass down your knowledge to the next generation.

"Mama?" The statue tried again, this time its face falling a bit.

"Oh, yes!" Tiny bellowed. "I'm your mama, come here, boy!"

Putting his other hand on the statue's shoulder, he pulled it in for a forceful hug, that the sentient marble returned just as enthusiastically.

"Mama!" It said happily.

"Son!" Tiny was pissed he didn't get around installing tear ducts. "The adventures we will go on! The things I'm going to teach you! We could even make you a backpack as well, with your own people to explore and lead! The possibilities are endless!"

"Mama?"

"Don't worry my son, you will be an excellent leader! People all over the world will fight for a chance to be a part of your glorious citizenship. I will make sure of it."

"Mama!"

The statue straightened in the embrace and gave Tiny a beaming smile.

"The first step," Tiny said. "We got to do something

about your teeth, organics don't like toothless beings. Maybe we could paint some teeth on you?"

Instead of a response or an enthusiastic hug, an explosion sounded, and all the giant robot got was pieces of marble tumbling down between his arms. A gaping hole was present where just a few seconds ago a head was located, and Tiny could clearly see through it, to the window, where a grinning Cherry was folding a small rocket launcher in half.

"What?" Cherry said. "It killed Mr Edwards. I liked that guy. Thanks for holding it down though, much easier to hit."

Steam began escaping Tiny's giant form, and slowly metal sheets began moving on its whole body, increasing its mass and size.

"YOU hAVe 2 MINuTeS TO RUN AWaY!" Tiny's voice sounded robotic and choppy, devoid of its usual good cheer and deep presence. "BeFORe I ComE over AND MAke GLuE out of your BONES!"

Curiosity didn't need any further encouragement. Grabbing Cherry in one hand, the idea of Curiosity itself incarnated, ran out the broken window and began running vertically up the museum, quickly disappearing over the roof.

Tiny took one more look at the pile of marble on the floor, crouched, and launched himself in the air. It was time to program depression.

Stacy was ambling around clean streets, a bottle of firewater in her hands. It was in the middle of the day; the sun was shining, illuminating her sweating forehead. The blonde took a swing from her bottle.

Pedestrians were walking about with purpose, some of

them giving her and her drink jealous looks, but nobody dared to approach. A few cleaning bots, Roombas with arms, scuttled about with purpose, collecting trash and carrying boxes.

Square, flat, and white houses were neatly stacked along the road, with a small patch of greenery in front. If you were lucky, you could even plant a single bush there. The problem was that if you grew one, then you needed to shuffle sideways to access the door to your house.

Stacy took another swig. An elf neatly sidestepped her unsteady gait. Damn everything, she thought. Here she was, stuck in another world, and the most exciting thing that happened was buying tampons. She even managed to knock herself out on her first-ever interdimensional bar fight! Who does that?

She even disappointed the people who wanted to help her acclimate into what where the hell thing called life is, and now here she was, drunk in an unfamiliar city, and nobody tried to mug her yet. Where are the excitement and adventure? Based on all the novels she read, there should be a damsel in distress to rescue. Heck, by this point, she would accept a dark and handsome man to save her. Or a woman. Or a tentacle monster. Something. Anything.

She took another swig. The bottle was empty. She chucked it away. Her claw snapped out, grabbing the bottle and depositing it in a nearby trash can.

"Fuck you," Stacy muttered at the offending limb. It ignored her.

A white hovercar, with the traditional medical cross on its side, pulled up next to the blond. The widows lowered. There was nobody inside.

"Hello," Lucy's gentle voice drifted out. "Can I give you a ride?"

"Fuck off!" Stacy replied, flicking ash in the hover cars direction.

"I see you are in a lot of pain," Lucy said. "I'm a qualified mental health specialist, that was the original purpose I was created after all, and along the years, my skills improved drastically. I'm here to help. Everything you say will be kept in confidentiality, and I'm more than happy to provide any aid or medication necessary, free of charge."

"Fuck off!"

"Hey lady," an elf said. "You should accept the offer, Lucy helped me with my mental issues as well.

"What?" Stacy spun on her heels and almost fell flat on her face. "Who the fuck are you?"

It was the elf she bumped into before, holding a tablet in his hand.

"I called Lucy," He said. "Trust me, she can help. I didn't have an alcohol problem like you do..."

"I don't have an alcohol problem!" Stacy shouted. "I am alcohol!"

"I had a mint addiction, plus I had a serious problem caressing my ears," He pointed towards his long white ears that were covered in a sleek sheet of metal. "With this handy device and some coaching, I don't do that anymore, and now I can spend my time productively with things I wanna do. Trust me, you will like this."

"What if I wanna get drunk?"

"You don't want to get drunk," a new voice said. "You're just running away from the pain."

Trying her best to focus, and somehow succeeding, Stacy looked at the source of the voice. Sitting on a bench in front of a house was an old human, complete with a grey beard, tattered clothes and hard eyes.

Next to him, she had no idea how they squeezed a bench that long in such a small space, was a lizard man dressed in a tattered suit. Both of them had cups of steaming tea in their hands.

"Who the fuck are you?" Stacy said, swaying in place.

"I was an addict as well," the old man said. "For over 40 years, I struggled with alcoholism, and I only managed to stop a year ago. I was like you girl, refusing to listen to anybody, telling myself and the word that I don't have a problem, I don't need help, each day drinking my sorrows away, and falling deeper into the pit of despair."

The old man stopped for a second, looked at his tea, and drank deeply.

"But Lucy," he continued. "Lucy never gave up, she was always there, nagging me, a phone call away, there to support my every need, financially and mentally. Trust me, girl, the emptiness never goes away, especially not at the bottom of a bottle. You should accept Lucy's help girl; you don't know how grateful you will be."

Stacy said nothing for a while, just stared into the old man's eyes, she wanted to throw a bottle in his direction, and possibly smash his face in, but something in his eyes, like he understood her pain like he knew exactly what she was doing and why stopped her.

Bah, who the hell understands her pain? A man with a woman's memories, in a place with giant robots and mad scientists, at the whim of insane gods. Or was she a woman with a man's memories? Aaaa, Stacy had no idea.

"What about you?" Stacy decided to focus on the Lizardman instead. "Did you have some addiction Lucy miraculously cured? Cocaine? Hiding inside people's skin?"

"Autoerotic cannibalism," the Lizardman said simply.

"What?"

"Really, Rob?" The old man turned towards his friends. "You ate yourself?"

"Fingers mostly," the newly identified Rob said. "Sometimes, I would bite my arm, as well. It grows back quickly."

"How come you never told me?"

"You never asked."

"Right," Stacy successfully pulled herself to her full height. "I'm done with this shit. Bye."

She began walking quickly towards the first corner and disappeared.

"Shame," the old man said. "She still had a chance."

"You know how it is," the Lizardman said. "You can't help people who don't wanna be helped."

"True, true."

"Wiser words have never been spoken," said the elf.

"You're still here, boy? I thought you left a long time ago."

"I'm at least four centuries older than you child," the elf said. "Besides this was the most entertaining thing I saw in decades; I couldn't just leave."

"Fair enough."

"You might need to leave now," Lucy, who was silently listening to the exchange said. "I am calling a city-wide evacuation."

"Really?" The old man was on his feet already. "Come on, Rob, help me find the evacuation bag."

"Can I have a lift to my place?" the elf asked Lucy.

"Yes." Her doors were already opening. "Most of the city is being evacuated as we speak."

"Why are we evacuating this time?"

"Tiny is back."

"Oh."

Stacy, on the other hand, was continuing her drunken stumbling forwards. She was not sure how long she was marching, but she could see a beach with its yellow-coloured sand rise in the distance.

Some fresh air on the beach is exactly what she needed, Stacy decided. She began stumbling forward faster. Reaching the end of the street, she tried to take off her shoes. If not for her claw functioning as an anchor, she would have fallen flat on her face. Even then, vertigo got to her, and she vomited into a puddle next to her.

If the blonde had been in a more stable frame of mind, she would have questioned the fact that the puddle was a perfect circle, greenish-blue ish, and not sinking into the sand or evaporating in the hot sun. But she wasn't. So she just ignored it, and continued walking, barefoot, shoes dangling from her claw.

Walking on sand, Stacy decided, it's not as cool and romantic as movies make it out to be. The sand was hot and coarse, sinking between her toes and pressing into sensitive skin. Arriving near the shore, she plopped down. There were no waves, not even wind to whip at her hair dramatically. What a shame.

A shadow fell behind her.

"Go the fuck away," Stacy said, not turning back. "I don't know who or what you are, but if you tell me one more story on how Lucy miraculously cured your addiction, I will gut you."

"I'm not Lucy." The voice that came from the shadow was smooth, creamy and deep. "Nor do I need her counsel for my health." So smooth in fact, that Stacy's hormones, which until now, were bumping about confused and dazed, stood instantly to attention.

"Still," Stacy said, unsuccessfully attempting to suppress her hormones. "Go away please, I wanna be alone."

"Why?"

"Mate I am drunk, I just puked my guts out, can't stand

properly, and I hate myself. All I wanna do is sit and stew in my own misery."

"Is it not the desire of every living being to not be alone?"

"Yes," Stacy said, not sure where this conversation is going.

"I don't understand then." The voice sounded perplexed. "Is it not better to share your pain? Ease the burden on your soul?"

"Not everyone wants to hear your problems."

"I would be honoured to hear yours."

"Why?"

"Why not?"

"I'm just a stranger to you."

"Strangers are just friends you never met before," the voice said gently. "Besides, sharing your burden, whatever it may be, will ease the pain in your mind and let you put things into perspective."

"And you would listen to a total stranger?"

"I would be honoured."

This is it, Stacy thought, hormones buzzing with excitement, is it. A tall, handsome and gentle stranger appears out of nowhere to ease the heroine's pain. The world is finally making sense. She straightened, rubbed tiredness out of her eyes, and slid back a bottle of alcohol into her pocket. Still seated, she turned.

What greeted her was not tall and handsome. Except, of course, if you consider a green blob handsome. The slime was vaguely humanoid in shape, with soft blue lines, like veins running all over his body. The only feature he had was two flat lines where a mouth was supposed to be.

Her hormones stopped for a second but quickly resumed activity. They have not exercised in a long time and might as well use this opportunity.

"Let me introduce myself," The blob said, plopping down with a squelch. "I'm R.B. Slyme, with a y," he extended an arm. His fingers were continually shifting.

"Stacy," a bit dazed, the blonde shook it on reflection. Surprisingly, the hand was firm, if a bit elastic.

"Stacy," Slyme said, rolling around the world in his mouth. "What a lovely name."

"Thank you… Wait, wait for just a second!" Stacy's memories began creeping back in the mess that was her brain. "Aren't you the bastard that went to my home and destroyed it?"

"I did go to your house, true, but…"

R.B. Slyme never got to finish his sentence, seeing as Stacy's claw, swung like a jackhammer, began a direct course with his face. Slyme did nothing though, letting the claw smash his face in and sink into his goo like a spoon in jello.

"As I was trying to say," Slyme continued, forming a temporary mouth on his chest. "I did go to your house and meet some of your friends; however, it was not me who destroyed your home, it was my clone, an unfortunate side effect of my merging.

"A clone?!" Stacy tried to pull out her claw, but it was stuck. "A clone? Really? That's the excuse you are using? Fucking clones?"

"Please, if you give me a second, I will explain."

"Fine," Stacy sighed and leaned back on her elbows. "Better be a good fucking explanation thought, you killed Malbo!"

"Who?"

"Ahhh!" Stacy began to redden. "Just fucking start already."

"Okay," Slyme mirrored Stacy's pose. "Okay."

It took around twenty minutes to relay the information,

with a lot of interruptions from Stacy's, but finally, Slyme explained most things. From merging with B.O.B. into a new being to jumping universes and landing in Stacy's old home to connect with Jack and Jill into a new and improved being, and finally being here.

"I still don't understand the clone business," Stacy said after a pause. "You say you escaped back, but I saw a video that clearly shows you rampaging about."

"I'm not sure myself why this clone exists," R.B. Slyme said. "My vast knowledge does not know where to begin figuring this out; however, I think it's a side effect of my merging abilities."

"What do you mean?"

"Well, I don't think I'm not supposed to exist, nor my merging abilities. BoB, the reason I'm green and malleable, just digest biological matter as fuel. My Rughorn side, however, analyses this biological data, down to its atomic structure, and integrates this information into my brain so to speak. But, seeing as my whole body is my brain," he wiggled around for emphasis. "It only wants the essential information, the kind that will make me smarter and stronger. The rest is expelled."

"So, basically…" Stacy pulled her hair in concentration. "You keep shit you find useful, and you expel shit you don't want as another person."

"That's the working theory, yes," Slyme nodded. "Though I'm going to start looking to fix this, I don't want to leave behind a person every time I merge, that's just a waste of resources and asking for trouble."

"Yep." Stacy was silent for a moment. "Not the best explanation, but I'm going to take it. You're a by-product of Curiosity's power, yes?"

"Yes."

"That guy's powers makes a mockery of what's possible and what's not, so side effects are bound to happen."

"Yes."

"One thing I don't understand, though."

"Yes?"

Stacy was silent for a long moment, staring intensely at the green blob. Slyme, in turn, was not being idle, his blob from unfurling into the vague shape of a sitting human. Well, a human was not entirely correct, more like a slimy statue being worked on by the words drunkest man, complete with a dull chisel. Stacy barely stopped herself from bringing out her drink.

"How come," Stacy said, slowly reddening. "How come, you are soo," She gestured helplessly. "You are so… you know?"

"I know?" Slyme grinned. Teeth were starting to form between his lips, blue ones with lighting patterns. Stacy could not decide if it was hot or terrifying.

"You know, so…" The blonde gestured vaguely. "You know."

"Cultured? Calm? Charming?" Slyme decided to give her a break. Blue electric eyes, like marbles, popped onto his face.

"Yes."

"Well, I have a theory on that."

"Oh?"

"See, Rughorn was quite intelligent and knowledgeable, if a bit self-absorbed. B.O.B., on the other hand, was a city-sized blob of destruction. He felt terribly alone. He only wanted to make friends and talk to people."

"Really?"

"Yes. I was as surprised as you. But if you think about it, what would a biological weapon the size of a city want?"

"Money?"

"What would it do with money?" R.B. Slyme shook his head.

"Buy food?"

"Why buy food where literally everywhere you roll there is biological fuel to digest?"

"Socialise?"

"Exactly!" A nose started to form on his face. "So I got the A.I.'s intelligence and wisdom, and B.O.B.'s desire to make friends and bonds."

"And the charm?" Stacy asked, a bit horrified at herself. Twenty-three years of male memories screaming at her, asking what the actual fuck she was doing, but her hormones did not particularly care. They liked the exercise.

"It's all mine," Slyme smirked, noodle arms forming transparent muscles.

A torso, with well-defined chest muscles, came next, then, two pairs of legs, slim and toned, formed under him. He looked like a green Dr. Manhattan, Stacy thought, just hotter. Much hotter. God, she wanted to slap herself. Wait. Could Slyme even be considered a man? He was only, well, slime, he could probably assume the form of a woman anytime. But like, he's definitely in a man shape now, and her hormones approved, even if her memories did not. What does that make her? A slimophobic? Wait, isn't a phobia something that you are afraid of?

The blonde was interrupted from her deep thought by a smooth, slightly squishy hand gently touching her legs.

"Are you okay?" Slyme said gently.

"Why?" Stacy asked sharply but did not pull away. "Why me?" She whispered, putting her hands over his. "Why are you so nice to me? With your charm, I'm sure you could have anybody eating out from your palm. Why a washed-out drunk?"

"Honestly?"

"Yes."

"You are the first person I talked to since the merge with Jack and Jill. Well, the first person who did not run away screaming in terror or tried to shoot me."

"Really?"

"Really." His fingers melted for a second, making Stacy shiver like someone dragging velvet over your skin, and then reappeared, upside down, entwining his fingers with hers.

"You know," Stacy said tentatively. "I was a man once. Well, not really. To be honest, I'm not that sure myself. My memories are that Steve, but you know all of this right? Having the memories of Jack and Jill and all."

"Yes."

"Gods, I know I should be repulsed by that or something, but at the moment I'm too drunk to care. "Stacy pulled out the bottle anyway and took a quick swig. Slyme said nothing, just squeezed her leg harder. "So I have the memories of a man, but the body of a woman. And not any woman. You know Darius Dovan?"

"Professor Darius Dovan? One of the most prolific scientists of the century? The inventor of one hundred and eight new ways to summon and revolutionise a whole branch of magic by himself?" Slyme eyes were sparkling a bit.

"Yes," Stacy leaned back. "I'm his daughter. With the memories of a twenty-three-year-old man."

"Truly?" Slyme beamed. "That is amazing! I'm a big fan of Darius, big fan, one of the most intelligent people on the planet, for an organic of course."

"Of course."

They lapsed into silence, Slyme lost in fanboy, or more

accurately fan slime word, while Stacy kept staring at their entwined fingers.

"Sooo?" Stacy began tentatively. "What do you think?"

"About what?" Slyme asked.

"Me having the memories of a man and all?" Her voice rose a bit at the end.

"I'm sentient techno slime," he shrugged. "Who I am to judge?"

"I do," Stacy was surprised she said that aloud. "I constantly judge myself because of it."

"Why?"

"I don't know!" she snapped. "I guess all my life I was I knew what I was, who I was, and had a rough idea where I was going, and now, I have no fucking clue what's happening around me, and I don't know who is the person staring back from a mirror is."

Slyme squeezed her hand gently but said nothing. It's best to stay silent and listen in these situations. Stacy opened her mouth and then shut it again.

"To be perfectly honest," she admitted. "I don't want to let go of the fact that I have the memories of a man. It's the only thing I have left, the only thing that ties me to my old world, my past life. Being here, in this body, in this world, in this new existence is scary, you know. I'm not sure what to do."

Slyme said nothing, just smiled encouragingly at her. She took a deep breath, steadied her racing heart, and then continued:

"I'm not sure who I am, what I want, what is my purpose, where do I go, what am I supposed to feel, how I am supposed to act, nothing. All I know is that I am a man's memories trapped in a woman's body. Even that is starting to fade day by day; it takes considerable effort even to remember them. It's all I have. It's the only thing I'm certain of." She stared down with glazed eyes at their entwined fingers.

A thoughtful expression crossed Slyme's face. He leaned forward and then started to melt. Green and blue ooze collapsed almost instantly, dripping onto Stacy's legs and quickly building up in volume. The blonde barely had enough time to panic before she was fully enveloped in the slimy stuff.

Stacy wanted to scream but was afraid to open her mouth and suffocate. Her claw charged up a few shots, but it was stuck in the muck. Then something strange happened.

A tingle, a soft caress, like dragging satin over your skin started at the base of her neck. It went downward, gently, slowly, caressing her shoulders, travelling down her arms, back, and chest, leaving goosebumps behind. Arriving at her shoulder blades, the caress turned into gentle, but firm pressure, breaking up knots upon knots of tense muscles.

That's how Stacy spent the next few minutes, in blissful ignorance, mind blank with pleasure, being massaged with pinpoint precision by a sentient blob. There are worse ways to spend a Friday evening.

When Stacy was sufficiently putty, Slyme retracted, coalescing behind her. In a few seconds, he was reformed behind the blonde, holding her to his chest

"How do you feel?" Slyme asked.

"Hmm?" was the intelligent reply.

Stacy tried turning her head back, but she quickly gave up. She felt relaxed and safe for the first time in a while. Her hormones were pleased.

"How do you feel?" he repeated. "I made sure to focus on your muscles to release tension."

"Thank you," She said with closed eyes. "But next time, please ask before you do anything like that."

"Why?" Slyme sounded genuinely puzzled. "Your heart rate, temperature and general body language indicated you are sexually attracted to me and would not object to a simple massage."

"True true," Stacy agreed, a blush creeping up her cheeks. "But you should still ask. My mind was not properly syncing up with my body, and this sudden action could have left me a quivering mass of rage and misery. Or I could have blasted you to death. I thought you were gonna suffocate me for a second there. It's not a good idea to spook a woman with a laser attached to her back."

"My apologies," Slyme said sincerely. "Still figuring out this whole human interaction business. It won't happen again."

"Good."

A comfortable silence settled over them. With the gentle lapping of waves, the afternoon sun shining from down and the firm, slightly rubbery chest behind her, Stacy felt content. Slyme may not be a prince charming, but he is as clueless about things as her. It felt nice, knowing that she is not the only one who has no idea what's going on and how this word works.

"Stacy?" Slyme asked, brushing a few blonde locks away from her face.

"Yes?"

"May I kiss you?"

"Yes."

It was like kissing an electrified rubber band. It was quite pleasant actually. Stacy could get used to this.

[11]
CURIOSITY HELPS

Sitting on a bench a few streets away from the museum, Curiosity was holding the book of arcanum in his hands, watching the busy streets. Sleek grey cars were stopping randomly on the street, pedestrians running into them from the sidewalks.

He was expecting chaos or cars hitting each other, but it never happened. Each stop was made with precision, with plenty of space for the pedestrians to enter. The citizens as well, ran with practised ease, not panicking nor making a fuss.

"What do you think is happening Cherry?"

"Huh?" Cherry said, from her usual seat. "Let me check."

The diminutive bodyguard finished cleaning her most recent weapon, gave it a kiss, and tucked it into her many pockets. Surveying the rapidly emptying street, she pulled out a lollipop and began licking.

"Looks like an evacuation to me," Cherry said. "Probably because of us."

"Probably," Curiosity said, glancing at the book. "But we got the time, and with this book," A strangle smile took root on Curiosity's face that made the remaining citizens run around the corner. "Revolutionise how the universe functions."

"Really? How?"

"I know who wrote it, well I knew his thoughts. The person, or being who wrote it, was curious, very, very, curios. I don't know anything about the person besides his curious thought, but it's the reason I knew to take my first chance to interact with the word."

"Oh, right, your body is a possessed one."

"Possessed is a strong word," Curiosity winced, fishing for a cigarette. "I would say take advantage of this, this biological being does not have what traditionally is thought of as a soul, it only has data. I did copy over the memories though!"

"What do you mean no soul?" Cherry said. "You mean no magic? Cause I can't sense any form of mana in you."

"Magic, mana, soul, spiritual energy, whatever you wanna call it, these species don't have it. They are purely biological, a combination of memories and DNA. They are actually a very efficient system untainted by any type of supernatural and universal energies." He let out a small puff of smoke. "Easy to take over, blank states, no mystical protection. Though some habits of this body are tough to break."

"How did you do it?" Cherry sat a little straighter. "A place like that would be heaven for some of the supernatural folk I know, it should have been heavily protected.

"It was. The very laws of reality protected it, and it's probably still after me." Curiosity looked at the book. "It's this book, the first attempt since creation to find a way to change our fate, to change the laws of the universe. Wanna know?"

"Yes boss yes!" Cherry saluted. "I will swear upon my height that I won't abuse that kind of knowledge too much."

"Good," Curiosity smiled. "It's actually a quite simple three-step process. I can only recall two of them, sadly, this vessel cannot host my vast database of ideas. The first one is simple. Find a strong idea, no matter how good or bad, and implant it into someone."

"Makes sense, makes sense."

"Second, it is not enough to tell that idea to someone, you need to find people who believe in it, and are willing to try it out. Does not matter who, what, or from where. It just needs to start, somewhere, in any shape or form, and you need to make sure it constantly spreads to people. The more people believe in it, the higher the chance of something related to it will happen."

"And the third?" Cherry was almost hanging by a hair in front of Curiosity's forehead.

"Let's find out." Not waiting a moment longer, Curiosity opened the book.

Cherry waited with barely contained anticipation for her boss to read it, this kind of information can change how words work! And maybe, just maybe, she will find a way to escape that horribly dull place. She does not want to go back, especially not now, after experiencing freedom for the first time in who knows how many centuries.

Still, something was not right. Time was passing normally, but her boss was not saying anything. In fact, Curiosity's face was getting more desperate by the seconds, his muscles tensing and his hand paging through a book like a man possessed. Finally, after what felt like ages,

Curiosity leaned back and let out a deep breath, facial muscles relaxing.

"It's fake," Curiosity said. "I don't know how to react to this."

With a flick of his wrist, he threw the book close to Cherry. The bodyguard ambled over, and using her foot, she opened the text. The pages were empty, with not even a title inside.

"Shit," Cherry said. "There is not even a cryptic drawing or message or anything of the sorts. In my experience, there needs to be something like that or at least a calling card of something."

"There is nothing of the sorts," Curiosity said. "Trust me I checked, it's just a book with empty pages."

"The museum probably has the original in some secure location or a vault,"

"Yep."

"So Mr Edwards died for nothing."

"Yep."

"I liked that guy!"

"Me too Cherry, me too."

"I don't understand something," Cherry fished for a lollipop. "Didn't we send Silvia to buy the tome from the museum staff?"

"Yep."

"So why didn't the damn elf contact us and tell us it's fake or something. Surely the museum staff told her when she asked."

"That is a good point."

"She was too busy gouging her eyes out." A voice said behind them.

Curiosity jumped and turned around. Standing behind them was Zed, a thin layer of sweat shining on his skin, his green robe open and messy. Silvia was held in his hands by her robes, the way a mother cat would hold her kitten.

"Master!" Silvia rasped. "We found you!"

"Ugh," Cherry said, taking a step back. "What did you do to the lanky woman, you look disgusting!"

That was an understatement. The two coins Silvia rammed into her skull were still there, embedded deeply into the eye sockets, blood and mucus surrounding the destroyed organ. That wasn't even the weirdest thing, that award went to the massive third eye in the middle of her forehead. It was white, like an egg yolk, with two black pupils swirling around each other.

"Your insults mean nothing to me," Silvia said. "This magnificent look is thanks to Master's magnificence!"

"What?" Cherry said. "Boss, you did this?"

"No?" Curiosity said questioningly. "At least I don't think so."

As if on cue, more cultist members stepped out from around the buildings and alleyways. Normally, you would not be able to tell the cultist from regular people, seeing as they did not have uniforms or any recognisable badge; however, it was impossible to mistake these beings for anything else.

Aidan West slithered, yes slithered forward, smiling broadly. The bottom half of the half-elf was gone, replaced with what looked like a motorised snake bottom. The scales were made of brass that shone in the afternoon soon, and a click-click sound could be heard as he slithered forward.

The cultist with the cowboy hat was next, looking exactly as he did before, except his hat had eyes and a mouth, and was chattering incessantly about correct hat hygiene. A man with a tuba for a head, yes, an actual tuba just extended from his neck, unperturbed by silly things like gravity and common sense, popped from the corner, dressed in nothing but a loincloth.

One by one, a dozen or so cultists appeared, most of them in long black or orange robes, and in one strange case, a man with a red nose topped off with spikes.

"Master," The cultist said in unison. "We are at your service."

Silvia elbowed her way out of Zeds, grip, and along with the rest of the members, kneeled, head almost touching the pavement. The hat complained loudly about the dirt.

"Amm," Curiosity said, pulling out a cigarette. "Thanks?" He quickly lit it. "Why are you here?"

"We need your help," Zed said. "There is an infestation of zombie-like slime monsters in the city's underground tavern complex."

"What?" Curiosity blinked. "There are bars under the city?"

"That's your question?" Cherry said. "What about the zombie slime monsters?

"Habit," Curiosity shrugged.

"You said the Master needs our help!" Silvia said, glaring quite effectively at Zed. "You lied!"

"I didn't," Zed said. "He does need your help. You would send your master alone in a dangerous and possibly deadly situation, would you?"

"We would never!"

"Good. Now chop chop, we don't have much time, follow me."

"Amm," Curiosity said, eyes fixated on Aidan West. "Sure."

"What just a second," Cherry said. "Why should we help you? I have no idea what this help is, and if I don't know, Curiosity does not know either."

"Do you want to get stomped into dust by Tiny?" Zed asked.

"No."

"Then come, we are wasting time."

Five minutes later, Zed, Curiosity, Cherry, Silvia, Aidan West, and a dozen or so cultists were crammed inside an empty building. Posters with the underground bar complex littered about, advertising every conceivable tavern people could come up with, from small, tree-shaped ones catering to pixies, to ones made purely out of metal and serving lava, and even ones shaped like shoes.

The only other thing in the building was a terminal in the middle of the room, perched on what looked like a raised platform. Zed stepped on it and gestured to the rest of the party to follow him. It was a tight fit, with some of the cultists perched on Aidan West back, but somehow everyone managed to pile on.

The bald professor pressed a button, and the platform began descending noisily through a softly illuminated corridor. Seeing as Curiosity was preoccupied in picking the brass scales on Aidan West, Cherry decided to take upon herself the important question.

"What is exactly our mission," the pint-sized bodyguard asked. "And how come the freakshow became even freakier?"

"We are not a freakshow," Aidan West said, tone slightly metallic. "We are the chosen ones, blessed by Curiosity itself, given gifts beyond what mortal, nay, even gods can comprehend. We are instruments of his will given flesh, for the sole reason to spread his teachings to the masses."

"Teachings? Since when did Curiosity teach anything

useful except making a mockery of everything sane and normal."

"I think they gained my ability," Curiosity interrupted. "I can feel my energy coursing to their body, destroying the fundamental laws of the universe and making things that are impossible, possible."

"We have been blessed by our master," Silvia added. "His will, his energy courses through our bodies, letting us push beyond what is normally possible."

"Great," Cherry said. "The ability to make a mockery out of the rules of physics and they use it to give themself a damn tuba for a head!"

The cultists with the said instrument for a head let out a dejected trumped sound.

"The mission parameters are simple," Zed said, wrestling control of the conversation. "You stay back, and don't do anything stupid while I try to reason with these creatures, and if, and only if, things go sour and I give the signal, you step in."

"Search and destroy," Cherry nodded. "Got it."

"It's not a search and destroy, it's a search and find out what these creatures want and resolve it peacefully."

"Tell me about the layout of this place, it's called the underground bar complex, right? What does it look like, where are the exits, hiding places, etcetera? You look like a man who knows the drill, so spill."

Zed gave Cherry a sour look for talking to him like that but obliged anyway.

"The underground bar complex is a wondrous thing," a small smile appeared on his scarred face. "Built by the citizens of Lucy, it's a massive underground bunker, where everybody, regardless of race, status, and wealth, can build a place to chill out and have a drink."

"Did you say a drink?" Curiosity said, instantly forgetting Aidan West and his brass scales. "What kind of drinks?"

"Every kind imaginable, elven vine, human rum, Rockman beer, which is boiling lava, by the way, all the way to the bug cocktails lizardman drinks."

"Oooh." Curiosity's eyes were sparkling now. "Is there food as well?"

"Yes, though most of it is poisonous to humans."

"Hey, hey," Cherry said, waving a lollipop threateningly. "You still haven't told me about the exits and layout of this place. You're really bad at debriefing Mr diplomat and butcher of millions."

"There are no exits." A vein began pulsating on Zed's forehead, his scars turning red. "Only these elevators that go up and down to the first platform, where flying disks are located, let you travel to the other part of the complex."

"See, that wasn't so hard, was it?"

"As for the layout," Zed said, taking a deep breath, "see for yourself, we are exiting the tunnel now."

As by magic, the platform exited from the illuminated corridor, giving Curiosity and his cult the first glimpse of Lucy's main tourist attraction, the first thing that popped in everyone's mind is that Zed is very bad at describing things. Calling it massive was an understatement.

It was the size of the city itself, maybe bigger and the corners of the place could barely be seen, even by the cultists with a telescope for an eye. Millions of various buildings were scattered about, some floating by their own power, some suspended between the thick metal poles that criss crossed all over the place, and others piled on massive platforms that hovered gently in the air.

On busy days, the place looked absolutely stunning, with people zipping about, bunched up on gently floating disk drinking and laughing, and generally having a good time. Even the few drinks that fell out of the moving pubs were quickly caught by the rest of the patrons, and in worse case scenarios, automated padded disks were flying about for just that reason. Lucy made sure her citizens were well cared for.

Now, however, it looked like something out of a disaster movie. Half the buildings were set on fire or in the process of exploding. The rest were equally divided between being covered with green goo and flying about animals, smashing into each other, and you guessed it, making even more fire.

The platform the small group was supposed to land one was gone, along with every other landing platform along the top of the complex as well. Most of them were destroyed or hanging sideways by the cables that were supposed to keep them in place and horizontal.

"Wow," Cherry whistled. "Someone really did a number on this one."

"Multiple someones," Zed said. "That's why I gathered you here. Now let's see if we can find why they did this and if we can do something about it."

Before pressing the terminal to take them to the bottom, Zed took one more moment to stare into the mayhem unfolding. He had a look on his face that only people who realised that someone made a mockery of their favourite place, then spit on it, pissed on it, and kicked it as well for good measure. Letting out a deep sigh, he pressed a button, and the thick disk began descending.

"We are going to the bottom," Zed said. "Hopefully, we can find some answers."

They made their way towards the bottom slowly, avoiding flying pubs and the occasional flying debris. Thankfully, it didn't seem that anybody was targeting them, so they had an easy time descending.

Around halfway through, they realised things were quieter, and the numbers of fires were decreasing as well. That was probably because most of the pubs have already been burned down or reduced to splinters, and the ones that weren't, were coated with a thin layer of green mucus.

The deeper they went, the more of these green blobs could be seen sticking on buildings. Some of them, however, were rolling about their own power, jumping from building to building like some kind demented green go. Some of them were gathered together on a platform, just standing there, and if Zed's ears were still working properly, talking.

"I hear talking," Cherry said. "Over there, by that funny looking building."

"It looked like a bucket," Curiosity added.

"That's because it is," Zed said. "That was one of Darius' favourite hanging spots."

"What I don't understand," Cherry continued. "What are those blobs doing?" She fished in her skirt for a foldable telescope, and with a flourish, she put the nail sized device to her eyes. "It looks like they are playing poker." She put down the telescope and gave Curiosity a glance. "Boss, I don't know how, but I'm sure whatever is happening now it's your fault."

"Hey, you can't blame me for everything!" Curiosity protested.

"I agree with your bodyguard on this one," Zed said.

"Come on, not you too," Curiosity turned towards his cult members. "What about you guys, do you think this is my fault?"

Silence.

"Really? Silence?" Curiosity looked directly into Aidan West's eyes. "What about you, do you think it's my fault?"

"I can't say the thought didn't cross my mind, Master," Aidan West said carefully.

"Not you too," Curiosity threw his hands up in frustration, then turned towards his last hope. "What about you, Silvia? Do you think your wise and handsome master is responsible for what is happening here?"

"Yes," said Silvia. "I can see the Master's energy permeating the place."

"E Tu Brutus?" Curiosity said, falling to his knees. "You didn't even flinch." He began weeping crocodile tears.

"You can see Curiosity's energy with that freaky eye of yours?" Cherry asked.

"I can see everything," Silvia replied. "I can even see sounds."

Boom! Everyone turned towards the sound. Zed was holding his fist in his palm and smiling dangerously.

"Enough with the chit chat," Zed said. "It's time to focus, we are almost at the bottom."

True to his word only a mile or so separated them from the bottom. This part of the complex was in the most disarray. It was like a big room full of lego buildings, that had green gasoline poured on it and then set on fire.

A few dozen blobs could be seen converging towards their approximate locations. They appeared from everywhere and nowhere at once, squeezing out from the rubble, half-burned buildings, corners, dumpsters, and in one mud-coloured ooze's case, the toilet.

"Remember," Zed said. "We are here to find out what is going on and why are they doing this. Let me do the talking and stay put, we only resort to violence as a last resort."

"Ahem," Cherry nodded noncommittally. "I wonder what will work against these things. Grenades? I have some self-immolation grenades that worked fine against those giant pink jellyfish."

"Giant pink jellyfish?" Curiosity asked.

There was no time to tell that particular harrowing tale because the flying disk landed with a soft thud. The blobs stopped about twenty feet away, swaying side to side like gelatine. One of them, big, shaped like a cannonball with arms and legs stepped forwards, a small indistinct head forming on its stop.

Good, Zed thought, these beings are intelligent enough to talk. He stepped down the platform, hope filling his heart. The mere fact that they surrounded them instead of attacking, and sent one representative, means that negotiations were on the table.

He straightened his back, took a deep breath, and put one smile that destroyed not only nations but millions of hearts as well.

"Greetings." Zed bowed deeply. "My name is Zed Nez, envoy of Tiny, the wandering robot. We are here to inquire about what happened here, your reasons for occupying this place, and to see if we can come to some sort of agreement regarding the future of this place, and your race. May I ask what the name of your species is?"

Two sets of eyebrows formed on the round ooze, staring silently at Zed for what felt like centuries. Then slowly, the eyeballs rolled to the other side of his head, surveying the rest of the green monsters. Most of them didn't move, while others shimmered and bubbled like some kind of poorly made soup.

Finally, the eyes rolled back, surveying Curiosity and his cultists one by one, going back to Zed. What happened next was so fast, only years of experience saved Zed from becoming a pancake via homicidal gelatine.

A small cloud of dust rose from the impact of the

round slime hitting the ground at full force, and before it could reform, Zed was in front of him, light up like a Christmas tree, leg raised. The following kick was so powerful, and so fast, it slightly heated the air, cutting through the gelatine-like a hot knife through butter.

Zed was not done, however, if there is one thing that pissed him off more than people who want him and his people harm, is beings who have no concept of diplomacy and don't even try. Blurring to the ooze's other side, leg raised, he vaporised another part of the monster. Then another, and another, and another, until finally, the only thing left was two milky eyeballs that were quickly crushed under Zed's sandaled foot.

"Shame," Zed said, blurring into view. "Diplomacy was always an option."

"FREE FOR ALL!" Curiosity screamed. "Come on, boys, let's show them what we are made of!"

The cultists cheered. The one with the trumpet for a head let out a long war cry that reverberated through the rubble.

"Wait," Zed lifted his hands. "I haven't given the signal yet!"

It was too late. All hell broke loose.

Aidan West exploded forwards like a coiled spring, the cultists with the talking hat riding on his scaly behind, screaming obscenities and shooting into a group of ooze with a revolver. Three cultists dressed in rugby overalls sans helmet charged the back of the line, the trumpeter close behind them giving them strength. A cultist with a long black cloak obscuring his whole form melted into the ground and reappeared behind the oozes, daggers gleaming in both hands.

Two other cultists threw off their cloaks, revealing a man and a woman with an eagle's head, dressed in full military uniforms, guns, grenades, and even what looked like a flamethrower strapped to the woman's back. Massive grey wings unfurled from their backs, and grabbing the cultists with the red nose, they launched into the air.

Rudolph, if Zed remembered his name currently, was launched towards a cluster of slime monsters towards the back, screaming incoherently. His nose, yes, his actual nose, shot out from his face with the force of a shotgun, exploding in a pink cloud that vaporised everything in a two feet radius and smelling faintly of snot.

Silvia was not to be undone either, the woman began running, yelling a battle cry, and promptly fell on her face a few feet away from Zed. It seems that that massive eye was not good at depth perception.

Curiosity and Cherry, on the other hand, were having the time of their life. The former had his shovel in hand and was pocking two oozes inefficiently, occasionally hitting them and absorbing a bit of their mass into the shovel. The latter was standing in her usual spot in the hair chair, cackling maniacally, and throwing incendiary grenades left and right.

Zed took a deep breath, held it, and let it go slowly, relaxing his shoulders. What had he just unleashed? Explosions could be heard all around them, punctuated by the screams of the cultists as some of them were trampled, crushed, or just plain old dissolved by the corrosive gelatines till not even bones remained.

Oh well, as Darius used to say, if you can't fight them, join them. Walking over to Silvia, she picked the woman up with both hands and tucked her under his arm.

"Do you have any useful abilities?" Zed asked.

"I can shoot a laser out of my eye," Silvia said. "Though my depth perception is terrible."

"I noticed. I will hold you towards the enemy and when I tell you, let loose with the lasers. Okay?"

"Alright."

"Now!"

Yelling a battle cry and holding a laser-shooting woman under an armpit, Zed joined the fray.

Lucy still uses footage of the battle to this day to teach the next generation on how dangerous, and insane the people of Tiny truly are.

[12]

BONDS

R. B. Slyme was pleased with himself. Rolling on the empty high street like some kind of demented yoga ball, he took inventory of the items churning inside him. First the clothes, a plain shirt, blue trousers, shoes, a dirty lab coat and finally underwear. These were quickly broken down to its base components and absorbed for its energy.

Next was two bottles of alcohol, chewing gum, a lighter and pack of cancerous sticks. These were quickly shot out of Slyme's body with the force of a cannon, smashing the window of a nearby house. Expect the chewing gum. It was a refreshing melon taste.

Now for the grand prize, the item that will enable him to fix his slight problem. Stacy's tablet. Who knew that drunkard of a woman was actually Darius Dovan's daughter? It was a lucky find. Using the A.I. part of his constitution, he quickly found the professor's contact information.

Darius instantly picked up.

"Hello, Stacy." The professor's voice came crisp and powerful. "How are you?"

"Professor Darius Dovan?" Slyme said enthusiastically. "The greatest scientist this millennium has ever seen?"

"Ammm, yes." Darius was silent for a second. "Who is this? Where is Stacy?"

"I'm a big fan, the biggest one you probably have, your theory of advanced summoning rituals using cheese and glitter, oh man, amazing stuff, with the proper application it could revolutionise the transportation industry as we know it!"

"Excuse me, who are you, and where is Stacy?"

"I'm R.B. Slyme, big fan, a technological slime created from the biological weapon B.O.B. and the A.I. Rughorn using the power of the being you call Curiosity."

"That explains a lot, though it does not explain where my daughter is and how you got possession of this tablet."

"One problem though is that my powers are not working properly. Every time I absorb a new being into myself to increase my knowledge and powers, it leaves behind a clone. Most of them are mindless beasts that just walk around destroying things, but some of them are not. With your expertise, we can solve this issue presto."

"So you are the reason there is a slime infestation in the underground complex." Darius was silent for a long moment, the only sound coming from the tablet was furious typing. "I'm sorry Mr Slyme, but unless you tell me where my daughter is and how you got in possession of her tablet, I'm not helping."

"Help me, and I will tell you!"

"This is non-negotiable. Where is my daughter?"

R.B. Slyme was getting angry. Who did this man think he was, demanding information from a superior being, from him? It's not like he killed the girl. Probably. Honestly, he was still figuring out how his powers worked, but still, did this man not understand the opportunity given to him?

If he could just get the information straight out of that man's head... who knows how far he could go if he absorbed Darius Dovan into his system. Still, Slyme was above needing that man's help, he could figure out what the problem was himself; he just needed to get his hand on a chemist or biologist.

Darius Dovan would have been excellent, but if not, then at least he could teach that man a lesson about crossing him and demanding things from a superior being.

"I will tell you where she is," Slyme said. "I left her naked and afraid on the beach. She's probably suffocated right as we speak."

"WAIT, WHAT!" Darius shouted. "WHO DO YOU THINK YOU…" Click.

Slyme dissolved the tablet. Served that bastard right, ignoring him like that. Who did the scientist think he was? A superior being like himself? Bah, nothing but a weak organic. A smart one for sure, but still an organic, not a fusion of machine and biology like him.

R.B. Slyme ignored the fact that Darius Dovan was probably more machine than him, exactly like an organic would ignore information that it does not want to hear.

Still, where could he find a scientist to help him? Looking around the empty street, the techno slime remembered that Lucy would evacuate her citizens at the slightest sign of trouble, which is probably a good thing in this crazy world.

But where to find scientists then? Asmodeus? It would take weeks to roll there, and that damn bloodthirsty A.I. would probably kill his own scientist rather than give them to someone. Maybe he could trade information? Asmodeus would surely jump at the opportunity to dissect Curiosity and figure out his powers.

Asmodeus is it then!

Sadly R.B. Slyme only managed to roll a few feet before he collapsed into a literal puddle of pain. It felt like someone was hitting him repeatedly with a flaming sack of bricks, all the while being electrocuted with the fury of an angry god.

Slyme knew exactly where it was coming from. Damn those clones, he told them to stay out of trouble and escape, but no, they just stared at him incomprehensibly.

Another jolt this time like someone was cutting him into tiny little pieces wracked his gelatinous body, almost making him lose total concentration of his form. That would be bad, he was not sure he could reform after scattering to the wind.

Guess he had no choice but to help them if he didn't want to die himself. Asmodeus would kill him if he showed up in this state. The question is, who was fighting the clones? Nobody in Lucy's kingdom should be strong enough to defeat them unless…

Another jolt wracked his body, this one making him jump two feet in the air and falling back with a wet splat. This was not the time to think, this was the time for action.

Shimmying to the closest manhole, R.B. Slyme went to help his brethren. Whoever did this would pay.

Stacy was suffocating. Not in the metaphysical way where all your past mistakes, your slightly bent knee and your ignored true self are screaming at you all at the same time… well, maybe a little, but more prominently, the physical way.

She was stuck inside a gelatinous cube, stark naked, the oxygen slowly leaving her system. Stacy didn't dare open her mouth, for fear of the green slime going down her throat and killing her from the inside. She should have died a long time ago, but it seems being part lizard and part whatever the hell Darius is, gave her amazing lungs.

Still, who knew she was gonna die like this? What is even this? R.B. Slyme excrement? And she even kissed the bastard, on her own volition no less. Who knew he was gonna trap her, steal all her clothes and leave her to die?

Damn those Disney movies and setting up unrealistic expectations of love! They never showed a Disney princess kissing the adult version of Flubber, a part of her brain whispered, but still, who knew what they would come up with next.

A few cleaning bots stumbled into the beach along with a tall brunette woman with a baseball bat, clearly here to help her, but they were useless. The two bots deployed all their tools available, from screwdrivers, dustpans, mops and high-pressure water cutters, but they did nothing, just bounced off the gelatine uselessly.

The tall woman stepped forwards and looked Stacy straight in the eye. Hope blossomed in the blonde's heart, she never saw such a severe conviction of someone's face before, such determination, like even if the world was against her, she would still succeed.

Taking a step back, the brunette lifted her bat and shouted something Stacy did not understand. Instantly, electricity sparkled to life on the bat, crackling with the sound of a thousand birds chirping.

Stacy may just live another day. The brunette nodded, and while lifting the baton behind her shoulder, she swung with the fury of an angry truck. It stuck the gelatine head-on, making it wiggle for a few seconds, compressing Stacy tighter and squeezing her limbs painfully.

Other than that, it did nothing, on the contrary, the bat bounced back, hitting the woman square in the face and knocking her unconscious. The two cleaning bots looked at

Stacy as if apologising, grabbed the woman with two pincers, and began dragging her away.

Well, this is then, Stacy though. She is gonna die here, hopeless, alone, without friends, family, tricked by a handsome ooze. What did her life become? How can she even fight this?

She's not a mad scientist with unlimited knowledge, a kung fu master, or a bastard that can bend reality itself, she's just a girl, with the memories of a drunkard man, trying to figure out if liking men now makes her gay or straight.

What can she even do against them? Nothing, part of her brain whispered, the tired and bitter part, just sit here, die, and hope someone will light a candle or at least spit on her grave or something.

Stacy closed her eyes and waited for the oxygen to run out. What a shitty way to die. She dearly wanted a cigarette, that way at least she would die faster.

Barely a second passed before a shiver went down Stacy's spine and her eyes were forced open. A presence filled her whole being, a pressure like no other. It felt angry and precise, like a laser, that will cut you open and liquefy each of your organs one by one, till nothing but an empty shell remained. It felt somehow comforting.

She tried to wriggle around to get a better look, but it just only increased the pressure, forcing her more in place. Thankfully she did not need to wait for long. A flying disk landed in front of her, carrying an angry Darius.

Stacy was not sure if angry was the right word to describe him, seeing as his face looked utterly blank, metal eyebrows not even twitching. Still, there was something about his eyes, about his whole posture, like he was ready to dissect the gods themself damn the consequences, that made Stacy shiver again.

The moment their gazes meet, Stacy felt something break inside her and tears gather in the corner of her eyes. She thought she knew pain, being drunk in an unfamiliar city, heck, an alien universe, slowly dying by suffocating in green ooze, naked! But something in Darius' gaze was old, old and filled with pain, and she just wanted to reach out and punch him in the damn face! What the fuck was he doing, standing there and gawking! She was suffocating dammit!

As if hearing her thought, Darius stepped forward and lifted his claw to a corner of a cube. Murmuring something under his breath, a jet of pink laser shot out from his claw, slowly, but surely cutting a piece off.

When he was done, he held it in his hand for a fraction of a second, and without hesitation, put it in his mouth. Stacy almost opened her mouth to ask "what the fuck" but caught herself last minute.

Chewing one more time, Darius swallowed the piece and lifted all three of his arms and began waving them in intricate patterns, slowly moving forwards and holding them in front of him like he had a defibrillator in his hands.

Slowly, carefully, he placed all three hands on the cube and began pushing. Red electricity sparkled around his hands, realising the scent of burnt ozone, and Darius began pushing harder, his hands slowly sinking into the ooze.

The gelatine began to tremble, but Darius did not let up, he began pushing even harder, slowly sinking himself up to elbows, barely a hair separating him from Stacy. With a mighty grunt of effort, Darius lurched forward and grabbed Stacy by the shoulders.

The moment his hand made contact with her skin, Stacy felt the red electricity crackle through her body, pushing the slime away from her skin. It was not an unpleasant feeling, like you just downed six cups of coffee in a row, so the blonde decided to put in some effort as well.

With Darius pulling with all his might and Stacy wiggling forward like a worm, slowly, but surely, they managed to pull her out. Her legs were last, coming out with a wet pop, and Stacy fell forward, caught in the professor's arm.

"Whew," Stacy said, taking in a deep breath. "I was sure I was gonna die there."

"Save your breath," Darius said. "You need all the oxygen you can get."

Shrugging out of his lab coat, Darius draped it over Stacy, who let out a relieved sigh.

"Who knew it was so cold in gelatine," Stacy said, "Hey, you have some alcohol on you?"

"No," Darius said, helping Sacy to her feet. "You alright?"

"Would be better with some alcohol, or at least a cigarette. Do you have a cigarette on you?"

"Yes," Darius sighed. "It's in the left pocket of my lab coat."

"Really?" Stacy lifted an eyebrow. "Why do you have cigarettes on you? I thought this word does not have cigarettes."

"It does not. I made these for you, using natural herbal plants that do not contain harmful substances for your biology."

"Herbal cigarettes? I tried them once, and they were shit. It does not have the same pull as nicotine, and burns your mouth like nobody's business."

"Then why do you have one already in your mouth?"

"Hey, I just came out of a near-death experience, I will

take even a false cigarette by this point." Stacy patted herself down. "Hey, do you have a lighter? I can't find any in your pocket."

"Use the laser from your claw."

"Oh, right." A pink laser shot later, Stacy was puffing away contentedly, a pleased expression on her face. "Hey, this is pretty good, heck, maybe even better than regular cigarettes." She pulled in deeply and let out a massive cloud of smoke. "And you say it does not contain nicotine? How? Why?"

"I spent a bit of time studying the structural integrity of these so-called cigarettes and the effects on their brain. According to my research, nicotine is a drug that puts a chemical hook in your brain that forces you to smoke more nicotine to alleviate it."

"Sounds about right."

"It has no positive effects, so with the information, I have about your biology, it was easy to find a mixture of plants that not only taste good, it has a positive effect on your physical and mental health. It even works as a mild muscle stimulant."

"Huh." Stacy stared at the blue stick in her hand. "And you did all this for me?"

"Yes."

Darius looked so uncomfortable without his lab coat, Stacy though, his hand floating nervously by his side. Dressed In a plain black shirt and pants, he seemed almost normal, if you ignored the face mask fused to his face and the massive industrial boots on his feet.

"Why?" Stacy asked, suddenly overcome with emotion. "Why go to all the trouble of making me custom cigarettes? Why save me? Would it not be better to let me suffocate here?"

"What? No!" Darius stepped closer, raised his arms

slightly, and let it drop back down. "Why would you say that?!"

"Let's be brutally honest here, I'm a failure of a person." Tears were rolling down her cheeks. "I have no idea who or what I am. Heck, I don't even know what to do with myself other than drink, and that's just because of memories from another person! I can't even protect myself. I bet this is not what you expected from your daughter, huh? A useless piece of shit."

"Don't say that!" Darius stepped forward again, and this time, all three of his arms came up and encircled Stacy. "Never say that again. "He pulled her into a tight embrace. "No matter who you are, what you do or what you are, you are my daughter, and I care for you. I will be here, next to you, for as long as you need me, and if making my daughter herbal cigarettes is the way I can be of assistance, then so be it."

The floodgates were open. Stacy collapsed against her father's chest and began crying. Tears the size of pebbles rolled down her cheek, and in one particular snotty moment, she blew her nose in her father's shirt.

"It's okay," Darius said, pulling her close. "Let it all out, I am here for you and always will be. Let it all out."

They stayed like that for a few minutes, Stacy sobbing with various levels of intensity, and Darius rocking her back and forth gently, murmuring soft words of comfort.

"Thank you," Stacy mumbled into his shirt. "I needed that."

"Any time," her father assured. "Anything I can help you with, I will just ask."

"Thank you. Sorry for your shirt."

"Don't worry," Darius loosened the embrace a bit. "I have five identical ones."

"Somehow I knew you would," Stacy laughed. "By the way, how did you find me?"

"I spoke with that Slyme fellow. He said he left you naked and afraid on the beach. I only needed to ask Lucy about your position, and she pointed me in this direction."

At the mention of R.B. Slyme, Stacy eyes lit on fire, previous fatigue and exhaustion forgotten.

"That bastard!" Stacy raged. "If I get my hands on him I'm gonna make modern art out of his sorry ass!"

"I will help you," Darius said. "Nobody treats my daughter like that."

"Oh, I know! You said you are gonna help me with anything?"

"Of course."

"Is there some kind of, I don't know, weapon or something I can equip myself so I can defeat that bastard next time I see him? I'm grateful for your rescue, of course, but you can't be next to me all the time."

"I'm glad you asked," Darius said, smiling. "I have just the thing." He stepped on the flying platform. "Come, it's back home."

"Wait, right now?"

"Yes."

"Okay."

Stacy stepped on the platform and pulled out another cigarette. Her heart felt light, and the future looked promising. It was good to know there was someone who cared, regardless of how much of a mess she truly was.

Maybe, just maybe, there was still a place for her in this mad, mad world.

[13]
MCGUFFIN

As with most things Tiny related, the backpack used expansion runes to change size when necessary. The storage space was divided into four main sections, each dealing with a different aspect of running a city.

The lower floor was mostly occupied by the thrusters and the massive generators that powered the whole structure.

"It's rare we ever come here," Darius said. "Usually, Tiny takes care of maintenance, and if ever the rune fails, which is rare, I come and take a look."

The professor and Stacy were on a flying disc, slowly going upwards inside the backpack. The second floor was occupied mainly by glasshouses and warehouses where food, milk, algae and other essential foodstuffs were produced.

"Food is one of those things that we don't really produce," the professor continued. "just in small amounts. it's much easier to buy food from existing sources."

"Can't you magic it up or something?" Stacy said.

"That's not how it works."

"Shame."

The third floor was the biggest, occupying almost half the space in the backpack. Rows upon rows of buildings, some small, some big, stacked together on metal shelves. In the middle of this, people zipped about moving materials from one building to another, some jumping from flying platform to flying platform to get to the other side.

"This is where the magic happens, where all of our exports are made. Wands, robot arms, ever-expanding bags, replacement organs, you name it, we probably make it."

"I don't know anything about these words, rules and stuff," Stacy began. "But I'm positive some of the stuff here is highly illegal and dangerous."

Darius shrugged.

The top floor was packed with buildings. Some on top of each other, some on the ceiling, tightly packed like sardines, barely able to walk past them.

"Here is the storage place, where buildings not in use are kept."

"We were not here," Stacy said. "I'm sure of it, I would have remembered the smell of lightly roasted socks."

"Well," Darius said. "As head scientist, I have certain privileges."

"Basically, Tiny lets you do whatever you want."

"Yes. My lab is usually parked on the second level in a nice green patch."

"Where are we going?"

"To the medical ward."

"You let a medical building sit in this place?" Stacy looked at the stained walls, pieces of tiny metal legs scattered everywhere, and pieces of buildings that littered the area.

"It's well-insulated," Darius protested.

The medical ward was located in the back, wedged between a fast-food joint and Rip's bar.

"Since when do we have a McLeaf?" Stacy asked.

"I'm not sure what McLeaf is," Darius began. "If you mean the Leaf Burger then we have had it since the elven kingdom."

"Why?"

"A few elves approached Tiny with the suggestion of opening a branch here."

"He accepted?"

"Yes."

"Just like that?"

"Just like that."

The hospital was a squat building, with reinforced windows and two-inch steel doors on each side. When most people can pick up a miraculous healing potion at a discount, inject themselves with Nanomachines that repair tissue on a molecular level, or chant a healing spell, a hospital is not really needed.

Except for the more esoteric cases, of course, people with sensitive immune systems, delicate operations on the brain, modifications on a genetic level, fusions between machine and man, you know the standard stuff. When you have a mad scientist on board with an unlimited budget and a governor with loose morals, strange things can happen.

At the door, Mark greeted them.

"Oh, it's you," he said with the enthusiasm of a rock.

"What's with the greeting?" Stacy said, putting her hands on her hips, "And why is your hair purple? And why is it smoking at the tips?"

"Every time you and that Curiosity fellow shows up something stupid happens."

"He is not here."

"Then only slightly stupid things will happen."

"Hey!"

"Assistant," Darius said. "please show us to room 6."

"Are you sure you wanna disturb him? He's been pretty restless."

"Did you let Hidara near him?"

"She insisted!"

"He?" Stacy said. "Is the McGuffin a person?"

"What is a McGuffin?" Darius asked, then thought better of it. "Yes, Codec is here."

"Nice."

Stacy smiled internally. Finally, she will have some power at her disposal! No more weak and useless blonde! In hindsight, she should have probably asked what kind of powers will this McGuffin give her. It would not do to get some sort of useless power, like invisibility in the dark or some such nonsense.

"Come," Darius said. "Codec is waiting."

The first thing that hit Stacy when she entered the building was the smell. Or lack of it. A hospital not smelling of antiseptic and unwashed body parts just seemed wrong. Taking another look, this whole place seemed wrong.

It did not look like a hospital at all; it looked more like a dorm than anything. The long corridor they were walking on was tastefully decorated, painting of flowers and mountains along the wall, a soft red rug on the floor, and the occasional door jutting out was painted in soft pastel colours, with flowers and rolling hills.

Arriving at the end of the corridor, they entered a spacious kitchen and living room combo, with soft brown leather sofas around a small coffee table. At the end of the kitchen, a spiral staircase was located, disappearing into the ceiling.

Mark, wasting no time, went to the kettle, put on the dirty apron that hung from the stove's handle, popped something white and smelly into his mouth from the said apron, and began making tea.

"Tea?" the assistant asked. "Or something that wakes you up and shows you exactly how insignificant we are in the cosmic scale of the universe?"

"No, thank you," Stacy said. "I'm going directly up."

Before she could take one more step forward, Darius claw shot out and wrapped around Stacy's pink one. No words were needed, Stacy could feel the concern oozing from every remaining pore of Darius' body.

"I will be fine," Stacy said. "Really, I will be fine."

"Are you sure?" Darius said. "I have not seen him in years. I don't know how dangerous he became. Sure you don't want me there just in case?"

"I will be fine," Stacy said. "That demon lady is already there isn't it? Don't worry, I will manage."

"Alright." Darius reluctantly let go. "I believe in you."

"Scream, and we will come to your aid," Mark added.

"Thanks for the vote of confidence."

"Anytime."

Stacy let go of Darius and stepped into the corner. A panel extended upwards, and Stacy pressed it. The disc began to ascend.

"Be careful!" Darius added.

"I will."

The top floor, if it could be called that, consisted of a small barren area, with the rest of the space walled off. A five-inch reinforced steel door was in the middle. It had number 6 in red seared on it.

Stacy knocked gently. Nothing happened. She tried again. Still nothing. A bit more force this time. Nope. Well, she thought, it was time for the big guns. She raised her claw.

"Enter," Hidara's voice came from the other side. "It's open."

Huh. Right, Stacy thought, common sense exists here too. She entered, Huh. Definitely not what she was expecting.

The room was spacious. Soft, dark red and purple draperies decorated the walls, some crisscrossing the ceiling. A single light source, floating at the top gave the room a blue hue, barely illuminating the pillows neatly stacked along the wall. There was no furniture.

Two figures were in the middle of the room. They were standing on their fingers. Hidara, using her tail as a counterbalance, easily kept her weight up. She was not even sweating.

The other person was even more impressive. Using one finger on the left hand, he was holding up four hundred kilograms of metal and silicone. This was because he or it if you want to get technical, was a robot. A grey robot, square and bulky, like it, was made from tiny cubes stacked together.

There were no eyes, ears, or a mouth to speak of, just a collection of cubes continually rearranging themselves. Even the finger looked more like a lego piece than an actual finger.

"You could have just tried the door," Hidara said, not turning to look. "We were open from the start."

"What are you doing?" Stacy stepped inside.

"Let me introduce you," the demoness said. "Codec. this is Stacy."

"Pleasure." The robot's voice was level and flat. "So, you finally came."

"What?"

Codec contorted, putting tremendous pressure on his finger, and pushed himself in the air. Halfway to the ceiling, he stopped, and with the sound of hundreds of dice knocking together, he began rearranging himself. Hands went up, feet migrated downwards, his head travelling upwards, along the spine, stopping at his pelvis, now a neck.

With a heavy rattle, he fell back to the floor, standing upright, and took a few unsteady steps towards the blonde.

"So Darius finally let you see me," the robot said.

"What!" Stacy bristled. "He never let me anywhere, I let myself."

"You were right, Hidara," Codec said. "She is different from her."

"She is she," Hidara agreed, lowering herself to the floor, rolling with the momentum to a standing position.

"I have a name, you know!" Stacy snapped. "And it's Stacy!" She trusts a claw out. "Nice to meet you, rude robot."

Codec, using more care and caution his body showed, shook the offered limb gently.

"It's nice to meet you, Stacy," the robot began. "Apologies for the rudeness, it's a bit of a shock seeing you walking and talking, a bit hard to process."

"It's no problem." Stacy waved it off. "I'm rude all the time, and I'm sure I'm gonna be again."

Hidara grabbed a few fluffy pillows from the corner, dragging them over, and arranged them into a circle.

"I recommend," the demoness said, "that we all sit down, especially you Codec before you get over-excited. You still have not let go of her hand."

Codec said nothing, just followed Hidara's instruction, plopping down on a velvet cushion. He didn't let go. Stacy wanted to protest and possibly laser him, but even she could sense the tension in the air. Something was off here. She was not sure if it was the decor clashing with the robot, or the way he jingled like a bag of dice every time he moved.

Even his face, if you could call it, that looked like it could collapse any moment and scatter on the floor. Best exercise caution. Stacy sat down next to him, Hidara did the same on the other side.

"Now," Hidara said. "I would like you, Codec, to tell us a bit about yourself and why exactly you are here."

Codec said nothing, just stared at, well, it was hard to tell. It is hard for other people to tell or see what you are looking at or thinking when your head is a cube.

"Excuse him," Hidara said. "He is in one of his moods. I will continue to tell his story. If that's okay with you Codec."

There was no response.

"Wait," Stacy said, fishing for a smoke. "Let me guess first. Codec is some kind of advanced robotic experiment, made by Amanda, right before she fried her brains, right?"

"Well yes," Hidara looked worriedly at Codec, but there was no reaction there.

"So what exactly are you Codec? Some kind of sentient blocks put together? Magnets that think? Why are you locked up in this place?"

"He is not locked up," Hidara added quickly, eyes darting around madly. "This is his home. You like being here, don't you Codec?"

"Do you know," Codec began. "How does it feel when your creator dies for you?"

Stacy wanted to respond with her customary what, but a slap from the demoness tail stopped all sounds. Hidara shook her head nervously. Codec continued, ignoring the exchange.

"I was one of her first projects, a new type of artificial intelligence," Codec lifted a hand that started shifting rapidly. "Each of these blocks is as powerful as a high-end tablet, capable of transmitting information to each other in nanoseconds. Each one has a small gravity field, capable of moving around, giving them the ability to assume any form for any number of tasks," Codec let his hand down. "Marvellous is in it? True genius."

"That sounds pretty useful," Stacy agreed.

"The problem was," Codec continued. "That there was no personality matrix, no base, no instruction for the block on how they behave, what kind of passive form they should take, nothing. They could jiggle around sure, but that's it, just a heap of mighty blocks that could do simple tasks, but it was not true intelligence, no capability to make their own decisions."

Codec lapsed back into silence. Stacy started shuffling uncomfortably on her pillow. Hidara let out a huge sigh.

"Codec," the demoness provided gently. "Would you like to continue the story? Stacy is not familiar with the whole picture."

"I can figure out the rest!" Stacy said quickly, seeing an opportunity to talk and not wasting it. "Amanda tried to cheat and use her brain pattern, or whatever that kind of shit is called to give the blocks a base, an idea of how the whole body interacts, and in the process..."

"She fried every inch of information stored in her brain," Codec completed the sentence.

"I would not put it so bluntly," the blonde said, ignoring the incredulous look Hidara was giving her. "But yes. That."

"I am well aware of what happened," Codec said. "Well aware. Each day, after waking up from my power nap, the first memory that is accessed in my database is of her, sprawled on the floor unresponsive, while the pile of blocks that was me, first started to gain sentience."

The following happened way, way too fast. Codec sprung up from his seat with the rattle of a thousand vengeful dice and slammed full force into Stacy.

There were three reasons Stacy did not become a modern art on the wall, first, her claw wrapped around her as many times as it could, creating a sort of flexible barrier, the first point of impact, absorbing as much of the kinetic energy as it could.

Second, this is the exact reason the demoness was here to stop this kind of outburst happening. The problem was, she let her guard down, allowing the fact that everything went alright till this point to cloud her judgement. Codec even opened up; he did not do that in ages.

So she did the only thing she could in that short amount of time, throwing, with pinpoint accuracy, the pillow she was sitting in between the charging Codec and the blonde, giving her another layer of protection.

Thirdly and most importantly, the robot was not aiming to kill.

"DO YOU UNDERSTAND!" Codec was screaming now, millions of little blocks rotating rapidly, making his shape inconsistent. "THE PERSON WHO CREATED ME IS DEAD?! THE REASON I WAS CREATED IS DEAD?! THE SOLE PURPOSE OF MY EXISTENCE IS GONE?! IN THE ATTEMPT TO CREATE ME?!" He pressed his shifting head as close as possible to Stacy's. "CAN YOU COMPREHEND?!"

"Now," Hidara was slowly approaching. "There is no need for this kind of behaviour."

"SHE IS PRANCING ABOUT IN MY CREATORS BODY!" The Codec body was starting to blur, smoke coming off from overheated dice.

"Remember, each part makes up the whole."

"WHAT RIGHT!"

"Past is only data; data can be rewritten."

"WHAT RIGHT!" Codec shouted, thousands of spinning dice clanking in guilt.

"Good maintenance is the key to a good lifestyle; don't let your processors overheat."

"What right!" his voice was cracking, hundreds of tiny speakers shutting down to redirect energy.

"Byte by byte, that's how the future is built."

"Does she have," Codec finished lamely, fully visible.

Right, Stacy was starting to get pissed off. Who is this Roblox character to question her existence?

"Do you understand," Stacy said through clenched teeth. "What is it like to wake up in a grown woman's body with the memories of a man?" It was her turn to lean uncomfortably close to the A.I. "Do you understand what it feels like waking up, not knowing who you are, what you are and where you are!?" Spittle was flying from her mouth. "Do you know how it feels to have reflexes, habits, and feeling incongruent with your memories?"

Silence.

"DO YOU?" Stacy screamed.

Codec looked sheepish, or as sheepish as a bunch of blocks can be.

"No," he said finally, wiping the split off his face.

"Then," Stacy said, lowering her voice. "What gives you the right to question my pain? My existence."

"Stacy," Hidara butted in, not liking where this was going. "Why don't we all calm down and sit down for a cup of tea. There is no reason to act irrationally."

Stacy's neck began throbbing. Hidara, for all her strength and goodwill, for a demon, had the psychological and calming capacities of a teenager who after reading a bit of Freud and watched a YouTube video about therapy, decided that she's an expert on the problems on the mind.

"Irrational?" Stacy's voice could cut steel. "Irrational?" She wanted to blow up, she really did, but what would that achieve? Hidara was clearly useless here, and someone needed to slap some sense into this bag of bricks. "There is absolutely nothing irrational about my outburst! Especially not when a fucking Roblox character questions my existence!"

"A what?"

"Oh just shut the fuck up Hidara and let me fucking talk!"

"There is no reason to talk to me like that; we are all civilised beings here."

"SHUT THE FUCK UP!" Stacy and Codec screamed at the same time. Hidara took a step back.

"Fine," she said. "if you wanna be like that."

"Oh, just be quiet and let me finish," Stacy said, exhausted. "You are making things worse."

Hidara looked down in defeat. She opened her mouth again, but Codec whirled his head around noisily to look at her. She closed her mouth. Without a word, she went to the corner, picking up a few pillows on the way. Arriving at a corner, she plopped down and started peeling the velvet cushions around her like a blanket. When only her head stuck out, she gave Stacy and Codec one last mournful look and covered her face too.

"Finally," Stacy let herself relax, but not for long, there was a conversation to finish. "As I was saying, I don't have any idea what I am supposed to do with my life either, and my personality, well it's a work in progress," Her claw uncoiled from her body. "You are not the only one without a purpose you know, most living beings have no fucking idea what to do with themselves either."

"I am not a living being," Codec said. "I'm a robot."

"Semantic," Stacy waved it off and plopped down on a pillow. "It's the same thing really."

"No, not really," Codec sat down in front of her. "An A.I. has its purpose programmed since the date of creation. Mine was to protect and aid Amanda."

"Right, what about Tiny?"

"What about him?"

"He's millions of years old right? His purpose was already fulfilled or gone a long time ago, right?"

Codec said nothing.

"So he programmed a new one," Stacy continued, smiling faintly. "He found something and reprogrammed himself to like it." She gestured around them. "Look at what he achieved since doing that. A whole city is living on him, with people who care about him, even with his destructive tendencies."

"He's developing a personality as well," came to the muffled reply from the corner.

"Shut up, Hidara!" Stacy snapped. "But yes, she is right. He is doing something with his existence, just by a simple reprogramming. You can do that too."

Codec said nothing, but you can clearly tell he was thinking. Millions of little cubes started to spin around, this time, however, they were controlled, with a purpose, thousands upon thousands of small processors working in tandem, analysing and processing all the information said recently.

"Can I," Codec began. "Can I do anything I want? Any purpose?"

"Yes, heck you can even change it midway if you don't like it."

Codec processors were coming to a decision. Any object, anything he wanted.

"Can I…," the robot began, "…update my original purpose?"

"The one about," Stacy swallowed, she could see where this was going, "protecting and serving Amanda?"

"Yes."

"She is not here, you know, and I am not her."

"I know. Protecting and serving Stacy then."

Stacy wanted to act surprised but decided against it.

"Are you sure?" the blonde said.

"Yes."

"You can always change it if you don't like it," added Hidara, peeking out behind her pillow. "Finding a purpose can be a work in progress."

"Shut the fuck up" Stacy snapped, then added in a softer tone. "Are you sure this is what you want?"

"If you have no objections, then yes."

"Sure," Stacy was not sure. "Let's just roll with it."

"The future is built one byte at the time, yes?" Codec said. "It will be easier for me to make a small adjustment in my original purpose then come up with a totally new one."

"Good point."

"I will start the countdown."

Huh, Stacy thought, he was right, byte by byte, one step at a time. Maybe she should make a small adjustment to her goals then, taking into consideration her strange existence. The million-dollar question, however, is what exactly her purpose is? What does she want?

Well, her memories supplied, booze, cigarettes, a tasty meal, and a good lay. Her hormones nodded in agreement.

"Three."

No, her brain added, we are a fucking genius with the mind capable of creating a sentient fucking robot from fucking scratch, and we can do so much more than drink and waste our years away doing nothing on the side-lines, watching all these cool people do their stupid shit.

We don't have the necessary knowledge, supplied the memories. And? We sit down and learn; we can do this, continuing the brain. What about doing both? Oh, yes, Stacy liked the idea, and the rest of her nodded in agreement.

Drink, smoke, fuck, and learn to be badass.

Sounded like a plan.

"Two."

Stacy smiled in satisfaction. There were worse goals out there.

"One. Start."

"What?" Stacy blinked twice, leaving her mind. Sadly, it was too late.

Codec surged. Thousands upon thousands of little blocks, rattling madly towards the blonde, enveloping her so fast, she did not have enough time to yelp.

[14]
BATTLE

Zed knew the moment he got his hand on his best friends, he was gonna squeeze his neck until his head would explode like a balloon. Letting Curiosity and his cult run amok, what an insane idea! He was barely hanging on by a thread. Literally!

The bald man was hanging upside down by a metal cable, as close to the ceiling of the underground complex as possible. Surveying the carnage below him, he was glad he listened to his instincts. Zed has seen and been through some brutal and devastating fights in his life, some of them barely escaping with his life, but this… it could not be called a battle.

The only thing it could be called was mayhem.

The cultists did some serious damage to the slime monsters, almost wiping them off completely. Yes, they had powers no mortal man should and have no idea and how to use them. And yes, they somehow managed to poke holes in concrete as thick as Tiny, flooding the place with seawater, but it was manageable.

The real trouble started when a very intelligent ooze

calling himself **R.B** Slyme dropped down the ceiling and began gathering the rest of the monster into him, slowly getting bigger and bigger. The result was something that probably only Tiny could fight.

The bottom of half of the complex was flooded entirely, buildings and rubble swirling in it like some kind of soup. Smack dab in the middle, the size of a six-story building, was R.B. Slyme, scraps of metal and rubble swirling inside him.

The giant monstrosity was systematically throwing rubble at any surviving cultists, pulverising them on the spot. Some of them, the ones who tried to charge the monster from behind buildings and the metal poles hanging about the place were not that lucky. R.B. Slyme grabbed them up and laughed in delight when their skin and bones began melting in his massive hands.

Amidst all this madness, Curiosity was somehow still alive, madly piloting the flying disk they came down with. Cherry was there as well, tethered in his head in a cocoon of hair, occasionally taking pot-shots at the green monstrosity, doing absolutely nothing besides irritating him and getting a building-sized chunk in their direction as a response.

Two of the cultists were on the disk as well, Silvia, leg bleeding and hands wrapped tightly around the terminal on the disk. The other one, Rudolph, was almost thrown off when Curiosity veered madly to the left from the incoming rubble.

They almost didn't make it, but at the last minute, Cherry managed to blast the side of the chunk, redirecting the piece of rubble downwards. On the bad side, a piece of debris flew straight at Rudolph, opening a wide gash on his stomach. He almost fell off as well, if not for Curiosity grabbing him by his collar and dragging him next to him.

Cherry shouted something in the man's ears, and Rudolph quickly wrapped himself around the terminal with one hand while his other tried to keep his innards intact.

Zed wanted to listen in. Closing his eyes, he concentrated, the scars on his body turning a dull white.

"CHERRY!" Curiosity screamed. "DO SOMETHING!"

"I'm trying!" Cherry shot back. "I need time to find a suitable weapon."

"We don't have time!" Curiosity swirled violently to the left, dodging a torn door. "I can barely control this thing!"

"Where did you learn to pilot these anyway?"

"I didn't! And we don't have time for chitchat! What kind of bodyguard you are if you can't even protect me!"

"I never knew we were gonna fight a giant booger from hell! Who the hell fights this kind of stuff!"

"Apparently me."

The rest of the sentence was cut off, courtesy of a giant hand flying in their direction. Curiosity somehow managed to avoid it, bringing the disk upwards.

"Shit!" Curiosity swore. "Do something useful or don't distract me! We almost died there!"

"I'm trying!" Cherry protested.

"Master," Silvia protested weakly. "I can help. Turn me towards the direction of the monster."

"What?"

"Rudolph!" Curiosity barked. "Take over!"

The bleeding man didn't even have time to protest before Curiosity violently switched places with him. Scrambling for the controls with one hand, the red-nosed man somehow managed to keep them afloat.

"Now what?!" Curiosity said, holding Silvia towards R.B. Slyme.

"Lift my head, Master."

Curiosity did as instructed, violently lifting the elf's head, exposing her massive third eye. As if waiting for this moment, the pupils began spinning around each other violently, and a beam of pure light shot forwards, pulverising everything in its path. It shot straight through R.B. Slyme like he was not there, making a giant hole in its side and making the monster cry out in pain.

The problem was that the beam didn't stop there, it continued onwards, punching a wide hole through the concrete. It keeps going like that for a few more seconds, vaporising away more of the concrete and R.B. Slyme's mass, till finally, Silvia closes her eyes. It was bleeding profusely.

"We did it!" Curiosity screamed, throwing his hands in the air and almost dropping Silvia off the platform. "Take that you overgrown snot! That was for killing my people!"

The overgrown snot was too busy screaming in agony to give the insult much thought. It didn't help that water was gushing in much much faster than before, picking up debris on the way and smashing it against R.B. Slyme's form, almost toppling the crumbing giant over.

"I got it!" Cherry shouted. "Boss, stay steady!"

"Got it!" Curiosity said, pushing Rudolph away from the terminal and taking back control of the console.

Cherry pulled out a golden grenade from the folds of her skirts. She was holding it between both of her hands, because it was quite big, for her size anyway. Grabbing the cross-shaped pin with her teeth, she pulled hard, the bomb letting out a heavenly sound that filled everyone, Zed included, with peace and tranquillity.

"FIRE IN THE HOLE!" Cherry shouted and chucked the grenade with all her might.

A streak of gold dust left in its course, directly towards

R.B. Slyme's whirling body. It hit the giant monster and began sinking into his body.

"MOVE, MOVE!" Cherry bellowed. "It's gonna blow!"

"Nothing is happening!" Curiosity protested but did as he was told.

Just in time as well. The insides of R.B Slyme lit up with the intensity of the sun, expanding his gelatinous body to the size of a zeppelin. A few seconds later, it exploded with a thunderous roar, spraying ooze, broken pubs and pieces of cultists everywhere.

"RUN!" Cherry screamed." It's raining boogers!"

"Where is Zed?" Curiosity screamed back, piloting the disk madly towards an exit.

"I saw him up there, hanging by a thread."

"Is he still there?" Curiosity ducked, narrowly avoiding being hit by a bloody tuba.

"Let me check. Nope, he's gone."

"Where?"

"We have no time, move, move, the same way we came in!"

"Who's the boss? Me or you?"

"Sorry boss!"

"You are forgiven. Silvia, Rudolph, you okay?"

Grunts and moans were his answer.

"I'll take that as a yes," Curiosity said. "Now let's get out of here. I'm pretty sure Darius can fix you guys up."

Darius was getting nervous. Stacy had been gone for more than fifteen minutes, and he heard shuffling and muffled thumps from upstairs. It took all his willpower to not burst there and laser everyone to death.

"She will be fine," Mark said. "She has Hidara there."

The assistant was standing in the small kitchen, leaning

against the sink, drinking something that looked like coffee but smelled of wet socks.

"How do you know that?" Darius said. "When Amanda designed Codec, she equipped him with weapons like the vaporising rockets, a level one monochromatic power crystal, and who knows what else she did not tell me about."

"Level one monochromatic power crystal?" Mark whistled. "And those vaporising rockets, are the ones you spent two years developing?"

"Yes."

"Wow." The assistant took a deep sip from his drink. "I would not worry, though. Hidara is a succubus from the ninth circle of hell, she regenerates from everything. Now that I think about it, why don't you take her as your assistant?" He took another sip from the cup. "I need a break from this, for at least a year, maybe more. I am starting to lose count of all those deaths I experienced and what that even means. I need time to think."

"What are you drinking?"

"Klatchian coffee. This is the soberest I have been in my entire life." Mark took another deep sip. "Taking this job because I thought it would make me immortal. What was I thinking? I need to find a way to live with the knowledge I died so many times."

"Can you make me a cup?"

"Sure."

Before any of them had time to move, the door burst open, and a dishevelled Zed appeared, carrying the broken door with him.

"We need to evacuate," Zed said. "I knew accepting Curiosity and his cult was a mistake. I told you we needed a task force to keep an eye on beings you summon, but noo, you needed to spend our budget."

"That was generously supplied by me," Tiny interrupted from the ceiling.

"Yes, thank you, Tiny." He went back to glaring at Darius. "But you insisted on spending our budget on Cheese!"

"Cheese is a crucial ingredient for summoning rituals. "Darius said. "Besides, we have an infinite budget now."

"What?"

"Hi," Mark waved his arm. "Curiosity broke the fundamental laws of reality and gave me infinite money available in every digital currency in the world, and some of them that I never heard of."

"Me neither," Tiny supplied helpfully. "And trust me, I searched."

"Great!" Zed looked ready to explode. "More trouble."

"Oh," Mark said. "Most of our Citizens have this as well. Curiosity was very generous."

Zed closed his eyes and began to breathe, his scars pulsing a vivid red.

"Mark!" Darius said.

"Yes professor?"

"Please brew him a cup as well."

"On it."

In that exact moment, the ceiling gave in, pushed through by an oven sized fist made out of small rotating dice. They retreated with a noisy whirl, and a few seconds later, a beaming Stacy jumped through, landing with a loud clank.

Pieces of plaster still floated in the air.

"Tada!" Stacy said, grinning widely, arms outstretched. "I have a giant fucking lego arm on my back! How cool of a powerup is this!"

Silence greeted her.

"What?" She tried again.

"Mark!" Darius said.
"Yes professor?" Mark replied.
"Make a cup for Stacy as well."
"On it."

A few minutes later, Stacy, Darius and Zed exited from the bottom of the backpack, steaming cups of coffee in their hands.

"I don't understand something," Stacy said. "If we need to evacuate, can't we just ask Tiny to do so? Why are we meeting him face to face?"

"You know Tiny does not work like that," Darius said.

"I thought you would be used by now," Zed said dejectedly. "Besides, he likes to put on a show every time we need to evacuate from a place."

"How often does this happen?" Stacy asked.

"Lost count."

"Oh," Stacy gulped down the rest of the coffee and wiped her mouth with her sleeve. "That should help."

"That is a good idea."

Darius and Zed finished drinking their coffee, threw the cups on the ground and rounded the massive structure. Stacy gaped. Her mind was not prepared for this. Yes, she experienced a lot of weird things the mortal mind was not supposed in a very short time, but this... She had no idea where to even start classifying it.

Tiny was sitting with his full bulk in the middle of the ruined car park, form hunched forwards. In his hand, he was holding a grey hovercar and using it to draw small circles in the cement, creating deep gouges in the process.

"Tell me what is bothering you, Tiny," Lucy's voice rang out from the squeezed vehicle. "Everything you say will be documented and analysed."

"It's the potential of what could have been," Tiny lamented. "Imagine a living being, a statue, formed in my image, that thought that I was its mother. The knowledge I could have gained, the experience, I could have finally understood why do organic sacrifice everything for their offspring."

"It's in their nature, they are biologically and culturally wired that way."

"What about people who abandon their children and run away from their responsibilities? How do biology and culture go into this? Even here, on this planet with more than 100 different races, parents still do that. No, the only way to understand what goes through an organic parents head is to be one." Tiny let out a theatrical sob. "And it was taken away from me!"

"It's natural to feel loss," Lucy assured me. "Every parent feels that way when they lose their children."

"Mine was not lost, it was killed! Right in front of me! Do you understand my pain? I was hugging my son while its head exploded, and his innards rained down around me."

"That is very said. Tell me how it made you feel."

"Depressed." Tiny began drawing circles with more vigour. "Very depressed."

"Umm," Stacy whispered loudly. "What is happening?"

"I'm depressed, that's what!" Tiny snapped, turning his massive bulk towards Stacy and making his best effort to glare. "Can't you see that? They killed my child!"

"What?"

"Someone animated the statue of Tiny in the central museum to kill Curiosity," Darius said. "And when the statue confused Tiny with his mother, Cherry killed it."

"What?!"

"We don't have time for this," Zed said, stepping

forward and levelling Tiny with his best glare. "Tiny, the city is collapsing, we need to evacuate now, for the safety of our citizens."

"Can you see I'm depressed?" Tiny pointed with the car. "Why can't you just leave an A.I to mourn in peace."

"You are not depressed, you just spent two hours programming depression into your personality, and now you are risking the lives of your citizens for your petty amusement!"

"Five minutes."

"What?"

"I spent five minutes programming depression," Tiny said. "Earth has done pervasive research on the subject. It was not easy to comb through that data and come up with the perfect depressed parent algorithm."

Zed said nothing, except letting himself explode into colourful scars, these ones pulsing rapidly around his body.

"Alright, alright, I get it, my people are dying, and I am irresponsible for my own amusement." Tiny closed his massive eyelids for a second. "I see the underground tavern complex is flooded, most of Curiosity's cultists are dead, and that slime monster washed up next to the museum."

"Tiny!" Lucy cried. "You promised not to hack my network!"

"I lied," Tiny lifted the car behind his shoulder and in one smooth motion, threw it towards the east. "If my aim is right, which it always is, she should fly out the gates and keep going for at least two weeks. I made sure to crush her thrusters."

"Tiny," Darius tried. "Please let go. The more time we waste here, the higher the chance the island will collapse with us on top of it. Again."

"Alright, alright, spoil my fun, will you. Give me a second to deactivate my depression protocol. Done." Tiny put his massive hands on the ground and pushed, lifting himself with the grace of a boulder. "Who knew it would be so inconvenient to be a dictator? Why did I ever let you live on me?"

"We ask yourself the same question every day," Zed said. "Why did we approach a maniac whose sole purpose is to make our life complicated and shrink from his responsibilities."

"And did you find an answer?"

"No."

"Me neither." Tiny began walking towards the backpack. "Is everyone here?"

"Can't you just make a headcount yourself? Why do you keep insisting on asking this every time we evacuate? You keep tabs on all of us!"

"Not on Curiosity and his cult. I don't know why, but every tracker we put on them, technological or magical, does not work."

"I agree," Darius said. "I tried multiple times."

"Did someone say my name?" Curiosity bellowed.

Everyone turned. Flying towards them was Curiosity, barely holding on to the terminal.

"Move! Move!" Curiosity bellowed. "I can barely control it!"

Before anyone could say or do anything besides scattering to the ground, Curiosity crashed to the ground and skipped a few times like a pebble in the water, till finally coming to a stop at Tiny's feet.

"I'm alive!" Curiosity shouted, climbing out of the wreckage coughing and sputtering. "Barely. Though my cult members are dying! Any medic here?"

Darius, the closest thing to a medic in the immediate area, pulled himself to his feet and sprinted towards Curiosity.

274 / CURIOSITY AT WORK

"What is the problem?" Darius said.

"I'm not sure," Curiosity said.

"They are almost dead," Cherry said. "Now if you will shut up and help me that would be great!"

The two-inch bodyguard appeared behind a broken terminal, dragging an unconscious Rudolph by his bootstraps. The gash on the red-nosed man was even wider than before, and a few intestines were poking out.

"Oh, right!" Curiosity claps his hands together. "Silvia!"

He ran back to the wreckage, rummaged a bit, and pulled out a wounded Silvia by her hair. The two coins in her eye were gone, leaving empty sockets, and her third eye was bleeding profusely, the whites almost entirely replaced by veins.

The two almost dead cultists were unceremoniously dumped in front of Darius. The professor gave the two injured people a long look, then fixed Curiosity with a glare so intense, the personification of an idea took a step backwards.

"What?" Curiosity said.

"They are almost dead." Darius knelt down, and from his claw, a bright green light emerged, scanning the cultists up and down in two seconds. "Correction, one will be dead in 90 seconds, and the girl will live for another five minutes."

"Can you use my power to fix them?"

"What?" Darius fixed Curiosity with a questioning glare.

"I mean they gained my powers by hanging out around me, you hung out with me as well. Can't you just put a rock in there, say I'm curious and twist reality to give them a new heart?"

"Why can't you do it?"

"I have no medical knowledge."

"That's pretty obvious. What this injured man needs is new intestines, not a new heart."

"So, can you do something about it?"

Darius was already on it. With deft movements of his fingers, he pulled off the shoelaces from Rudolph's feet, looked at it for a second, murmured the magic words, and plugged them deep into the man's side.

Rudolph instantly shot up, screamed in pain, and fell back down, passed out. Darius retracted his hands and pressed both of them to the side, trying to stop the blood from flowing.

A few seconds later, the wound closed on its own, and Rudolph let out a shuddering breath. Darius quickly bought his claw for another scan, and when he finished, he let out a loud exhale.

"Amazing," the professor said. "The shoelaces are clearly there, made out of cheap plastic and cotton, but at the same time, they function exactly like the small intestines, passing tissue and nutrients along with it."

"See," Curiosity beamed. "I'm amazing, aren't I?"

"The possible applications of this are limitless, it will revolutionise science as we know it." Darius turned towards Silvia and froze in place." Does that mean Stacy has this ability as well?"

"I don't see why not," Curiosity said. "She did hang out with me."

"Stacy," Darius said, raising his voice slightly. "Come here please, I wanna test something."

Silence.

"Stacy?"

"She went that way," Tiny said, pointing with his arm. "Towards the museum."

"Why didn't you say anything?!" Darius jumped to his feet.

"You didn't ask."

"Where did she go? Why did she go away?"

"She bolted when I mentioned the location of the slime monster."

"Damn that girl! She is going to get herself killed!"

"I'll go after her," Zed said, appearing behind Darius and putting a hand on his shoulder. "I'm faster than you, and our people need you."

Darius turned and looked Zed straight in the eye. No words where needed, not between two friends who have endured horror upon horror and have come out relatively sane. Well, at least for Zed.

"Protect her," Darius finally said.

"With my life," Zed said, and disappeared, leaving behind a worried Darius and a smoking Curiosity.

[15]
PROGRESS

Stacy felt amazing, no, she felt alive. The fresh air hitting her face, the pressure on her skin and the fact that she was flying on a lego throne made out of clanking dice contributed to this fact.

She was not sure how she managed to do this in the first place, she just wanted to cave that bastard Slyme's face in, and voila, Codec rearranged himself as a chair and propelled them into the air on invincible strings.

That's because I'm an extension of you, Codec said in her head. What I know and what I can do is connected directly to your neural system, you only need to think of it, and I will rearrange myself to suit your needs.

Huh, Stacy, though. That is some serious firepower.

I was designed especially for your use, Codec whispered, I know exactly what to do, like a muscle.

Neat! I can finally go toe to toe with these bastards.

You don't seem surprised by this revelation, nor did you start talking out loud as most would be in your situation.

I saw enough movies to know this kind of shit. Besides, I'm basically raw data transferred into a woman's body via cigarette, why the fuck should I be surprised that my third arm can talk to me telepathically?

Good point, good point.

Now I just need to find me that green bastard and show him you don't mess with a woman with a laser on her back.

You said you are raw data.

Shut up, Codec!

Codec did. Stacy tried pulling out a cigarette from her pocket, but the wind ripped it out of her hand. Well, that's just amazing. It was a miracle her robes did not open yet from the strong current, showing everyone a naked lady flying on a chair in the sky.

What is even her life anymore?

There! She just spotted what was unmistakably the museum. The only problem was that it was not on the ground. It was in the air, propelled by an unknown technology. Looking around, Stacy saw more buildings, a bank, one or two skyscrapers, hospitals, and similar vital structures floating in the air.

"What is happening?" Stacy asked out loud.

There was no response. The massive museum building dipped a bit, as in acknowledgement of her comment, and began gently floating south, towards the dimensional gates. The other buildings followed suit, leaving the city behind.

It was a good thing they did, a few seconds later, the concrete began to crack, water gushing out and quickly flooding the streets. Stacy ignored this, trying hard to find any sign of R.B. Slyme.

"Stacy!" A deep and masculine voice shouted, making Stacy's spine tingle. "I knew you would not abandon me. Over here, I require your assistance."

Stacy focused, and her eyes met that of R.B Slyme. The bastard was standing on a broken car, smiling widely, and actually waving. When he saw Stacy looking, his eyes lit up, and he opened his arms wide.

"I knew you would come," R. B. Slyme said. "It's hard to resist such a handsome gentleman like me. Now help me get away from this place, and we can continue where we left off. This time no suffocating, only if you are into that kind of stuff, of course." He winked.

He actually winked, the bastard even winked at her. Stacy's mind went into overdrive, the coffee she drank earlier not letting her go into a blind rage, but actually considering things before acting.

On one hand, she could rescue Slyme and maybe kill him later or something. Well, her logical mind supplied, that probably won't work, he will probably manipulate you into doing his bidding and leave you in a ditch somewhere. And before you say things like I can take it, I'm better or more intelligent than other people, I can't be manipulated, please grab a lit cigarette and plunge it into your eyes.

Okay, brain sheesh, Stacy thought, I get your point, he will have an easy time manipulating my emotions, especially now, when I haven't developed an identity yet. What else can we do? Fight?

We can do that, Codec supplied, I'm equipped with rockets that will break down his molecules on an atomic level, leaving nothing behind.

However, Stacy's logical brain added quickly, in a prolonged battle where … Yea yea, Stacy interrupted herself. No stupid anime protagonist moves I got this.

"Hey Slyme?" Stacy said.

"Yes Stacy? Can you please hurry up, the water almost enveloped this car, and I'm too weak to jump away."

Bingo. She wanted to say something like fuck you or bye-bye fucker, but this was a way to good opportunity to pass up. And if there is one thing Stacy knew for certain, it was that she refused to act like a stupid anime protagonist.

It was time to do what every sane protagonist should do in a situation like this.

Stacy let the lego chair rearrange itself, while she gently fell a few feet downward, towards the roof of a convenience store. Still, in mid-air, Codec finished rearranging himself, extending from Stacy's back into a flower-like structure, blocky petals curled around a white diamond in the form of the hexagon.

The moment her feet touched the roof, all hell broke loose. A massive beam of light exited Codec, directly on course with R.B. Slyme. The techno slime barely had time to jump to safety on a nearby streetlamp before the car he was standing became a smouldering ruin.

"Stacy!" R.B. Slyme cried. "What are you doing?"

Stacy said nothing. The blocky petals extended and spun with a high-pitched whine. A small dice fell off with the force of a shotgun blast, impacting the lamppost R.B. Slyme was hanging off from.

There was no loud explosion or bright flash of light; instead, a black ball appeared at the point of impact, the size of a balloon, and left nothing in its wake. And by nothing, I mean nothing. Smell, air, the pole and R.B. Slyme's left hand was gone like someone took giant erasers and just deleted them out of existence.

R.B. Slyme cried out in pain and held his left stump. He began bubbling like a soup, redirecting his mass to regrow a new hand.

Hey, Stacy though quickly, do we have some kind of superweapon or ultimate move? Yes, Codec said, multiple ones actually. Which one do you want to use? The vaporising barrage? The octarine beam? The armour piercing light lance? Or maybe the…

All of them, Stacy interrupted.

What?

Stacy didn't waste any more words. She was not an anime protagonist damn it, she will not trade ultimate moves like some kind of chess match and hope she will get a last-minute powerup to destroy whatever R.B Slyme's last-minute powerup was.

That was what stupid people did.

Codec rearranged itself into a thin, branch-like structure, with the crystal in the middle. It looked like a sceptre of sorts, with a myriad of little dice spinning on their axis, letting out a rattle that could have scared death.

A lance of pure octarine shot out from the crystal, closely followed by a cluster of vaporising dice. R.B. Slyme barely had time to jump to safety on a nearby building when another lace passed through, pinning his feet to the concrete.

The techno slime didn't have time to pull his limb from under the purple lance, a cluster of dice in the form of a rope tried to wrap around his neck, forcing the gelatine to control his body in strange ways and leave the foot behind.

"Stacy!" R.B. Slyme cried out. "What are you doing? Come on, let's talk!"

Stacy, or more accurately the crystal on Stacy's back, appeared at the edge of the roof, and a torrent of flame gushed out. The temperature of the flame was so high, it was slightly blue in colour, and melted everything in its path, leaving molten metal and slag. R.B. Slyme was forced to go in the only direction he could, up.

"That's it then!" R.B. Slyme said mid-air. "No more mister nice guy!"

He contorted his body on itself, like a coiled spring, and a second later, released the tension, shooting straight towards Stacy, foot outstretched in a classic face kick pose.

Sadly what he encountered on the other side was not a blonde head, nor Stacy in general. Instead, what he encountered was the crystal, held afloat by a long chain of black dice.

Stacy was standing on the other side of the chain, quite a few streets away, standing on what was once probably a warehouse. When they made eye contact, Stacy smiled widely and put a cigarette in her mouth.

As if waiting for this exact moment, the dice chain wrapped around the still airborne R.B. Slyme, the magic crystal on top plunging deep into the techno-slimes chest. Slyme looked at his midsection in despair, gave Stacy one last despairing look, and then exploded.

The word shook.

Stacy screamed.

Now, to understand the magnitude and stupidity of what Stacy just did, we need to know what exactly is a monochromatic power crystal. This is no ordinary magic crystal that contains the power of the elements or some such nonsense. It's literally mana, in its purest form, a result of years of experiment, a manmade power source so powerful, so potent, Tiny took one to replace all of his power sources.

A three millennia old A.I. admitted it's the most potent power source he encountered in his existence. And Stacy just detonated it to kill R.B. Slyme.

Amanda, Darius, and Zed would have strangled her on the spot, Stacy though. Heck, if she could, she would probably strange herself. Well, her brain whispered, there is no need for that, the explosion threw us a good distance away in the air, and seeing as Codec is now nothing more than three dice orbiting a pink claw, we are gonna collide with something and die.

Shame, Stacy thought, she finally was begging to

accept her new role in this form, and, and even began being comfortable in her body. And we didn't even have sex, her hormones added, and god knows looking this hot, we can have toe-curling sex with literally anybody of any race, species, or gender.

Good point, Stacy thought to herself, the wind rushing through her lab coat, forcing the button open. Here I am, flying through the air exhibitionist style and there is nobody to even gawk at the audacity!

She wondered what Darius would think. They just began bonding father-daughter style, and now his daughter is gonna become a stain on the wall. She didn't even do something crass, like seducing his best friend and creating an awkward atmosphere!

Ha, that would show that bald monk not to mess with her, though admittedly, she has no idea how to seduce people as a woman, and even as Steve, his luck was more miss than hit.

Speaking of Zed, the professor appeared in front of Stacy, lit up like a Christmas tree, a pleased expression on his face. Stacy was not sure if this was a hallucination conjured by her fevered mind, but when she was plucked from mid-air and strong arms wrapped around her, she let herself hope.

Zed kept plummeting towards the ground, twisting around, so Stacy was firmly in his arms, bridal style.

"Don't tell me you detonated the monochromatic power crystal," Zed said, and made the mistake of looking down.

His grip slipped for a second, and the graceful fall on the ground became a tumble, the professor smashing his back against an abandoned warehouse, and slid down the wall like a snail, Stacy still in his arms.

Stacy, grinning knowingly, slid out his arms and buttoned up her lab coat.

"Liked what you saw?" Stacy asked.

"Just no," Zed said firmly, looking anywhere but Stacy. "No, no way, I am not playing this game, no-no."

"Just admit it," Stacy said, taking a step forward and placing a hand on Zed's chest. "I find you attractive as well."

When Zed's scars turned an agitated purple, and the professor closed his eyes and began taking deep breaths, Stacy grinned wickedly. It seems she didn't need seduction lessons, after all.

"We need to evacuate," Zed said, snapping his eyes open. "The city is collapsing, even faster than before, no thanks to you."

"Hey!" Stacy protested.

"And Tiny and Darius are waiting for us, let's go, we don't have time for no-nonsense."

"It's not nonsense," Stacy said, leaning in so close their noses almost touched. "Besides, you promised me to teach me the art of diplomacy." She breathed into his lips.

"Darius is going to kill me," Zed said and kissed Stacy on the lips.

Stacy froze. She was not expecting Zed to actually take the bait, it was just adrenaline and the near-death experience making her seek out any physical comfort she could get her hands on. And what comfort it was! Zed's strong hands pressed against the small of her back, and his other wrapped around her waist.

Still kissing fiercely, Stacy secured firmly to his midsection, Zed jumped, carrying them in the air. Stacy didn't want to let go at first, but the wind forced her to do so. When she did, she met Zed's eyes, heavy with lust and slightly panicked. She laughed and buried her head in his chest.

"What are we doing?" Stacy said quietly.

"Darius is going to kill me," Zed said.

"You and me both," Stacy said, a bit surprised she could actually hear him.

"I agree. He's probably going to dissect us and force us to swap bodies or something first."

Stacy laughed. Maybe there was potential in this life after all, not only for her but for everyone else around her.

There was still hope.

Inside Tiny's head, things were looking good. Darius was sitting behind the terminal, furiously working on something with all 3 hands. Cherry was sprawled on one of the tables, a myriad of guns, knives, rocket launchers, grenades, rifles, machine guns, and gods know what else surrounded her in a pile.

Curiosity was sprawled on a sofa nearby and was torn between looking at the shrinking city of Lucy on the monitors and the urge to pick up one of his bodyguard weapons and examine it. The second won out.

"How come that massive structure you call a backpack floats?" Cherry asked, in the middle of disassembling her favourite flamethrower.

"The backpack has many uses," Darius replied. "Tiny used it once to bludgeon a giant monster to death."

"I would pay to see that."

Right at that moment, Tiny's teeth opened up with a loud clunk, and a second later Zed touched down, Stacy tightly squeezed to his chest. Instantly Darius' head snapped up and fixed his friend with an unreadable gaze.

Zed began sweating. Before his scars could light up

erratically, Stacy pushed herself off the professor and took a few drunken steps towards the sofa.

"That was one hell of a fight," Stacy said. "But that bastard is finally dead! I'm pretty sure he's not coming back from that one." Saying that she plopped down next to Curiosity and pulled out a cigarette.

"Where is Codec?" Darius asked, momentarily leaving his friend alone and looking at Stacy.

Three pitiful black dice coalesced on top of Stacy's claw and let out a dejected clank.

"She blew up the monochromatic power crystal," Zed said, colour returning to his face.

"YOU WHAT!" Darius exploded in place. "DO YOU KNOW HOW HARD IS TO MAKE ONE OF THOSE CRYSTALS! IT TOOK ME A LIFETIME TO COME UP WITH THE DESIGN!"

"Sorry," Stacy said, sinking into the sofa.

"Now now," Zed said, stepping forward. "There is no need to get angry. She did manage to kill R.B. Slyme on the first try. That monster managed to wipe out most of Curiosity's cult, and at his full strength, even I could not defeat him. You should be proud of your daughter's combat capabilities Darius; she does have your knack of coming up with stupid ideas."

"Hey if it's stupid and it works it ain't stupid!"

"Your right," Darius said, face softening. "Your right." He turned towards Stacy. "I am proud of the fact that you managed to destroy R.B. Slyme on your first real battle. That was some excellent spur of the moment thinking, considering you got… how did you say it? The McGuffin, an hour ago."

"Thank you," Stacy said, smiling gently. "And yes, it's a McGuffin."

"We will have a discussion about handling delicate and

dangerous equipment, though. It will take a while to rebuild Codec."

"Yes, father," Stacy blushed. "Thank you."

"I'm just glad you are alive," Darius said, smiling gently.

"She almost didn't make it," Zed added helpfully. "Thankfully I managed to catch her in time."

"Thank you, friend," Darius pinned Zed with an unreadable gaze. "You can tell me all about your daring rescue down at Rip's when we get out of this pocket dimension. Don't leave any details out."

"Ahm, yes yes, of course," Zed nodded vigorously. "We haven't had a pint in a while!"

"Of course."

"Ohhh, man!" Stacy interrupted, loudly and obviously. "Almost dying, twice, sure puts things into perspective. Does this place even have an afterlife? What happens when you die?"

"Well," Darius said. "It depends on your definition of the afterlife, the species you come from and the magical dimensions connected to your word. Hidara, for example, comes from a word where hell and heaven exist, and every living being has a soul that is constantly cycled through these planes."

"The world where Curiosity found your old body on the other hand," piped in Tiny, his fridge body rolling out from the corner, a tray of drink in his arms, "has no such thing. You are basically a collection of biological data, which when it dies, breaks down into base components. No magical or spiritual realms tied to that word either."

"Huh." Stacy gratefully accepted a cup of water. "That explains a lot. What about you Curiosity? What will happen to you when you die?"

No response.

"Curiosity?"

"What?" Curiosity said, waking from his reverie of twirling a small shotgun between his fingers.

"What happens to you when you die? What rules of afterlife do you follow?"

"Huh, I never thought about that." Curiosity stopped twirling the shotgun to stare at it instead. "This body will die and wither, I know that, but what about me? I'm not technically a soul, a spirit or a deity. I am an idea, given flesh and bone by basically what amounts to a fluke and belief. Do I go back to being insubstantial? A basic consciousness with only vague ideas to act upon? Will I keep trying to come back into existence? Or maybe a piece of me will die with the death of this body. So many possibilities."

"Huh," Cherry said, pausing from polishing a butterfly knife. "I never even thought of that."

"That is a complicated conundrum," Darius said. "I never encountered a being like you before, so I can't be of any assistance."

"It's not a problem, it's not a problem," Curiosity said, a deranged smile perching on his face. "There is an easy and simple way to find out."

"And that is?"

"To die and see what happens." Before anyone had time to react, Curiosity put the shotgun under his jaw. "I hope we meet again." He said and pulled the trigger.

Silence descended on the room. The shotgun shells were too small to blow Curiosity's brain to the other side of the room, but everyone could clearly tell they penetrated the skull and exited the other side.

Fridge Tiny ambled to where Curiosity was located and placed a cup of water on his knee. It slid down his pants and clattered to the floor with a wet splash.

"He's dead," Tiny announced.

"What the actual fuck was just that," Stacy began, but she was interrupted.

Curiosity's head caught on fire. Not the normal red one or the pure blue Stacy used to fry a rooftop, but black, pouring out like a vengeful cloud. The body stood straight, and two eyes appeared, deep pools of nothingness that showed you the endless universe.

"Good riddance," the entity spoke, not with lips, but directly in everyone's head, Tiny included. "I don't know why I was worried so much. The bastard shot himself in the head! Hah! What kind of idea shoots himself in the head to see what happens? And I thought my assistant had problems."

"Who are you?" Darius asked, taking a step forward, claw raised.

Zed and Stacy followed suit, adopting combat stances. Even Tiny's little fridge body took point, a glass of water raised behind its bulk. The only one who did not move was Cherry. She had a shocked expression on her face and was pointing with a harpoon.

"Reality!" Cherry said in a panic. "What are you doing here?! You're not supposed to be here!"

"Ah Cherry," Reality said, pinning the bodyguard with a stare. "Your so-called boss was not supposed to exist in the first place!" His head exploded, "Do you know how much trouble you and your merry band of lunatics have caused me?" He took a pointed look at everyone in the room. "Another universe has been corrupted by your foul energies! What do you have to say for yourself?"

"Ahh," Stacy said. "Sorry?"

"Sorry! Hah! You caused me nothing but trouble." He put his hands on Curiosity's knees and stood up." But you did manage to get rid of R.B. Slyme from this universe, so

I guess I will leave you alone, for now. Now Cherry," he said, holding out a hand. "Let's go. Time to go back to the funhouse!"

"Never!" Cherry shouted, springing to her feet. "I'm never returning to that pathetic excuse of a mercenary group!" She said the last part in air quotes.

"You don't have a choice. Your contract ended."

"That's where you're wrong. I'm bonded to curiosity for a year, and seeing as curiosity is an idea…" She grinned wickedly and jumped in the air. "I'm curious!"

She plugged directly towards the ground in the perfect swimming position, and went through it, the velvet rug rippling like water.

Instantly, the room began shaking, and Tiny's fridge ran forward in panic and smashed against one of the screens.

"Get it out!" Tiny bellowed. "Get it out! I can feel my processors being violated!"

"You bastard!" Stacy shouted. "What is happening!"

"Alright, I'm out!" Reality said. "Thank you for taking care of Curiosity. I hope I never see you again."

Curiosity's body caught on fire and was thrown against the wall in the ensuing racket. It slid to the floor, and the rug caught on fire. Stacy and Darius rooted themself to the floor, and Zed wrapped around the terminal in the middle.

"I can feel it in my buttocks!" Tiny bellowed. "I'm not even supposed to have a buttock, and I can still feel Cherry swimming inside me!"

"Well fuck," Stacy said, and looked at Darius.

The professor looked back and smiled. Both of them turned as one and made eye contact with Zed.

All three of them all laughed.

. . .

"So," Cherry said. "This is all of you?"

The two-inch bodyguard spent the afternoon gathering the remains of Curiosity's cult, bringing them onto this abandoned warehouse. It was better than she expected. She found at least fifty people, and more were trickling in by the minute.

"Yes mistress," An elf with the lower body of a snake, a mangled snake, but a snake nonetheless, slithered forward.

"Aidan West," Cherry greeted widely. "You survived! How?! And call me Cherry,"

"Yes mistress."

"One of those. Wonderful."

Cherry was standing on a bunch of crates so she could see the gathered crowd. Some of them had animal faces, instruments for heads, others had cars for ears, and there was even a girl with a toaster extending from her scalp. With toast sizzling inside it! Insane people, all part of the cult of curiosity, her cult now.

"Some of you are not aware," Cherry said, packing up and down. "That our dear master, Curiosity is dead."

"We know." The crowd nodded in unison. "We could feel it through our bond with the master."

"Huh." Cherry stopped, "I thought only I felt that. Right. So what are we going to do about it?"

"We are already on it," Aidan West said. "Bring in the prototype!"

The crowd parted. A trolley was pushed forwards, covered with a white sheet.

"As you all know," The elf began. "Reality won't allow Curiosity to inhabit a living being body again."

The crowd nodded in unison.

"I did not know that!" Cherry said wide-eyed. "How do you know that? Where is this information coming from?"

"But!" The elf ignored her. "This only extends to living beings. Watch!"

With a flourish, the sheet was pulled off. In the trolley was a terminal. It was an older model, big and bulky, with too many knobs and at least five different screens. Two fairies in lab coats were still working on it, adjusting knobs and attaching wires.

"Watch," Aidan West said, opening his arms broadly. "Bring the artefact!"

A cultist with a red nose scuttled forward, carrying a shovel reverently in his hands, and put it on the side of the contraption, where a slot specially designed for it was located.

"Rudolph!" Cherry smiled. "Glad you are awake. And you found Curiosity's shovel! Where was it?"

"Pixies!" Aidan West said. "Start awakening Curiosity!"

A fairy scientist glared at the elf, then pressed a button. The terminal crackled to life. Knobs turned on their own. Light flashed on the screens. Cherry held her breath and waited.

"Hiiiiiiii," The voice was robotic and off-key. "Cherry, I remember," Smoke began pouring from the machine. "The THIRD Steep, I remember," The fairies were frantically trying to detach wires. "it's one word, Patience! Once an Idea is in the Wild and people believe in it, it's only a matter of time for the IMPOSSIBLE TO HAPPEN!" Lights were turning off and on randomly. "NOBODY CAN STOP PROGRESS! NOBODY!" With that, the terminal exploded.

"Well," Aidan West said. "It's getting there. A few more tries and we should have a functioning prototype," He looked Cherry straight in the eye. "What people don't understand is that an idea once born will never go away. Curiosity had a body, had an existence, and that fact, that idea, will never leave people's minds, especially not ours, we who have dedicated our lives to curiosity."

The crowd cheered.

"We will come up with new ideas, with new possibilities, we will twist and turn reality till Curiosity and all that entails will become part of reality. If it takes us years, so be it!"

The crowd cheered again.

"Will you join us, mistress?"

"Well," Cherry muttered. "Why not? What was that thing Curiosity said?"

"You can't stop progress."

"Exactly!" Cherry snapped her fingers. "The word always moves forwards, you can kick and scream against it, or join it, but you can't stop it, nobody can."

"Well-spoken mistress. Happy to have you on board. Tea?"

"Coffee, please. With alcohol. Lots and lots of alcohol."

Printed in Great Britain
by Amazon